CHASING
ENDLESS
SUMMER

V.C. Andrews® Books

The Dollanganger Family
Flowers in the Attic
Petals on the Wind
If There Be Thorns
Seeds of Yesterday
Garden of Shadows
Christopher's Diary:
   Secrets of Foxworth
Christopher's Diary:
   Echoes of Dollanganger
Secret Brother
Beneath the Attic
Out of the Attic
Shadows of Foxworth

The Audrina Series
My Sweet Audrina
Whitefern

The Casteel Family
Heaven
Dark Angel
Fallen Hearts
Gates of Paradise
Web of Dreams

The Cutler Family
Dawn
Secrets of the Morning
Twilight's Child
Midnight Whispers
Darkest Hour

The Landry Family
Ruby
Pearl in the Mist
All That Glitters
Hidden Jewel
Tarnished Gold

The Logan Family
Melody
Heart Song
Unfinished Symphony
Music in the Night
Olivia

The Orphans Series
Butterfly
Crystal
Brooke
Raven
Runaways

The Wildflowers Series
Misty
Star
Jade
Cat
Into the Garden

The Hudson Family
Rain
Lightning Strikes
Eye of the Storm
The End of the
   Rainbow

The Shooting Stars
Cinnamon
Ice
Rose
Honey
Falling Stars

The De Beers Family
"Dark Seed"
Willow
Wicked Forest
Twisted Roots
Into the Woods
Hidden Leaves

The Broken Wings Series
Broken Wings
Midnight Flight

The Gemini Series
Celeste
Black Cat
Child of Darkness

The Shadows Series
April Shadows
Girl in the Shadows

The Early Spring Series
Broken Flower
Scattered Leaves

The Secrets Series
Secrets in the Attic
Secrets in the Shadows

The Delia Series
Delia's Crossing
Delia's Heart
Delia's Gift

The Heavenstone Series
The Heavenstone Secrets
Secret Whispers

The March Family
Family Storms
Cloudburst

The Kindred Series
Daughter of Darkness
Daughter of Light

The Forbidden Series
The Forbidden Sister
"The Forbidden Heart"
Roxy's Story

The Mirror Sisters
The Mirror Sisters
Broken Glass
Shattered Memories

The House of Secrets Series
House of Secrets
Echoes in the Walls

The Umbrella Series
Out of the Rain
The Umbrella Lady

The Eden Series
Eden's Children
Little Paula

The Sutherland Series
Losing Spring
Chasing Endless Summer

The Girls of Spindrift
Bittersweet Dreams
"Corliss"
"Donna"
"Mayfair"
"Spindrift"

Stand-alone Novels
Gods of Green
   Mountain
Into the Darkness
Capturing Angels
The Unwelcomed Child
Sage's Eyes
The Silhouette Girl
Whispering Hearts
Becoming My Sister

V.C. ANDREWS®

CHASING ENDLESS SUMMER

G

Gallery Books

New York   London   Toronto   Sydney   New Delhi

G

Gallery Books
An Imprint of Simon & Schuster, LLC
1230 Avenue of the Americas
New York, NY 10020

First Gallery Books trade paperback edition February 2024

V.C. ANDREWS® and VIRGINIA ANDREWS® are registered trademarks of A&E Television Networks, LLC

GALLERY BOOKS and colophon are registered trademarks of Simon & Schuster, LLC

Simon & Schuster: Celebrating 100 Years of Publishing in 2024

For information about special discounts for bulk purchases, please contact Simon & Schuster Special Sales at 1-866-506-1949 or business@simonandschuster.com.

Interior design by Erika R. Genova

Manufactured in the United States of America

10 9 8 7 6 5 4 3 2 1

Library of Congress Cataloging-in-Publication Data

Names: Andrews, V. C. (Virginia C.), author.
Title: Chasing endless summer / V.C. Andrews.
Description: First Gallery Books trade paperback edition. | New York : Gallery Books, 2024.
Identifiers: LCCN 2023031364 (print) | LCCN 2023031365 (ebook) | ISBN 9781668015940 (trade paperback) | ISBN 9781668015957 (hardcover) | ISBN 9781668015971 (ebook)
Subjects: LCGFT: Novels.
Classification: LCC PS3551.N454 C47 2024 (print) | LCC PS3551.N454 (ebook) | DDC 813/.54—dc23/eng/20230714
LC record available at https://lccn.loc.gov/2023031364
LC ebook record available at https://lccn.loc.gov/2023031365

ISBN 978-1-6680-1595-7
ISBN 978-1-6680-1594-0 (pbk)
ISBN 978-1-6680-1597-1 (ebook)

AUTHOR'S NOTE

At the time of the writing of this novel, Lahaina, Hawaii, was—and hopefully will once again be—a popular and exciting town and beach resort. It would be a disservice to the inhabitants and those who lost their lives to erase its existence from this story.

CHASING
ENDLESS
SUMMER

PROLOGUE

Grandmother Judith died today, but it should have been yesterday. My cousin Simon, who often claims to know just about anything, told me so in that arrogant tone of voice I suspect he's had since birth. His cry at delivery probably caused the doctors and nurses to step back. It probably sounded like "How dare you?"

"Grandmother died during the night, about eleven, but no one would wake Grandfather to tell him so because he had left a 'do not disturb' order as clearly as if it had been posted in large black-and-white letters on his bedroom door," Simon began. "He instructed his CEO, Franklin Butler, to announce her death as occurring today. And Dr. Immerman will put today's date on the death certificate. She died when Grandfather was told she had died and not before. Nothing happens here in Sutherland unless Grandfather says it happened," he said with his wry smile.

I never really knew if Simon's respect for Grandfather Sutherland was born out of absolute fear or absolute envy. I know he enjoyed our grandfather's control of everyone and everything. I remember he told me about when Grandfather attended school and the guidance counselor called him in to talk about his future, she asked him where his ambitions lay. He said he told her he intended to be a dictator of a country. He was twelve at the time.

Simon had come up to my room, which had been my mother's room upstairs in the southeast end of the great Sutherland mansion. When I arrived, Simon told me the mansion was nearly sixty thousand square feet with twenty-two rooms, eight of which were bedroom suites. All the furniture was one of a kind, expensive, and rich-looking. The dining room table, which could seat eighteen easily, was made of a dark piece of preserved wood. Wrought-iron chandeliers and candleholders were strewn about the house. Layers of thick, heavy textiles, fringed jabots, and valances were used to create the curtains. There were rich and dark colors, such as reds, blues, purples, emerald greens, and gold. Grandfather Sutherland preferred clear glass windows rather than his father's stained glass, which he had removed. Almost everywhere you looked you saw large, comfortable chairs and dark-colored oversize sofas. They made a statement. This was the owner's palace. Large furniture seemed to emphasize a large personality, a great man, the true lord of the manor. He was in everything.

However, there wasn't a hint that my mother had ever lived in this room. When I was brought to it, nearly four months ago, it looked and smelled like it had been scrubbed with Clorox or some other powerful antiseptic. I thought I was moving into an operating room in a hospital. There was nothing on the bureau or the night tables to suggest her, nothing of hers left in the closet or in the bureau drawers, and there were only my new bathroom necessities in the en suite bathroom.

I had no picture of her to put in a frame or at least to keep in the drawer of the night table so I could take it out and look at her before I went to sleep. In fact, there were no pictures of her anywhere in the den, the Sutherland Room, on the hallway walls, or in the dining room or library study of the great house now, so I wasn't really surprised that her old room had been scrubbed of the scent of her or even a strand of her hair. I hadn't been in Grandmother Judith's bedroom, so I wasn't sure if she had a picture of my mother or pictures that included her. I was confident I wouldn't find one in Grandfather's room, not that I would ever dare approach it, much less enter it without his permission. His room was toward the end of the northwest corner of the mansion on the first floor, at least half of the corridor away from Grandmother Judith's suite.

The hardwood floor of my mother's bedroom looked newly stained, and the walls repainted a light brown. The shine on the floor gave me the impression I could ice-skate on it. The only picture on the walls was one of a racehorse my grandfather had once owned, Cutter, a cinnamon-brown horse that nearly made it to the Kentucky Derby. The black mechanized window curtains were recently installed, as were the coffee-and-cream area rugs on both sides of the king-size oak bed with its nondescript starched white comforter and pillows. There were matching dark brown bedside tables and a matching bureau with an oval mirror above it in an oak frame. None of the furnishings had anything embossed on them, no birds or flowers, not even some squiggly design. They were as plain and simple as could be.

Mommy had told me that her room at Sutherland was deliberately dark and neutral. There was nothing feminine about it. "It was a subtle way for my father to say that what I wanted didn't matter. I guess that was equally true for my brother, Martin. We could have easily exchanged rooms. We had the exact same furniture! There was probably some sort of sale if you bought two of the same thing." And my mother wasn't permitted to add anything, especially to the room I was now using. Mommy claimed that back then, "Your grandmother was even afraid to spray her cologne in my room. I always suspected that my father wanted a second son.

"I think even Martin had that suspicion and fearfully imagined my father's dream boy hovering over his shoulder. Your grandmother's opinion wasn't important when it came to most things that involved our family and Sutherland," my mother said, "but I especially believed she hesitated to brag about compliments she had received for how pretty my hair was or how I looked in a new dress, because it reminded my father that she had given him a daughter and not another son."

"Why didn't they try to have another child, then?" I wondered aloud. I often wondered the same thing about my father and mother. I would have loved a sister or a brother. Maybe even as a little girl I should have realized that was a significant hint about the future of their marriage and our family.

"Truthfully? I think my father was afraid he'd have another daughter. It would have added to his manly embarrassment," my mother told me.

"But it seems unfair that she couldn't talk about how pretty you were, or how popular you were at school with your teachers and other students."

"She did that from time to time, but my father rarely mentioned it, or at least she did when I was present when he met with businesspeople or had friends over for dinners and parties. But whenever my mother did, he managed to change the conversation as if she hadn't even spoken. There were times when I felt he had hired me to fill a role, just like any other servant. Whenever my mother complained about his lack of attention to me, he had this way of looking off or at something he was reading as if her words literally evaporated before they reached his ears."

How could a mother's opinion about her child not be important?

I always wondered. I saw that servants and especially Uncle Martin and Aunt Holly were afraid of displeasing Grandfather Sutherland, but how could a woman still remain his wife if she was so shackled, right down to her very thoughts about her own daughter? How hard had she protested? What kept her from walking out the door? Was she so in love with my grandfather that she would forgive him anything?

I had not really gotten to know Grandmother Judith the way other kids my age knew their grandmothers. I had hoped we would become closer after all that had happened after my parents divorced and my mother was killed. I had anticipated that Grandmother Judith would protect me and finally care deeply for me. What was worse, a mother's loss of a daughter or a daughter's loss of a mother at a young age? Weren't they at least equal tragedies? I never got to ask her. In fact, I don't think I ever spoke with her privately for more than a minute or so after I was permitted to be a Sutherland again. And every time I merely mentioned Grandfather, she looked terrified that I might say something unpleasant about him. She looked more afraid than I was. She always appeared on the verge of crying whenever she saw me. I felt guilty even saying, "Hello, Grandmother. How are you today?"

According to Simon, Grandmother Judith had been sickly ever since my mother's funeral. Later, Simon would tell me her conscience smothered her. She rarely came to dinner because of how visibly irritated Grandfather Sutherland would get when she moaned about this pain or that. I suspected he had "advised" her to stay in her bedroom suite until she was stronger, which everyone knew would be never. I hadn't seen her for nearly a week, and early in the week, I had overheard one of the maids tell another that Grandmother Judith's heart was "ticking down like an antique clock that needs to be rewound. I swear she is fading and cracking just the way a flower does when it's pressed between the pages of a diary."

"Hush," the other said, and looked around as if she believed the entire mansion was filled with listening devices. They fled from each other like two guilty children. The house creaked from the weight of the fear the servants exhibited, especially when Grandfather appeared or his footsteps, accompanied by the tap of that mahogany walking stick, could be heard echoing through the halls. He always wore boots because he liked the added inch or so of height they gave him, not that he wasn't a tall man. Simon told me that he wasn't as tall as his father, which was something else he blamed on his mother. When I grimaced, Simon said, "The gene pool. He would have rather been cloned."

Now Simon stood there in my bedroom doorway like some proper servant himself, with my father's perfect posture. He resembled a town crier announcing the day's headlines in some nineteenth-century English pub. I had read the description in a young adult history novel.

"My parents and I just arrived. Summoned, I should say, to hear what Grandfather's plans are for Grandmother Judith's funeral. You're expected to be there at the family gathering occurring in a few minutes."

He said Grandfather immediately had sent him upstairs to tell me what had happened. He made it sound as if it was a very sought-after assignment and his getting it proved how important he was to Grandfather. His ego was like an air hose pumping up the shoulders of his nearly six-foot slim body.

Admittedly, I was surprised that Mrs. Lawson, the head housekeeper of Sutherland and something of a guardian as she had been for my mother, didn't come to wake me and tell me the news as well as how I should now behave. She lorded it over me with regard to just about everything else. Sometimes she made me feel as if everyone believed I would do or say the wrong thing and set off an explosion. After I had been permitted to rejoin the family, whenever I started to speak, everyone looked like they were holding their breath. Was I normal? Had I been turned into some sort of creature? Would I contaminate them? I heard whispering about me even when there was no one else in the room. Every ancestor frozen in a portrait looked at me coldly. Sometimes I felt like I was leaving dirty footprints on the sacred cold Sutherland floor tiles.

Since my mother's death in the car accident after my father had divorced her, Sutherland seemed never to lose its shroud of gloom. Grandfather Sutherland was afraid that because my mother had surprised everyone with her gay relationship and I had remained living with her and Natalie Gleeson, I would turn out to be gay, too, so he hired Dr. Kirkwell, an expert in the techniques of aversion therapy. For months, she was practically the only other person I had seen here at Sutherland. She was still my academic tutor and was constantly evaluating me. Sometimes it felt like she had crawled under my skin. Together, she and Mrs. Lawson were bookends on a shelf of nightmares.

For months, I had been kept in the gloomy big bedroom at the end of the darkest first-level corridor in Grandfather's large estate just outside Colonie, New York. Perhaps my incarceration and the hiring of Dr. Kirkwell were another one of my grandfather's ways to punish my mother after her death. From what I had learned and what she had told me about her life at Sutherland, my mother was often defiant when it came to my grandfather, who never made a suggestion to her or anyone. Instead, his comments were, and continued to be, orders, demands, and firm conclusions. Truthfully, I couldn't remember anyone challenging him the way my mother had even before her affair with Natalie, and I certainly didn't see anyone doing it now.

After months and months of treatments and tests designed to strip me of any thoughts or tendencies that could result in my becoming gay, Dr. Kirkwell was satisfied with what she called "your progress in becoming normal again." For a final test, she forced me to pretend to be my mother and write a letter of apology to my father. When Grandfather read it and approved of it, I was permitted to reenter the Sutherland world. The possibility of my father forgiving me and accepting me into his new family loomed because of the letter.

It had been so long since my parents and I were here for grand dinners and events, but apparently my father had been here to visit with Grandfather Sutherland often, sometimes without my mother knowing. My mother said he gave Grandfather reports about her. I knew he relied on Grandfather for family advice as well as for business advice, especially after my mother and Natalie Gleeson, the daughter of our neighbors, became close friends quickly and then fell in love.

Mother and I called her by her nickname, Nattie. From the first day he had met her at her father's funeral wake, Daddy never liked Nattie. He often ridiculed and criticized her. He could find fault in the smallest details about her, trying to prove she was a snob, full of herself because she was an assistant to the American ambassador to France, spoke French fluently, and had been to so many important places in the world, including the White House. Practically every time she mentioned one of the prestigious places in his presence, he would quip something like "Well, I've been to the motor vehicle bureau."

After Mommy brought her into our lives, he scrutinized everything that occurred at our house, questioned and studied it like a police detective, looking for ways to blame Nattie for this or that slight change in things, whether it was where flowers were put or a picture moved from this wall to that or even a book out of alphabetical order.

In the beginning of their marriage, when I was very young, my mother kidded Daddy about his obsession with perfection, especially about his own clothes and possessions. Everything had to be in its proper place. His clothes were spotless, his pants sharply creased, and his shoes spit shined. Mommy used to tease him about it, even saluting him and calling him "Captain Bryer." I remember her telling me she didn't mind it in the beginning because he made her feel safe. Avoiding changes was simply his nature, who he was, and how he was brought up in a military family. Order and discipline were how you kept protected.

The neighbors noticed and nicknamed us the "Robot Family" because of how organized we were, how perfectly coordinated our clothes were, and how neatly arranged everything was inside and outside our house. Mrs. Hingen across the street claimed she could take her daily blood pressure pill exactly when my mother opened the front curtains every day.

It seemed so natural, then, for Daddy to work as an FAA air traffic controller at the Albany International Airport. Lives depended on what he saw or anticipated and how clearly and quickly he reacted. He couldn't be anything less than a perfectionist, and for that reason he was quite intolerant of mistakes, accidents, and unawareness. From the very beginning of my mother's relationship with Nattie Gleeson, he analyzed anything or everything she said about her and did with her, no matter how small and insignificant it would seem to anyone else. When my mother protested and argued that he was being unfair, even ridiculous, he began to grow more and more suspicious of their relationship, sometimes even cross-examining me about it: "Where did they go? What were they talking about? What did you see them do?"

I tried to answer Daddy's questions as accurately as he would want, but I couldn't help feeling he was turning me into a spy and every answer I gave him was a small betrayal. My reluctance probably confirmed his suspicions, even about me.

Once my father had discovered them together in bed, he divorced my mother and went off with another air traffic controller to live with her son and daughter in Hawaii, where he worked in the airport tower at the Kahului Airport in Maui, doing the same thing he had done at Albany International: directing planes to land and to take off.

At the time, Daddy didn't want anything to do with me, either, because he now firmly believed I had kept my mother's secret from him and probably because, like my grandfather, he thought she and Nattie had influenced me and I'd corrupt his stepdaughter, maybe even his older stepson. Most of all, he thought I might continue to ruin his straight-arrow reputation. After my mother died, he approved of whatever my grandfather decided to do with me. He did idolize Grandfather Sutherland, more than I think he loved me. In fact, despite how beautiful my mother was, both she and Natalie came to believe that my grandfather had given my father financial incentives to marry her. He had chosen her husband, the path of her life.

"If he could, he would choose when I take a breath," Mommy had once said when she was complaining about her father.

When a tractor trailer jackknifed and instantly killed my mother, as well as seriously injured Nattie, my grandfather sent Mrs. Lawson to come get me at school. I was whisked off and locked away from anyone I knew. The only time I was permitted to go out was right at the start to attend my mother's funeral. I was at her grave site looking down at her coffin in disbelief when Simon stepped up to me and said, "She's not down there."

Before I could ask him what he meant and build up my hope, I was forced back into Grandfather's limousine and returned to Sutherland for my months of aversion therapy, which even included electric shock treatment. I couldn't get to Nattie to help me. After Simon snuck in, I finally learned about Nattie. No one else would tell me anything. I couldn't even mention her name. Simon revealed what he had overheard his parents, my uncle Martin and his wife, Holly, say about her. From Simon I learned that Nattie was paralyzed and couldn't talk or make much more than unintelligible sounds.

When he told me that, I wasn't going to believe him, but then he literally showed me the truth about my mother's funeral and burial to prove he wasn't making up anything. He snuck me out and to Grandfather's inner office, where I saw the urn. I understood that Grandfather had my mother cremated and held a burial in what was a false grave he had created to fool my grandmother, who had wanted her in the family cemetery. It was his way to avoid another family crisis, which could become just as public.

Getting the answers to the two big questions—what Simon had meant at the grave site when he said she wasn't down there, and what he knew about Natalie Gleeson—came only when I would cooperate with what he called quid pro quo. It was part of Simon's plan to get me to permit him to do sexual things to me. Later he claimed that he was doing these things only to help Dr. Kirkwell perform her aversion therapy. He had been sent in to test me. Would I react to a male's advances positively or not? He proudly called himself her intern.

I hadn't spoken to him since that last day in the dark and some-what hidden bedroom, when I drove him away from me before he could have his way. Now, whenever he and his parents came to Sutherland for dinner, I wouldn't even look at him. It didn't seem to bother him, or if it did, he would never show it. Simon had inherited all the Sutherland arrogance. He was brilliant and years ahead of others his age mentally and academically, and he was good-looking. I couldn't take any of that away from him. But I didn't have to like him or even consider him my cousin, no matter what his intellectual accomplishments were.

Simon was here often because he was in a special academic program; he didn't have to attend school except when he had to take an exam. He was taking college-level classes called Advanced Placement even though he was only in the tenth grade. He had moved into the special program a year ago when his teachers realized they couldn't keep up with him and his needs without ignoring everyone else in the class. At least, that was the way he described it.

I was not in a school, either. I was still being homeschooled by Dr. Kirkwell until I finished this school year and maybe would be able to see my father in Hawaii during the summer. I was told that he would decide then whether to keep me or send me back. I was awaiting his final okay to visit. It had been weeks since Dr. Kirkwell and my grandfather had agreed to send him my letter of apology, written the way, after Dr. Kirkwell's treatment, I imagined my mother would write it. In the exercise, I had to pretend to be her.

However, my father was not someone who changed his mind easily or quickly. And he was rarely forgiving. He was a lot like Grandfather Sutherland that way—"cemented in his ideas," as my mother would say. So many of her expressions and descriptions became mine. After all, I saw most of the world through her eyes when I was younger, actually right up to her death. And her expressions were all I had left of her now.

Simon didn't knock on my door when he came up to tell me about Grandmother Judith; he simply opened it. I was just getting dressed, which brought a smile to his face. He had caught me in my bra and panties. I pressed my skirt against myself to shield me. Before I could complain, he made his announcement about Grandmother Judith. I listened and then, probably to show him that he couldn't intimidate me, continued to dress as if he wasn't there. I didn't say a word, didn't acknowledge he had said a thing. Despite what he had told me, I still wanted to treat him as if he was invisible.

"Your ignoring me is a mistake. You should realize by now that I'm your best friend here," he said. He came the closest I'd heard him get to whining, which for Simon would be practically a sin.

I paused and looked at him.

"Best friend? You wanted to rape me, pretending you were doing something scientific or whatever Dr. Kirkwell calls it, and now you want me to think of you as my best friend?"

"Well, it wasn't exactly that. I wasn't going to rape you."

"You made me undress in front of you. You told me that stupid lie about your wanting to become a specialist doctor for women."

"It wasn't totally a lie. It's still a possibility."

"Please. Spare me, Simon."

"You'll never forget me. Whenever you do have a boyfriend, you'll think of me. Imprint," he said, pointing to his temple. "Anything you do with any other boy will trigger the memory of what you did with me."

"You mean what you did to me, not what I did with you."

He laughed. "Same thing in the end, the memory end."

"How can you sound so proud of it? I don't think you ever feel bad about anything you do, do you, Simon?"

"What?"

"Now I know why I pity you."

His smile faded. "You pity me? I'm not a prisoner of Sutherland," he said, and then smiled again. "You have a great deal to learn about yourself and this family, and if you were smart, you'd realize I could help you. Be mature about it, and we'll become friends."

"Mature? Besides, now you want me to believe that you really want to be friends?"

He shrugged. "I have no problem with it."

I sensed vulnerability. There was something desperate in the way he spoke. There weren't many opportunities for me to take advantage of anyone, let alone Simon, the family genius.

"If you want me to trust you as I would a friend, then you have to be more truthful," I said, folding my arms and glaring at him.

"About what? I told you everything."

"Not everything. What did Grandfather really know was going on in that horrid bedroom? I'm not stupid," I quickly followed, taking a step toward him. "I can sense things about him, too, sense what he's thinking and feeling when he looks at me and talks to me, especially if you're anywhere nearby at the time. We haven't had a private conversation about any of it yet, but I can still tell he didn't know exact details, and I don't think he knew what you did.

"I never stopped thinking that he has no idea how cruel aversion therapy is, even though Mrs. Lawson made it a point to tell me that was exactly why he hired and paid so much to Dr. Kirkwell, an expert. People who are supposed to love each other, share the same blood like parents and their children, can be angry with each other, even say terrible things to each other, but eventually those happier memories return. Did I imagine the sign of love in Grandfather's eyes when I was a little girl, a sign he couldn't stop me from seeing because it had its birth in his heart? It's time I heard the very truth, Simon. No sense lying," I quickly warned.

There was that wry smile. "Okay. Truth. The only reason I told you that he knew about my helping Dr. Kirkwell and taking you to see the urn was so you wouldn't mention it to him. I would get into trouble about the urn especially."

"So, he didn't know exactly what went on in that horrid bedroom?"

"Probably not in the detail you're suggesting, although I wouldn't swear to anything. He never shared anything about the treatment you were undergoing. I figured out most of it myself, researched it.

"I'm sorry about trying to deceive you," he said. "Truthfully, I didn't think much of what Dr. Kirkwell was doing. It's another form of voodoo. Don't ever tell anyone I said it," he whispered, "but Grandfather can be exploited, too, if he's not careful."

His confession and apology surprised me, and his honest feelings about what had been done definitely made it more difficult to dislike him.

I relaxed and sat to put on my shoes as I envisioned Grandmother Judith. My best memories of her were from when I was a little girl, maybe five years old. I always thought she was a pretty woman who seemed particularly proud of her looks, especially her button nose. I couldn't recall her not being dressed perfectly, with her hair styled and her makeup looking like it had been done by a cosmetician for movie stars. My mother took after her when it came to her appearance.

As if making an excuse for it, she once told me that she thought she had to dress perfectly and look like a model because she couldn't remember her mother not appearing so. "It just seemed that was how women should be. My mother was more of an example for me than a mother," she added, which took me a while to understand. From everything my mother had told me about her youth, it became clearer to me that Mrs. Lawson performed Grandmother Judith's daily motherly duties, whether she was specifically assigned to do them or not.

Her brother, my uncle Martin, didn't need a guardian. He lived in Grandfather Sutherland's shadow, mimicking everything he did or said, and from what my mother had told me, he rarely came to Grandmother's—his own mother's—defense when Grandfather criticized her or denied her something.

Grandmother Judith did have a warm smile for me all the time, but she had a habit of looking at Grandfather Sutherland first or right after, as if she wanted to be sure it was all right. He did control who loved whom in this house and how they did it. According to my mother, Grandmother Judith busied herself with social and charitable events, almost as if she was searching for ways to avoid Grandfather. Despite her not coming to my rescue when I was locked away, I couldn't help but feel sorry for and about her. I think my mother did, too, even though she was angry at her for not taking her side against Grandfather Sutherland's more as well.

"It's sad about Grandmother Judith. They were married a long time. Is Grandfather sad?" I asked Simon.

"Hardly."

"What?"

"You heard Grandfather say often that he thinks sadness is weakness. You don't get sad; you get mad."

"That's silly. You have to be sad when someone you love dies. If you don't have love, it doesn't matter how wealthy you are."

Simon laughed as if I had said something childish. "I don't think Grandfather ever loved Grandmother in the romantic sense you mean. He saw her as something that completed Sutherland."

"Saw her as *something*? *Something*?"

"Exactly. She fit his image of what the mistress of Sutherland should be, much better than his own mother did. He thought Great-grandmother Abigail was too casual about how she dressed. Great-grandfather didn't like many of her friends, and neither did Grandfather. They weren't rich or important enough. She didn't appreciate what it meant to be a Sutherland."

"You mean she wasn't arrogant enough, not enough of a snob."

"I'm just telling you what I know."

"Really? How do you know any of this? You weren't even born."

"You'll see. Maybe."

I grimaced in doubt, but it didn't stop him.

"To make sure Grandmother Judith was okay, Grandfather checked off a list before he asked her to marry him."

"Where are you coming up with these ideas? Who told you that?"

"You'll see."

"Stop saying that."

He shrugged.

"What list, anyway? What was on it?" I asked. I couldn't help but be curious. What did he really know?

"Her family background and status, her looks, her education, and her opinions, not that he really ever let her have any. He liked that his father was jealous of how perfectly Grandmother Judith fit, while his own wife, Abigail, was unfit to be the mistress of Sutherland in comparison. She didn't have the same values, especially when it came to how she presented herself at social events. He called his mother giddy and silly, even labeled her embarrassing at times.

"My father says that our great-grandfather and grandfather were very competitive about everything, even wives. Great-grandfather competed for Grandmother's attention right in front of Great-grandmother Abigail. He'd compliment her and not compliment his own wife. At Sutherland balls, he'd dance with Grandmother Judith and leave Great-grandmother Abigail standing on the sidelines."

"So our great-grandfather didn't love his own wife, either, or care about her feelings?"

"Her feelings? Remember, our great-grandfather Raymond Sutherland had an illegitimate child with a Black maid in this very house, practically right under our great-grandmother's nose. You don't do something like that to your wife if you love her. I told you about Prissy living in the room they locked you in. They gave you her old clothes."

"The girl who aged into an old woman quickly."

"She suffered from progeria. I think I gave you a pretty good description."

"I hate to think about it. Oh," I said, shaking myself as if ice water had dripped down my back. For months, I did wear her clothes.

Simon nodded. "Truth is, I don't think anyone ever loved anyone in this house when Great-grandfather was in charge. I heard my father once say that to my mother—admit it, I mean. That's the world our grandfather grew up in and was supposed to model his own life on."

"A world without love?"

"Loyalty and success were more important to the Sutherlands and always were to Grandfather. They still are and always will be."

"Then I don't pity you as much as I pity him."

"Don't ever let him think that," he warned, his eyes actually wide with fear, maybe because he thought I'd mention what he had said.

"You don't know him as well as I do. You could stumble right back into that locked room."

"You don't think he would do that again now, do you?"

"We can't be sure that he wouldn't. I don't think either of us has yet heard a word of regret about what was done to you, whether he knew all the details or not, right? Remember, Mrs. Lawson has his ear. I'm beginning to think she whispers into it even when he's asleep. She's very protective. No one dares criticize Grandfather within a mile of her. It's almost like she's waiting for you to screw up."

I could see he was enjoying frightening me.

"You make it sound like the floors of the mansion are really thin ice."

"They are, which is why what you have to do, Caroline, is consider me as more of a guide than anything else and follow my directions."

"Guide? Guiding what? I was just joking about the floor."

"Guiding you through this family, especially saying and doing the right things. You're just settling in. You've been here with your parents, but you haven't even seen this entire mansion. You don't know the secret places where the bodies are buried."

"Bodies?"

"Do you want my help or not?"

"Is there another quid pro quo?"

"As I said, I'm just trying to be a friend."

I studied him for a moment. He did look sincere. Did I want him for a friend now? Why was it so important to him?

"You don't have any friends, do you? I mean, you don't attend classes in school. Where would you meet someone, Simon?"

He simply stared at me. As Daddy would say, I had hit a raw nerve.

I rose. "I'm going downstairs. We should be thinking only about Grandmother Judith right now. And you were sent up to get me, weren't you?"

He followed me out and to the top of the stairway. The dark brown carpeted steps and thick mahogany banister wound down like a curling snake. Even the large wooden balls sitting atop the end of the railings below looked like raised snake heads. So much of this mansion seemed threatening, looming above and around me to remind me I was in the Sutherland world. Corridors echoed your footsteps. The house marked you, followed you. It still felt like it creeped up on me whenever I stopped to think about the family's past, the walls narrowing, the lights dimming, and the floor undulating under my feet. Because of how carefully Daddy would go up and down the eighteen steps at our house, I was always careful when I descended these thirty-two. How did you make a mansion fortified with angry ancestral spirits feel like a home, or at least feel safe?

Before I could take my first step, Simon seized my elbow. I turned to him.

"What?"

"You don't have any friends, either, Caroline. We're more alike than you think."

"There's a big difference between us, Simon."

"You're female and I'm male?" he joked.

"No. A lot more than that."

"What, then?"

"I want to go home. I'll always want to go home," I said, and continued downstairs.

CHAPTER ONE

The day after I was permitted to leave the bleak bedroom, Grandfather sent Mrs. Lawson out with me to buy new clothes. I had been told that everything I had owned before I was brought here, even things like dolls, books, and games, had been given to charities. Anyone would think that my grandfather had wanted to erase my previous existence just as he wanted to erase the memory of his daughter, my mother. Mrs. Lawson had told me that I would be reborn. She said that it was the only way Grandfather would accept me back as a Sutherland. It had nothing to do with Grandfather's spiritual beliefs. Mommy had told me that he believed religion was a refuge for failures. He didn't abide by church teachings. Nothing I had been doing or anything my mother had done was a sin to him, unless you could call defying him or damaging the Sutherland reputation evil.

I would almost have been happier if Mrs. Lawson had bought me nothing when she took me shopping. Practically everything fashionable for a girl my age, everything on display at the best department stores, was unacceptable to her. She bought me what she could stomach and then took me to one of her favorite thrift shops to find me the rest of my wardrobe. Some of the clothes and shoes were easily a decade old. When I protested, she warned me the way she warned me about anything, warned me the way Simon just had implied things were: "Do what I say, or I'll tell your grandfather you haven't changed a bit, and he'll put you right back in that bedroom." I couldn't even look down the dark hallway, where, at the end of it, the double doors hovered in my mind like some cloud full of thunder and lightning. I was still waking up at night when one slammed shut in a dream.

Emerson, my grandfather's driver and my mother's favorite person working at Sutherland, drove us about and kept quiet even though I knew he could clearly see my unhappiness. He helped bring everything up to my room, and when Mrs. Lawson was not nearby, he said, "Think of all this as temporary, Caroline. Once you are out of here and away from one of the witches from *Macbeth*, you'll blossom as you should. Cheers."

I hadn't read *Macbeth*, but I wasn't surprised to hear him refer to Shakespeare. Emerson was a tall, thin man who had been born in East Sussex, England. He was always immaculately dressed in his uniform and cap. He had a trimmed mustache, as gray as his full head of hair, and dark blue eyes. His face was lean, with sharp creases in his forehead. Ordinarily, he kept his thick lower lip over his upper lip so that it looked like he had only one. My mother had told me that while she was growing up at Sutherland, she spent more time talking to him than she did with any of the other servants, save the cook, Mrs. Wilson. She told me she would sit and watch him wash and polish the limousine, vacuuming the inside immaculately. He was so intense about it that he would pick up something with tweezers. While he worked, he told her about his life in England and how he had wanted to be a race car driver when he was younger. He often sang old English songs to her and read to her from books of poetry and loved quoting lines from Shakespeare's plays.

But even before everything terrible had happened, my mother warned me to be careful about what I said or told to him because he was very loyal to Grandfather. The truth was that I wished I could see whatever Emerson saw in Grandfather that made him willing to be so devoted to him and stay so long as his chauffeur. Mommy thought no one spent more time alone with Grandfather, not even his CEO, Franklin Butler, and certainly not Grandmother Judith.

Now Simon and I were headed to the discussion of her funeral. I walked slowly, dreading the thought of returning to that family cemetery and looking at what I knew was my mother's false grave. How could I stand there and not reveal that I knew the terrible truth, something only a few really knew?

Simon stepped ahead of me.

"We're going to the—"

"I know where we're going," I said. "It wasn't that long ago when we were all gathered in the Sutherland Room to discuss my mother."

He nodded and walked a few steps ahead of me. The doors were opened on the grand living room, with its large fieldstone fireplace and gray area rug over the slate floor. There was something special about it, royal, because it was where Grandfather either spent his relaxing time alone or demanded everyone's presence for some grand announcement. As soon as I stepped in, my memory of being summoned here for the announcements about my mother's funeral brought a rush of blood to my face. Everyone would surely think that the tears floating in my eyes were for Grandmother Judith, when they were really still for my mother.

Once again, I looked up at the family portraits and the family crest, which featured three stars. It was the symbol of Grandfather's company, Sutherland Enterprises. Ancestors seemed to come to life, looming above us with their familial authority. As a little girl, I recalled believing that their eyes moved along with us. Surprisingly, this time the gray window drapes were opened wide, the sunlight casting a glow around Grandfather Sutherland, who sat in his heavy-cushioned ruby-red chair that matched the semicircular sofa.

Everyone always had their assigned seat on that sofa. The last time there was a family gathering, for Grandfather's decisions about my mother's funeral, Grandmother Judith was sitting on his far right with her feet on the ottoman. A nurse had been attending to her because she had collapsed when she had heard the news of my mother's death. I remembered how exhausted she was from her sorrow. No one dared take her seat today. All glanced at it as if Death sat among us. For some reason, as frightening as it was to imagine him dark and ugly, I always saw a gleeful smile, too.

Uncle Martin looked the saddest of all in the family. He had his head bowed and clutched his hands as though there was still a possibility Grandfather Sutherland could declare Grandmother Judith alive. He was squeezing so hard that his fingers reddened. From the little I could see of his eyes, he had apparently been crying. Aunt Holly sat with her hands in her lap, looking down as well. Mrs. Lawson, appearing more impatient than somber, stood to the right of them, scowling. Did she approve of anything anyone else but Grandfather did in this house?

Emerson stood just behind her, looking, as my mother would say, like a guard at Buckingham Palace. Often he was the first person seen whenever any visitor came through the main gate. Emerson was always in uniform. Mrs. Wilson, the cook who had been hired when my mother was three, stood beside him. She was the only one dabbing away the tears in her eyes. I saw her risk a small smile when she glanced at me.

Franklin Butler was to Grandfather's right, his hands behind his back, staring ahead but not looking at anyone in particular. No one was apparently more important to Grandfather than this tall, stout man with a full head of completely white hair that contrasted sharply with his olive complexion. He had thin lips, a sharp nose, and high cheekbones. I had never looked at him carefully or with great interest but somehow noticed now that he had unusual brown eyes, closer to rust.

Even though he hadn't been unpleasant to her, my mother hadn't been very fond of him. She called him Grandfather's hit man because he carried out Grandfather's orders without delay, no matter who would suffer losses in their business or the loss of a career. He was an attorney to whom Grandfather had promised to someday award a judgeship.

This morning, Grandfather looked slightly pale, his freckles faded and the lines in his face chiseled deeper. He never sat with slumped shoulders, especially when he faced the family, but he did now. He had placed his mahogany walking stick beside him against the chair. His velvety blue eyes looked a little watery. Could he be very sad after all? Why should I believe what Simon had told me? How could he know so much and be so certain about Grandfather's feelings? What did he really know about this family's history?

"Take your seats," Mrs. Lawson whispered to us loudly enough for everyone to hear.

Simon glared back at her but sat quickly when I did.

Grandfather Sutherland stared at us so hard that my heart started to pound. Was he angry at me already? What had I done wrong? Did he think I wasn't dressed properly for the meeting in the grand room? *That's not my fault*, I wanted to say. *Mrs. Lawson bought my clothes.* Before he spoke, he stroked his thick silvery-gold mustache, something I remembered he often did when he made a major announcement.

"Your grandmother and I discussed the arrangements for her funeral," he began. Why was he was talking only to Simon and me? After a beat of silence, he looked at everyone else. "She was always worried about social gatherings, and for what it's worth, she saw her funeral as simply another."

He paused to pick up some papers and put on his dark brown reading glasses. They tottered on the bridge of his nose until he tucked the handles in behind his ears abruptly. I knew enough about Grandfather Sutherland to know he abhorred anything that made him appear old, something I knew Grandmother Judith had spent most of her days fighting, maybe because she didn't want to appear older to him. However, I really thought Grandfather was more concerned about any of us appearing in any way weaker. That was all he seemed to talk about. In fact, I remembered him saying recently that age wasn't an excuse for anything but death: "If you still have your wits, your mistakes carry your byline." Almost immediately, I thought of my father agreeing.

"These are her instructions. I don't approve of everything, but . . . they're hers, and I promised to carry them out. A Sutherland promise is as good as a constitutional amendment," he said in a louder voice as if he could hear someone questioning it in their thoughts. "All of you remember that before you ever make one."

He looked especially hard at Uncle Martin, whose face turned the color of a raspberry. When did a son stop being a little boy to his father, especially a father like Grandfather Sutherland, who demanded so much and expected so much from his family? I wondered. Would he ever?

My mother once said that if her brother defied their father, "at least once, he'd respect him more." My father disagreed. "You don't win respect with defiance, disobedience. You win it with accomplishment."

There was another long pause, and then abruptly, Grandfather raised his right arm with the papers clutched in his hand. Franklin Butler practically leaped forward to take them, putting on his own reading glasses.

"The funeral ceremony will begin at nine a.m. this Thursday at St. Michael's Episcopal Church. Reverend Joseph Vance officiating," he began.

"Didn't he retire?" Uncle Martin asked. When he grimaced, his cheeks bubbled.

"Mrs. Sutherland wished him to conduct the ceremony, and he's agreed," Franklin Butler said.

"I keep that church afloat," Grandfather practically grunted. "They'll do what we want. What's the difference to you anyway, Martin? You hardly go to church and went only to please your mother."

Aunt Holly looked like she was going to speak, perhaps to defend him, but then pressed her lips together tightly. She was keeping her light brown hair longer, probably because Grandfather Sutherland had said something critical about her keeping it so short. According to my mother, Aunt Holly was more gleeful and happy as a young woman, but when she and my uncle Martin lost their baby girl, Annabelle, at three months to sudden infant death syndrome, she became an entirely different person, meek and soft-spoken. She always looked thin and vulnerable to me. My mother told me Uncle Martin and Aunt Holly's infant's death rocked their marriage badly, too. She once told my father that they remained together only because Grandfather Sutherland wanted it that way. "Sutherlands don't divorce; they destroy," she said.

"Nothing, no difference," Uncle Martin muttered. "I just—"

"Just listen to your mother's instructions," Grandfather snapped, and Uncle Martin seemed to shrink back so much that his jacket and shirt looked a size or two too big for him, and he was stout but soft, with shoulders my father said were too small for a man of his size.

My father had the same disdain that Grandfather had for his own son. Daddy said he reminded him of putty. He told my mother that if he had two weeks with him, he'd turn him into a man.

"Following the burial at the family cemetery," Franklin continued, "we will return here, where the funeral reception will be held. Mrs. Lawson is in charge of all the arrangements: flowers, food, and the harpsichordist Vanesa Hume, Mrs. Sutherland's favorite, whom you might recall because she's been here a few times. The reception will be over sharply at three. At his discretion, Mr. Sutherland will discuss the disposal of Mrs. Sutherland's possessions. There is no will or any other document that will impact your lives. Mr. Sutherland has already chosen her clothes for her interment.

"The memorial cards will be arriving at the church and here for those who don't attend the church service. Mrs. Sutherland designed them herself, the colors, the eucalyptus borders, and chose the picture of herself.

"I will handle any press inquiries. Mrs. Sutherland approved of the obituary I was honored to write. Copies of that will be available at the reception as well."

"When did she ask you to write her obituary?" Uncle Martin asked. He looked and sounded upset that he wasn't asked to do it.

"Three days ago."

"I encouraged her to do it," Grandfather said. "What does the timeline for that have to do with anything?"

"I just—"

"Any more unnecessary questions?" Grandfather asked.

On the tip of my tongue was the biggest question of all: Wouldn't it be nice if we buried my mother's ashes in her grave the same day?

Of course I didn't ask it, but as if he could read my thoughts, Grandfather Sutherland nodded at me as a way of signaling Franklin Butler.

"Dr. Kirkwell will not return for your tutoring, Caroline, until the day after the funeral," Franklin Butler said, suddenly turning everyone's attention to me. "However, she left some instructions and work for you to do in the interim," he added.

Interim, I thought. *We're mourning my grandmother's death. How can that be called an interim?* It sounded so cold, indifferent, something to tolerate and get over. Grandfather was still staring hard at me, challenging me even to appear upset. I looked down. I couldn't imagine how my mother ever outstared him.

"Are any of her friends speaking for her at her funeral, in church or at the ceremony?" Aunt Holly asked.

Uncle Martin looked at her and then quickly and fearfully at his father.

"She didn't ask for anyone in particular, and no one has come forward, Holly," Grandfather said. "Most of her so-called close friends can't put a sentence together. Why? Do you want to speak?" His eyes sparkled. He enjoyed putting the question to her.

Her face flushed almost as red as Uncle Martin's. "Oh, no," she said. "I couldn't without . . . oh, no."

"Before you ask, I informed her older sister, Irene. It was your mother-in-law's wish, otherwise I wouldn't have done it. As you know, she ran off with the family's chauffeur and was three months pregnant at the time. I don't expect her to show her face, even for this. I'd put my foot down when it came to her and her husband staying here, as well as either of their children, before she could even consider it."

"Did Irene stay in touch with Mom?" Holly asked as if she had just become a member of this family.

"If she did, I certainly wasn't told, nor did I care to inquire."

Aunt Holly looked at me. I knew what she was wondering: Had my mother kept in touch with her disowned aunt? I really didn't know, and I didn't remember her even mentioning an aunt Irene. Aunt Holly could see it in my face.

Then I glanced at Simon, who didn't change expression, but in his eyes, I could see he was smiling. I really might need his help to understand and live with my family.

"Franklin and I have some things to do now," Grandfather said. "Business that can't wait." He used his walking stick to rise to his feet. "We've had our breakfast. Mrs. Lawson, come to my office in two hours to finalize details for the wake."

"Yes, Mr. Sutherland."

"Mrs. Wilson has prepared breakfast for you," he said, looking more at me than anyone else. "Just go to the breakfast nook. Clara Jean is waiting to serve it just like any other morning," Grandfather said, and walked out with Franklin Butler. No one got up until he was gone. Mrs. Wilson and Emerson left quickly after them, and then Aunt Holly rose.

"You can go have breakfast with Simon and Caroline, Martin. I'm not very hungry. I'm going to sit out in your mother's garden for a while."

She started out before Uncle Martin could respond.

"I'm hungry," Simon said. He looked at me. "It's warm enough to eat on the patio. No sense staying cooped up in here on such a warm spring day."

"It's not a time to play any games on the lawn or courts," Mrs. Lawson warned him, and fixed her eyes on me.

"I don't play games," Simon replied. "Nor do I need you to tell me what and what not to do on this occasion or any other."

She gave us both a mean look and left.

"I have some things to do that can't be delayed," Uncle Martin said. He looked stunned and confused. "I'll return in a few hours. Try to behave yourself," he told Simon, but looked away quickly and left.

I had always thought Simon's parents were afraid of him. It was almost like they weren't sure he was theirs. But I couldn't stop thinking about something else.

"I don't remember anything about a great-aunt Irene running off with the chauffeur," I said. "Why was that such a tragedy even if she was pregnant? They married, right?"

"It happened close to forty years ago, not that it would matter when to Great-grandfather or Grandfather. Let's just say people were a bit more intolerant and leave it at that. I'm warning you. Don't bring it up again in front of Grandfather."

"But my mother never said anything about her and—"

"Who knows what your mother knew? My father is certainly afraid to mention her. Everyone obviously is, as you can see. The halls of Sutherland are full of land mines."

"You're right," I said. "There is a lot to learn about this family."

Simon smiled. "Exactly. I'll tutor you when it comes to that education. Let's eat," he said. "Clara Jean will serve us outside."

He started for the door and stopped.

"Don't you want breakfast?"

"It doesn't seem right. It's almost like nothing happened. Grandmother just died, but Grandfather's going back to work. Even your father is doing something with the business, I bet."

"Yeah, well, life goes on, especially at Sutherland. Get used to it. Tell you what. I'll do all the homework Dr. Kirkwell left for you. Probably in less than an hour for me. And no quid pro quo," he quickly added.

"Then what?"

"We'll start the tour. I have some special things to show you in the basement."

"I don't know. I mean . . . exploring the mansion seems not the right thing to do right now."

What I really meant was I didn't trust him.

"Why not? What else would you want to do?"

"I don't know. I just . . ."

"Well, let's have some breakfast, and then you'll be able to think more clearly."

I followed him slowly. He told Clara Jean we were going to the patio, which had two tables, each with six chairs, and an awning that shaded it from the morning sun. When I stepped out, I saw that Aunt Holly was sitting on a bench in Grandmother Judith's garden. Apparently, Grandfather Sutherland had given her permission to design it and choose the plants and flowers early in their marriage. It had two fountains, both with tiered pots on a stack of field-stones.

I didn't stop to sit at the table Simon had chosen. I continued to walk toward the garden instead. I remembered my mother enjoyed it and took me to it most of the times we came to Sutherland. However, I couldn't remember my grandmother enjoying it with us more than twice. She was always busy with something. Mommy said her mother was the only person she knew who had devoted her life to ignoring it, whatever that meant.

"Hey, where you going?" Simon called after me. I ignored him.

He caught up with me and seized my right elbow. I turned sharply on him.

"I'm just going to talk to your mother, Simon. Get your breakfast. I'm not as hungry as you."

His eyes narrowed. "Don't tell her that I overheard anything between her and my father and then told you," he warned. "You'd be sorry if you did."

I pulled my arm from his grip.

"Take it easy," Simon continued. "I only mean I won't be able to find things out for you. No one else is going to tell you anything, especially Mrs. Lawson."

"You're not the only one with brains. I'm not stupid," I said, and walked on.

Aunt Holly didn't know I was there until I sat beside her on the bench.

"Oh, Caroline," she said, wiping the tears off her cheeks. "So much new grief so soon."

"Yes. I was hoping to spend more time with my grandmother."

"I'm sure after things settled down, she would have liked that."

"Why?"

"Why what, honey?"

"Why are you so sure?"

"Oh. Well, I think she reached a point where she would have defied anyone. She didn't have the strength, perhaps, but she had the will."

She looked straight into the garden and not at me.

"I'm sorry I didn't do more to help you, not that I have that much influence here or ever have. I was very fond of your mother. She was actually my best friend in so many ways. I also felt sorry about your grandmother, sorrier than her own son felt," she said, turning back to me with a flash of anger in her eyes. "Very often, especially in the earlier days, whenever I came here with Martin, I would spend my time with Judith. We were more like sisters comforting each other."

She smiled.

"I don't know which one of us had more complaints that we were afraid to voice to anyone else. For a long time, I blamed my weakness on the loss of my child, but I should have gotten stronger. Your grandfather is a force few can reckon with, especially not his son."

She looked back at Simon, who had just been given a glass of orange juice.

"It seems I'm failing everyone now." She looked at me again. "I'm hoping you'll be stronger as you get older. Or maybe you will live with your father and escape Sutherland."

"I don't think that even if I lived with him and his new family in

Hawaii, I would escape Sutherland," I said. From what well of knowledge I drew that, I couldn't say. It just felt like something my mother would say, because she had never truly escaped, either.

Aunt Holly smiled and stroked my hair.

"Maybe you'll surprise us all and be the strongest. My husband and, unfortunately, my son are servants. Both cherish my father-in-law's favor."

She looked back at Simon again.

"Be careful with Simon. He's grown into almost a stranger. I know he's brilliant, but most of the time, I wish he was just an average teenager. I think it was a mistake to let him become part of that Advanced Placement program. Young people need the company of other young people. Good grades and being ambitious are important, very important, but socializing is just as important. I missed out on it and grew up almost as isolated as Martin did, which was what attracted us to each other. I thought he'd get stronger after we married and had our own home."

She smiled.

"Actually, I thought your grandfather would get weaker with time and Martin would develop his self-confidence and his own self-image. Perhaps it's not too late. I guess we just have to wait and see," she said. "After the funeral, I'm going to try to be here more often for you. Maybe you'll be the daughter I lost. Would you like that?"

If I said yes, I felt I would be betraying my mother, but I could sense Aunt Holly might need me more than I'd need her.

I nodded.

She put her arm around my shoulders and kissed me on the forehead just the way Mommy would.

"The women have to stick together in this family," she said, and smiled.

"I'd like to know more about Great-aunt Irene," I said. "I never even heard her name mentioned."

She sighed. "In time. Too much about this family at once could smother you," she said.

We sat silently.

"Hey," we heard Simon say. He had gotten up and drawn closer to us. "Mrs. Wilson made a great breakfast. Everyone needs to eat something, right, Mother?" he asked. He sounded just like Grandfather Sutherland, enough like him to make Aunt Holly turn and nod.

"Yes, Simon's right. We don't want to get weak just when we need strength the most."

"Well, it's not the most, but it's important enough," Simon said, then turned and headed back toward the patio, satisfied he had made his point.

Aunt Holly rose, and I followed. She held my hand.

"Like I said, be careful with Simon," she said, and we started for the patio.

I almost stopped her to tell her what he had already done to me, but that would have revealed everything.

And Simon was right.

Once I told her, I might well be locked up in that horrible bedroom again.

CHAPTER TWO

I told Simon that I didn't need his help to do Dr. Kirkwell's work assignments, but he kept insisting he could do my work in minutes. I thought he just wanted to show off, and I was getting tired of it.

"If I don't do it and she questions me about it, I'll be in trouble not remembering what I supposedly had done," I told him firmly.

I walked away before he could respond, but he followed me to the study next to Grandfather Sutherland's office. I was tempted to let him do the assignment. I really didn't want to do any homework. I wanted to mourn Grandmother Judith's passing, maybe return to the garden where Aunt Holly had sat and think about my grandmother. I was sure my mother would want me to do that, but everyone else in this house was going on with his or her work as if nothing had happened. Immediately after a little breakfast, Aunt Holly had decided to go home and asked Emerson to take her. Uncle Martin still hadn't returned from wherever he had to go, and Grandfather hadn't come out of his office.

Except for the sound of vacuum cleaners and the footsteps of maids here and there, the enormous house echoed with deep silence. It expanded the emptiness hollowed out in my heart. I wanted to cry but somehow couldn't find the tears. It had been so long since I heard my grandmother speak, especially to me. How would I mourn her, someone I really didn't know? She never came to visit us, even when we were the Robot Family. She couldn't even sneak over, because Daddy would surely mention it to Grandfather. Because of Grandfather's attitude about birthdays, she never attended one of mine, and if I received any gifts from her, they seemed to come directly from a store with a generic card printed "Grandmother J." I suspected Mrs. Lawson was asked to do it and did so reluctantly. However, the more I learned about her and her life with Grandfather, the less I blamed her. She was still my grandmother.

Maybe all the sorrow will come later at night, the garden in which sadness grows so much more easily, I thought. When you're alone, your feelings have a better opportunity to overwhelm you. Very little is competing for your attention. That was surely true for me in the horrid bedroom for months where I spent almost all day and night by myself. It made it all so much more difficult. Mrs. Lawson enjoyed grinding that into me: "You young people aren't afraid of anything as much as you are of solitude. Without your constant music and chatter on those mobile phones, you'd wither like dried-out flowers. That's why you'll gladly obey and try to be reborn."

She wasn't wrong about people my age especially, except maybe when it applied to someone like Simon, who seemed to prefer his own company above the company of others his age. I couldn't imagine him listening to popular music or even watching television. Ironically, I thought, he was another Prissy, aging faster and faster. Maybe he was realizing it, and that was why he suddenly wanted me to like him, but I wouldn't let myself feel sorry for him. At least, I hoped I wouldn't.

Instinctively, I knew he might somehow take advantage of it. Really, how sad was that? Maybe nobody trusted him if his own mother didn't.

This was a mansion and a family where love could come from a spigot in drips and drabs. Like a beggar in a gutter, you held out your palms and hoped for a sign of affection or a kind word. It had been true for my mother and grandmother. It seemed to be true for my uncle and aunt as well. Why would it be any different for me? Where would I go unless my father decided he would give me another chance and invite me to his new home in Hawaii?

When I sat at the table and opened the math workbook, Simon stood behind me, looking over my shoulder, watching.

"You're making me nervous," I said.

"What did you and my mother talk about?" he asked. "You were talking quite a while before I interrupted."

"Grandmother Judith. Maybe you didn't notice, but your mother is quite upset. I don't know why your father didn't stay with her. He's the one who should have been in that garden with her."

He was quiet. I started working on the math problems.

"My parents hardly do anything together anymore," he suddenly said. "I hate eating dinner with them. It's like eating in a morgue sometimes. It's why I like spending more of my time here. They'll never stop feeling guilty about my sister."

"Well, what do you do to help them?"

"I've given them a lot to brag about."

"Oh boy. How generous," I said. I put my hands in my lap and turned to him. "Did you even cry about it?"

"Cry? What good would that have done?"

"Showed you cared and you felt sorry for them as well as your little sister. It's called compassion and sorrow. Didn't you read that in any of your textbooks?"

"Very funny."

I turned back to the work. "You're making me nervous. Why don't you go do what you do?" I said, but I couldn't really concentrate and stared at the same problem for minutes, thinking about the things Aunt Holly had said.

Finally, he took the pen out of my hand. "Just watch. You'll learn that way, too," he said. It was impossible to understand any of what he did. He zoomed through the answers as if they were already there and he had only to trace them.

"I can't keep up with you."

"When you have time, you can reread them."

He closed the math workbook and opened the English grammar one. With the same lightning speed, he finished the pages that Dr. Kirkwell had assigned.

"She knows I'm not that perfect with grammar."

"Don't worry. I deliberately chose the wrong answer twice."

He looked at the history assignment.

"Just pages to read. Do it to help put yourself to sleep tonight."

I watched him work the science assignment and questions. He closed the book.

"There. What would have taken you two days, I'm sure. Now you have no excuse."

"For what?"

"Like I said. We'll explore the mansion. First, we'll go down to the basement. There are things to show you, things you'll want to learn about the family history. You'll know what's right to say and what's not and why not. I had to teach it all to myself, make my own discoveries, but I think I did that pretty well."

"Do you ever stop patting yourself on the back?"

He smiled. "Well, my hope is you'll take over for me and do most of the patting."

"Oh, you do, do you? You're miles beyond help. I'm not sure you should take a chance and turn your back on me, either."

He laughed, and then we heard Grandfather's office door open and close. Neither of us moved or spoke.

"It's Lawson," he whispered. "I know her footsteps. She's coming here."

"So?"

"You never know what she'll make up about us."

He pressed himself to the wall by the door.

She opened it and looked in at me and around the room.

"Where's Simon?" she asked.

"How would I know? He doesn't tell me what he does. I don't even know if he's still here."

I saw Simon smile, but I quickly looked down so she wouldn't sense him standing there behind the opened door.

"Just don't get in anyone's way today," she said.

She closed the door.

"That was pretty good," he said. "Even I believed you. We make a good team."

"To do what?"

"Take over Sutherland. What else? C'mon. I'll even show you some of Grandmother's old things. You'll feel less guilty doing it."

He opened the door and peered out. When he looked back and gestured, I rose and joined him. Maybe he was right. Maybe I should know all I could about the family and about this place. Daddy still had not agreed to let me come visit, let alone take me back. Whether I liked it or not, Sutherland would be my home. I had better learn Grandfather's Ten Commandments. And I was eager to learn more about my great-grandparents and Grandmother Judith. Maybe there was even information about Great-aunt Irene.

I followed him down the corridor on the left to the basement door on our right.

"The basement is big, but it doesn't run under the whole house. Grandfather added on to the mansion but just had slabs under the new construction."

He opened the door and flipped a switch, illuminating the stairway, which seemed to disappear below as if it descended beneath the earth.

"Don't look so nervous about it. I spent a lot of time down there alone. I made it my private clubhouse. It would take us years to go through everything. You'll see."

He started down and then turned to me.

"Close the door," he said in a loud whisper when I stepped in and onto the top step. "Quickly."

At the bottom of the stairway, Simon flipped another switch, and the cavernous basement exploded in light. I started down reluctantly and stopped when I saw mice rush for places to hide.

"Mice," I said.

"They're as harmless as Mickey. You probably lived with a few when you were being treated by Dr. Kirkwell."

"Tortured, not treated."

He laughed, and I continued to the bottom. About halfway to the far wall, the floor was cracked with pitted cement that looked yellow and gray in places. The walls were concrete and the air was musty. I didn't see any windows. Already my lungs were complaining about dust and stale air. Spiderwebs hung from everywhere on the basement ceiling wall. They had an eerie design, as if each spider claimed a certain amount of inches and didn't invade the others'. Pipes running along the ceiling looked sweaty, and there was the hum of various equipment, some boxed in on the far right but something else groaning about midway.

"Ugh," I said. "Why would you want to come down here?"

"Like I told you: discoveries. I'm still making them. Come on," he said. "I have something very special to show you first."

"Why is there so much furniture down here, and from the looks of the dust on the sheets covering them, down here a long time?" I asked as I followed him.

"It's all Great-grandfather's furniture. After he died, Grandfather Sutherland replaced everything in the mansion except the portraits and some other paintings. One of these days, he'll sell everything to an antiques dealer and make a small fortune. That's how he thinks. It's all investments, even people."

"He likes to erase the memories of people," I said, "more than make money on them."

Simon paused to look back at me. "Exactly. If there's no evidence of them, there's no competition with their legacy. Lesson one: one of the worst things you can do is compliment Great-grandfather Sutherland for building the foundation of the Sutherland empire. All of Great-grandfather's plaques and awards are in that box over there," he said, pointing. "Grandfather doesn't like having them in his face. The less said about Great-grandfather, the more Grandfather likes it."

"Don't worry. I don't know enough about Sutherland Enterprises or him to compliment Great-grandfather."

"Grandfather hates anyone even suggesting he was born with a silver spoon in his mouth. If he says anything about his father, it will revolve around how he corrected and improved everything he did. According to him, he saved the Sutherland business. Great-grandfather was unable to adjust to more modern times. Grandfather says his father was mainly lucky."

"Was that true?"

Simon paused to think and then nodded. "Adjusting to more

modern times in business meant being more ruthless, getting there first. Grandfather loves to say, 'He who hesitates is lost.'"

He walked on, passing some black leather-bound trunks, all the same kinds of trunks with straps around them.

"What's in these?"

"I'll show you after I show you this," he said. "As I promised, a couple of them have Grandmother Judith's things as well as Great-grandmother Abigail's. Most of Grandmother Judith's are the things she had when she first married Grandfather. He eventually had her whole wardrobe replaced. My mother says he dressed her like a store mannequin at the start. Later she became very fashionable, as you might remember, and gradually replaced the wardrobe he liked with more expensive things. He was too embarrassed to cut off her credit. He tried to hold her to an allowance, but she enjoyed spending more. You'll read about it in the diaries that are stashed down here, how he would bellow at a new bill at dinner while she calmly ate and talked about this upcoming charity event or that. She wrote that if she spent an extraordinary amount, she would be sure to invite someone to dinner so he would have to swallow his complaints along with his food."

I looked back at the trunks. "I hope there are only clothes and diaries in them and not the remains of a servant or business associate," I muttered.

"Maybe there are. I haven't looked in all of them." He laughed. "Just wait. I'll satisfy your desire for the macabre."

"I'm not asking you to do that."

He walked on and then turned left past another stack of covered furniture. "I suppose I'm the one with the macabre taste. The basement is the most interesting place in Sutherland to me. It's another kind of family cemetery."

"I agree. You're mentally distorted."

He laughed and then stopped at the edge of the concrete floor.

There was a dirt floor and then a slab of additional concrete that looked about six feet long and a few feet wide. An inch or so of it was above the floor.

"There she is," he said.

"What? Who?"

"That's Prissy's grave."

For a few seconds, I didn't move, and then I approached slowly and looked at the slab.

"There's nothing written on it."

"Of course not."

"A grave, down here in the basement? Why?"

"Everything about her was kept secret, especially her birth and death. The fewer people who knew about her, the more our great-grandparents liked it."

I looked down at it again. A centipede came up at the right corner and started its slow journey across the slab. *The girl whose clothes I wore for months is under this?* I thought. *Why wouldn't they have put her in some cemetery?*

"I don't believe you. You're just trying to frighten me. There's probably some sort of equipment under there."

I stepped back.

"No, but there's nothing to be frightened about. It's a grave. There's no ghost. When I first discovered it, I was suspicious and didn't think it anything special. Then I noticed that something was buried on the other side of it."

He stepped around the slab. I followed, and he knelt and began to brush off the dirt until a metal box was visible. He smiled up at me and worked his fingers in on the sides of it until he could lift it out. He blew off the dirt and opened the box. I saw the papers.

"What is that?"

"Her death certificate," he said. "Signed by Dr. Samuel Mallen, who was the family doctor at the time. It describes the cause of her death. I imagine they wanted it just in case anyone accused them of murdering her or something."

He took the paper out and held it up so I could read it.

"See the date, June 12, 1959? Great-grandfather was twenty-five. He and Abigail were married two years. Grandfather Sutherland was born two years after. Abigail had two miscarriages prior. They didn't think she'd have any children. I'll show you Abigail's diary, too, where she moans and groans about it, cursing doctors. She had a lot of nasty words for Great-grandfather as well. Diaries are places where especially young, helpless women can be brave. It's in one of the trunks. I read the whole thing down here in one sitting."

He smiled and carefully reburied the metal box, spreading the dirt over it again.

"You'll like her diary. Great stuff. She suspected Great-grandfather fathered a few children and wasn't surprised he had gotten one of their maids pregnant with Prissy. She thought he was just trying to prove his manhood."

He looked up at me.

"Does that sound familiar?"

"What do you mean, familiar?" I asked.

He stood, sighed, and leaned his head back to show his impatience.

"Not everything is as clear to me as it is to you, Simon."

"You're right. But it's as simple as some of your math problems, Caroline. Pride. It explains what you and your mother went through, what really bothered Grandfather. How can a full-blooded man like Grandfather Sutherland have a gay daughter? No offense," he said quickly.

"That's—"

"Stupid, I know, but I'll never tell him, and it would be a small hurricane if you did. However, don't knock arrogance and pride so quickly. It makes it more difficult to lose, and Grandfather doesn't lose."

"Maybe you're talking about yourself, too."

He shrugged. "I could be accused of worse things than being consistently successful."

I looked at the cement slab and then at him, especially the way he was looking at me with his impish smile.

"How could they get away with this and get a doctor to sign those papers?"

"Everyone has a price, Caroline, and Grandfather Sutherland and his father could pay it. Besides, look at how many people work at and depend on Sutherland Enterprises. Grandfather has a majority interest in many businesses, just like our great-grandfather did. Both could hire and fire anyone, anytime, close a business down, determine to whom and when and where they sold. Both could ruin anyone's career, even a doctor's. Grandfather is even more powerful. He controls media, can spread fake news and distort what someone did or does. That's power. Kings didn't have as much power as our grandparents did and do."

"You are in awe of him."

He shrugged. "Better than worshipping rock stars or sports heroes. I can't hope to be either, but I can become as good as, if not better than, both Great-grandfather and Grandfather if I want."

The centipede stopped at the center of the slab as if it was claiming possession of it.

"I thought you wanted to be a doctor, even a surgeon. That's what you told me when you forced me to play your quid pro quo."

He looked away quickly.

"I feel sick," I said. "The smell down here is nauseating."

The air was even more stuffy this far in, and I could see many more spiders hanging on to their webs. Who knew what was crawling right around us, around and in between the old furniture and trunks?

"I don't want to breathe this air anymore, Simon." I looked at Prissy's grave. "I'm not sure I want to know any more about the Sutherlands anyway."

I turned to go back to the stairway.

"Wait. There's an outside basement door. It hasn't been used for decades, probably. It's old and rusted, but I think we can get it open."

"Why is it so important?"

"I told you. There's a lot to learn down here. I'm still learning, too. We're the grandchildren. We should know all we can. We'll get some fresh air into it."

"How come it never bothered you to stay so long down here?"

He had that arrogant smile again. "I have the power of concentration. When I focus on something, the world around me could be exploding and I wouldn't notice. It'll be fine. You'll see."

"We'd better go back upstairs. Mrs. Lawson will be looking for me. She practically breathes down my neck."

"She'll never come down here. Despite her tough act, she's afraid of creepy-crawlies. Besides, if anyone believes Prissy haunts this place, she does. She won't even open that basement door for fear that Prissy's spirit will come rushing up the stairs."

I looked around. He was right. There was so much down here. The history of Sutherland slept here like a family of vampires, never to see the light.

"C'mon. I'll show you some of Grandmother's old things and show you her diary. I'd be careful about taking it upstairs, though—about taking anything. It's better if Mrs. Lawson doesn't suspect we're sorting through these family secrets."

"Why should that matter to her? Why is she so concerned? She's not related to us, right?"

"I think Mrs. Lawson has been in love with Grandfather from the moment she walked into Sutherland. She's what you might call overprotective. And I have other suspicions about her, but let's not get ahead of ourselves—or ahead of you."

"Maybe I don't want to know anything about her."

"Of course you do," he said with that self-confidence that annoyed me. "You'd love to have something to hold over her. I would, too, but not for any specific reason other than I'm like Grandfather that way. I like the power to control people."

"Like you did me?"

"Sorta," he said, smiling.

He hurried down the corridor to a small stairway. I followed slowly. He went up and began to push and press on the metal doors. Dust fell all around him, but he wouldn't retreat.

I remained back a few feet.

"You're going to get sick or something," I said. "There could be all sorts of diseases."

That made him push harder. After a few more groans, he had one side opened slightly and took another step up, pushing the door until it fell back. Light and air rushed in as if it had been waiting to do so for decades.

"See?" he said, and opened the other side.

"I can't believe you stayed down here as long as you claim you did and never did that. For your own health, at least."

He shrugged. "You're a good influence."

He started down the steps, and I turned, and now that there was more light on this section of the basement, I saw it. It was lying next to one of the trunks as if someone had simply forgotten to put it in: the airplane my father had given me. I hurried to it.

"This was mine," I said as he approached.

"Yeah, this trunk looks new. Not that much dust caked on it."

He opened it, and we saw my things. I knelt and began sifting through them. Almost all of it was something my mother had given or bought me. There were even presents Nattie had bought me: blouses, a pair of pajamas, and some slippers.

"If you take any of that out and upstairs . . ."

"But why . . . why tell me they gave it all away? Mrs. Lawson said Grandfather wanted to get rid of everything and anything that had to do with my mother and especially Nattie."

He stared.

And then he said something I would probably never forget.

"Grandfather is obviously a lot more complex than even I thought. Maybe he even has a conscience."

"How could he have a conscience and then create an empty grave for my mother as well as hide her ashes in that urn?"

He stood there thinking.

"Well?"

"Maybe he's not exactly hiding it."

"I don't understand."

"I guess I have to qualify something I said. Maybe he did have deeper feelings for Grandmother Judith, and that's why he went through with the burial charade. Otherwise, he would have told her how it would be, and that would have been that. He's that way with most anything else. I was here having dinner when he first heard from your father about your mother. After he went off to call her, he came back to warn Grandmother Judith not to have anything to do with her. He told my father and mother the same thing, but maybe . . ."

"Maybe what?"

"Maybe he always wanted to be closer to your mother."

"But . . . all that he did to me . . ."

He nodded.

"Well?"

He smiled and then turned quickly serious again, with that older face I would someday call a "smug" face.

"We all have two personalities, I guess, one stronger than the other, but maybe not stronger all the time. Who knows, someday you might see that's true and even forgive Grandfather for the things he did but didn't want to do. There's an American poet who wrote, 'Do I contradict myself? Very well then, I contradict myself. I am large, I contain multitudes.'"

"Walt Whitman," I said. I would never forget overhearing Mommy tell Nattie his name when she used the same quote. Nattie was quite impressed with her.

"Wow. You do surprise me, Caroline."

"My mother was well educated, and so was Nattie. Sometimes you learn more by just listening to something else besides the sound of your own voice."

"Wow. You can snap the whip."

"Do you blame me? Do you think I'll really ever forgive Grandfather and, for that matter, you?" I asked.

His eyes seemed to brighten and then dim. "I don't know. I never really apologized. I guess I'd have to confess first."

"Confess what now?" I said, feeling stronger than him suddenly. He looked younger, more vulnerable.

"I lied about it all. I didn't do anything because Dr. Kirkwell told me to do it. I snuck in on my own and made all that up myself. I did it because . . ."

"Because what, Simon?"

He took a deep breath. "Because I wanted to."

He glanced at me and looked away quickly.

"You confuse me," I said. "But I appreciate your telling me the truth."

I couldn't help it. I wasn't sure I didn't like his confession. Was that wrong?

He nodded. "I'm sorry. Let's talk about that some other time. For now, let me show you Grandmother Judith's diary. She had great penmanship. It's almost artistic."

He hurried toward a trunk, more like fled from me.

The more I learn, the more unsure of myself and everyone around me I become, I thought. How I wished I was back in the Robot Family.

I looked at the plane my father had given me. I could see his face, I could feel his smile, and I could remember how firmly he would grip my hand, just tight enough to give me a sense of safety but not hurt. He was a perfectionist even at that.

For the first time in a long time, I felt the tears—tears not for myself and not even for Mommy.

They were for him.

I hoped Simon was right. There were two people in everyone, and the one who lived in Daddy and loved me would get stronger.

CHAPTER THREE

Simon wasn't wrong about Grandmother Judith's penmanship. The writing looked like a work of art. I didn't want to remain in the basement, but the moment I opened the diary and began reading, I sat on the trunk and lost track of time.

I had no idea that J. Willard Sutherland was interested in me. It was actually my father who told me, and very casually at that.

He lowered his Wall Street Journal and said it. Then he returned to whatever he had been reading. I remember my heart fluttered like the wings of a baby robin. J. Willard Sutherland was the most handsome man I knew. He wasn't pretty-boy good-looking, either. His handsomeness came from the manly firmness in his strong chin and perfect full lips, his high cheekbones, and his stunning velvety blue eyes that radiated self-confidence. He had the shoulders of one of his laborers and yet looked noble and almost statuesque in his tailored shirts, jackets, and pants. No other young man exuded as much self-assurance, which I could feel assured came from far more than his wealth. He possessed a different, more original sort of arrogance—the arrogance of someone who knew he belonged in his shoes. Unlike most young men, he knew himself thoroughly. There was no doubt about who he was and who he would be. It was as though every step he took, every glance, every word, had been well planned. How could any woman not fall in love with him?

I looked up at Simon, who was standing there and smiling at me. "What?"

"Not worried about stale air, mice, and spiders, I see."

"Very funny." I thought a moment. "You were right. There is something special about learning more about our family. They're not all puppets and cut-out dolls."

"I thought you might say something like that."

He looked so smugly satisfied with himself. I stood up, clutching the diary under my arm.

"But I'm not going to spend hours down here in this family cemetery, as you correctly described it. I'm taking this upstairs to read tonight, especially because we'll be attending Grandmother Judith's funeral shortly. I never really got to know her, and I'll never get to know her better than I will after reading this."

He shook his head. "They've deliberately taken the lock off your bedroom door, Caroline. Mrs. Lawson's sole purpose now is to confirm that you're 'normal' enough to be a Sutherland. I can tell you that I've observed her when Dr. Kirkwell was with Grandfather. She's jealous of Dr. Kirkwell's influence on him. And don't forget that Dr. Kirkwell kept her completely out of it during her performing aversion therapy on you. It's

Dr. Kirkwell's conclusions that convinced Grandfather to let you return to the kingdom. If it had been up to Mrs. Lawson, you'd still be in there.

"Personally, I never liked Mrs. Lawson, and I know she's not very fond of me," he continued. "I've contradicted her a number of times in front of Grandfather, and a number of those times, he sided with me. She's sickly jealous of anyone who commands Grandfather's respect, especially Franklin Butler. I've seen the way she smirks at him and speaks to him when Grandfather is not around."

"So?"

"So? If she sneaks up to your room and bursts in on you while you're lying there reading Grandmother's secret diary, something Grandfather buried here with so many other things, she'll scoop it out of your hands and run right to him with it. As you read more of that, you'll understand why I'm saying he wouldn't want you to be reading it. It's quite personal at times. I've never doubted that Mrs. Lawson read it before it was brought down here."

"I'll scratch her eyes out before I let her rip this out of my hands."

"But she'll know you have it, that you've gone through all these things and might know lots more. Now you know that they really didn't give away your personal possessions and gifts your mother and her girlfriend gave you."

"Good."

He paused, thought with his head raised and leaning back as if he was reading instructions written in one of the spiderwebs, and then looked at me again.

"If I'm asked about it, I'll have to say I have no idea how you got your hands on that. You snuck down here on your own. I might even be forced to say it's something your mother would have done. Got to protect the old rear end. Up to now, Grandfather has never been disappointed in me."

"Then why did you bother to do this and risk it?"

He shrugged. "A little excitement, and I felt sure you'd listen to my instructions."

"Well, I'm not," I said. "But don't worry about your precious place with Grandfather. You don't have to deny it. I'll say I came down here and found this on my own because my mother told me about some of it. And if Mrs. Lawson tries to convince Grandfather that I'm lying and it was you, I'll assure him that I didn't and don't want to have anything to do with you. Convincing them of that won't be difficult for me."

He winced. "That hurt," he said, rubbing his shoulder as if pretending I had punched him.

"And I'm taking the model jet plane my father gave me. I'll hide it in a drawer."

"She'll search your drawers, Caroline. She'll look under your bed. She'll even check the inside of your toilet bowl. She'll take a microscope to your room."

"Stop it. You're just trying to frighten me."

He shrugged again. "It's the one place where we're at a disadvantage as a species," he said in his arrogant, lecturer voice. "Put a puppy on a ledge ten stories high, and it'll whimper and cry; put a human baby there, and he or she will giggle right off the ledge. Fear is good."

I stared at him defiantly.

He sighed deeply. "All I can do is warn you, Caroline. I'm going up now. I have some reading to do myself."

He went to the outside basement door and began closing it quietly.

"All right," he said, returning. He saw how determined I was, even though what he had told me really did scare me. "I have a compromise for you."

"What?"

"That diary is thin enough. She doesn't know your reading assignments. We'll cut out the inside of a biology textbook I have in the study with some of my other books and insert the diary in it. If she pops open your door and sees you reading, she'll assume that's what it is. But you have to leave the model plane down here. Deal?"

I thought for a moment.

"I promise to sneak you down here again and again if you want, but we have to do it when I decide, when I am confident that it's safe."

"You're just like them: you're taking over my life."

"Self-preservation. You'll get used to it. It's what makes you a true Sutherland."

I stood, still deciding about whether to get the model plane or not.

"Give me the diary," he said. "I'll put it under my shirt until we fix the biology textbook. She won't dare touch me if she sees us."

He unbuttoned his shirt.

"Well? C'mon, Caroline. If she returns to the study and you're not there or in your room, she'll surely get suspicious and start searching for us, for you mainly. You said so yourself."

"Okay," I said, and handed it to him.

"Wise choice."

"Why do you want to spend so much time here at Sutherland anyway?" I asked. "You could have a lot more fun and less worry if you made some friends and did things together. I know I will."

There was a small twitch in his eyes when I brought up his lack of friends. I knew Aunt Holly wished he was more social.

"I like it here. Someday all this will be mine. It will be more important to be a friend of mine then."

"Those won't be true friends. They'll pretend to be so they can take advantage of you."

"That's all friends are: people who take advantage of each other. Some are just better at hiding it. I won't have any illusions about it, but it won't matter. I'll have Sutherland."

"That's a long way off, Simon. Your father would inherit it first, and you'll go to college, won't you?"

"My father will always need me," he said. "Maybe he won't inherit it first."

"What's that mean?"

"Nothing for you to worry about. Come on. Quietly. I'll check the hallway first," he said, and started for the stairway.

I looked back at it all, the trunks, the old furniture and paintings smothered in dusty gray sheets. I envisioned someone being tied, gagged, and, like my mother's ashes, shut up in an urn, stored in the darkness, all of it a futile attempt to erase the past that surely revisited everyone in this family often in dreams and nightmares. They were the true cobwebs in Sutherland.

Simon beckoned, and I hurried up and behind him to step out of the basement and close the door softly behind us. The house was as quiet as before, maybe even quieter.

When we reached the entrance lobby and turned toward the kitchen, we heard Grandfather call, "Simon."

Even my heart paused and then began to thump faster, the beat so loud in my ears that I was certain Grandfather could hear it, too.

"What are you two up to?" he asked. It seemed always true, but somehow even truer now, that the house grabbed the sound of his voice and echoed it through its veins, the corridors, upstairs and down. He didn't live in this mansion; he wore it like a suit of armor.

"Oh, hi, Grandfather," Simon said, so casually that he could have convinced even me how innocent we were. "I just helped Caroline with some of the assignments Dr. Kirkwell had left. We're trying to occupy our thoughts to keep from thinking about poor Grandmother Judith."

"Um," Grandfather said. His face seemed to soften, his eyes suddenly distant. "My grandmother used to open every window in the house when someone died in it." He was lost in a memory for a moment and then, thinking it made him less authoritative, perhaps, snapped out of it and in a louder, firmer voice said, "You two should go outside. Get some air. We'll be confined to churches and rooms full of sorrow soon enough. Go on," he ordered. "Just stay out of everyone's hair today especially."

As if she was always there to be the period or exclamation point to his statements, Mrs. Lawson appeared, stepping out of a shadow behind him.

"I'll keep an eye on them," she said.

Grandfather grunted his approval and walked off. She remained, glaring at us. Despite her being at most only two or three inches taller than I was, she always appeared to be towering over me. I had often seen how some of the maids cowered and shrank after she had snapped an order or had come upon them suddenly, probably when they least expected her. At times, she seemed to emerge from out of the walls. Was it her omnipresence, her seeming ability to appear suddenly when anything troubling happened, that gave her such authority? I wondered if the woman even slept. Simon wasn't exaggerating when he compared her eyes to two microscopes.

I had no doubt there was no love lost between her and Simon or anyone else in this mansion except Grandfather. When it came to Sutherland, she was truly his broom and mop. It was easy to see that all he had to do was glance at someone or something, and she would leap at it with a hatchet in her hand.

"How many eyes do you have, Mrs. Lawson," Simon quipped, "that you can afford to spend one on us?"

Her face reddened.

"We're going to get our textbooks and notebooks and, as Grandfather said, we're going to sit outside and read. You can follow us if you want."

She turned away and headed for the grand ballroom, where Grandmother Judith's funeral reception would be held.

Simon grinned at me. "Let's go to the study. I'll get a large enough textbook I use to carefully hide the diary. Then we'll go to lunch on the patio just as Grandfather told us."

He kept his left arm slightly up to press the diary closer to his body. I lowered my head, now admittedly a little nervous and frightened, and followed him. It wasn't twenty-four hours ago that I wanted to keep at least ten feet away from him, not look at him, and not even hear his voice. Somehow, whether he had planned it cleverly or not, he had me depending on him. I always knew he was much more intelligent than I was—or anyone else in the family, maybe. How would I know when he was sincere and when he was cleverly controlling me? Was I simply another game to him, simply amusement? When I did think harder about it, I did worry.

What if he had done all this not because he really wanted me to be his friend but because he eventually could reveal everything to our grandfather and become more important and more appreciated? He could show he was better than Mrs. Lawson, even better than Dr. Kirkwell. "She fooled everyone but me, Grandfather," he could say.

He hurried out ahead of me, not looking back once to see if I was following. We went to the study, and he found the textbook he wanted. I watched him cut a wide frame in the pages.

"It'll fit right in here," he said, inserting the diary and then proudly closing the book to show me. "Don't worry. She doesn't have X-ray eyes."

He took a book for himself.

"Adam Smith's *The Wealth of Nations*," he said, showing it to me. "Grandfather loves it when I quote from it. It's the foundation for modern economics . . . his Bible. Mine too, actually."

He handed me the textbook hiding Grandmother's diary.

"Let's go. And don't look back. Mrs. Lawson loves it when you show any fear."

I followed him out and tried not to watch for her.

We went out to the patio, but Simon suddenly started away.

"Where are you going?" I called when he turned left off the patio.

"To the pool. Let's get farther away from the house. She'll eavesdrop on us. We'll sit on lounge chairs and read. Actually, I'm probably just going to think."

"About what?"

"My future. I have to make some important decisions soon."

He kept walking. I hurried to catch up.

"What decisions?"

He paused and looked back at the house. "Just as I told you . . . she's watching us. The woman is a fanatic."

"What decisions?" I asked, glancing back.

Mrs. Lawson was standing at one of the sliding patio doors and looking at us; it was creepy how well Simon knew her.

"About my own immediate future. You're not going to be here forever, you know."

He walked faster. I had to jog to catch up with him.

"What are you saying?"

He didn't respond until we reached the pool.

"Well?"

He flopped onto a lounge chair.

"What did you mean?" I asked.

He looked up at me but still didn't answer.

"Simon?"

"Your father is going to let you visit, spend the summer, and maybe live with him and his new family," he said quickly.

"How do you know?"

"I know," he said.

I sat on the lounge chair beside him.

"Why didn't you tell me that earlier?"

He stared ahead. The gardeners were trimming bushes near the pool. Off in the distance, we could hear the sound of someone's car alarm going off, the beeping so annoying that even birds were flying away in every direction.

"Do I have to beg you to talk?" I said.

He turned to me, his eyes flashing anger. Why? "I thought if I did, you wouldn't care that much about learning all there is to know about our family. There really isn't anyone else with whom to share it. My mother doesn't really care about it, and my father . . . my father is afraid he'll say something I might repeat to my grandfather."

"But how do you know about my father? No one has said anything to me."

He looked at me so hard that I could see he was debating whether or not to tell me something I might use against him or accidentally mention and get him into trouble. What could be worse than what he had already done by showing me the urn?

"I can get into Grandfather's email, and often I do," he confessed.

"You spy on him?"

"Stay up-to-date, not spy. 'Spy' sounds too . . . evil."

"But he wouldn't like it."

"If you tell him . . ."

"I'm not interested in telling him. What did my father say, exactly?"

"He said if you continued to behave appropriately, he was willing to have you visit and see for himself. Something like that. I don't recall the exact words."

He opened his book and started to read or look like he was. It was surely like him to leave me hanging. Then I thought of something.

"If you got me into trouble, Grandfather would tell him, and he wouldn't invite me for the summer."

Simon lowered his book and gave me his wry smile. "You think I'm that desperate that I would get you into a trap to keep you here?"

Yes, I thought, but didn't say it.

I lay back and started to read Grandmother's diary again. For a man who was supposedly so formal and stiff, coldly analytical about women to the point where he would make a list of positives and negatives about one, Grandfather surely sounded more like a romantic man in these early diary pages. He always brought her flowers, took her to beautiful places, and began buying her jewelry. There were always love notes attached to the flowers and gifts. How could she not fall in love with him?

But was his love for her really nothing more than his putting on a new set of clothes? If not, what had changed him? Grandmother Judith described his proposal of marriage taking place here at Sutherland, and it seemed like such a beautiful love scene. It was a beautiful day, and he held her hand and had her look at the mountains while he spoke what sounded more like poetry. Grandfather Sutherland?

"Did you really read this?" I asked Simon.

He lowered his book. "Just skimmed it, I suppose. I saw that it was a girlie thing. Hard facts about our family were what I was after. Why?"

I stared at him so hard that he had to smile.

"What?"

"Maybe you don't really know who Grandfather is," I said.

A frightened bird couldn't leap off his face as quickly as did that smug smile.

"There is no one who knows Grandfather better than I do."

He snapped open his book and, I'm sure, pretended to return to his reading, but I could feel him watching me out of the corner of his eye.

I read on. Grandmother Judith was very excited to become the mistress of Sutherland. They also had their wedding right here, and from the way she described it in detail, it was probably one of the biggest weddings in upstate New York. Even the governor attended. Her subtle comments about Great-grandfather and Abigail Sutherland suggested she wasn't terribly fond of either of them. She clearly understood the rivalry between our grandfather and his father, but what Simon surely missed was how jealous Abigail was of Grandmother Judith. From her description, it seemed clear to me that she was constantly looking for ways to diminish her. After a while, I wondered how they all lived with each other, even in this mansion in which you could avoid seeing someone for days.

I don't know how much time actually passed, but Simon suddenly said, "Close the book. She's descending on us like some vulture."

I glanced back and saw Mrs. Lawson walking toward us at a surprisingly fast pace. I didn't think she was capable of moving that quickly. I closed the book, sipped what was left of my drink, and looked at Simon. Had she somehow discovered that we had been in the basement and I had Grandmother Judith's diary?

"Get up and go directly to the Sutherland Room," she said as soon as she was close enough.

"Why?" Simon asked, not even giving her the respect to look at her when he spoke.

"Reverend Vance is here to discuss the church service with the family. Your father asked me to fetch you."

"Fetch?" Simon said, smiling. "Who says 'fetch' anymore?"

Mrs. Lawson drew her shoulders back and widened her eyes to the point where I thought they would burst. Delight and laughter were sizzling so quickly inside me that I thought I wouldn't be able to smother even a giggle. She fixed her stone-cold eyes on me as if she knew how much I wanted to laugh. It had been so long since I had a good reason to or an opportunity.

"'A good thrashing' are some other words not often used today but are obviously in dire need here," she said in her familiar icy voice, and then spun on her heels so hard that they nearly caught in the grass and sent her sprawling. "You've been told," she declared, like someone staking a flag in the ground, and started for the house.

Simon stretched and stood.

"Let's go before she riles everyone up," he said. "Keep the textbook closed, and get it up to your room as soon as you can."

"I think you really enjoy teasing and poking at her."

He smiled. "Well, you can't, so I have to do it for you." His eyes were lit with delight. "Let's go."

He turned to walk to the house. Whether I liked it or not, he was going to be my guardian. He waited, and I walked with him. Out of the corner of my eye, I saw how his hand seemed to float toward and then away from mine. Maybe it was because I had just read Grandmother Judith's romantic feelings toward Grandfather, but I almost wished he had taken my hand. Was it wrong to want to feel wanted, to accept some token of affection? Or would all the Sutherland ancestors captured in portraits on all the walls glare down in a rainfall of rage and somehow send me back to the bedroom of darkness?

There was no question about what Mrs. Lawson would do.

She was waiting gleefully at the entrance to the Sutherland Room and nodded to Grandfather as we arrived. I looked into her face and saw the pleasure it gave her to do his bidding. It wasn't such a big accomplishment to "fetch" us, but her look of self-satisfaction made it seem so.

Aunt Holly and Uncle Martin, dressed more formally, both turned to watch us take our seats. Franklin Butler was standing in his usual place.

Reverend Vance sat on a black folding chair beside Grandfather, who, in his ruby-red heavy-cushioned chair, looked a foot taller. The reverend was a heavy man who looked like he was poured over the folding chair.

"I'm sorry that we all have to meet on such a solemn and sad occasion," he began in a rather thin, high-pitched voice that sounded more like a woman's. He then went on to describe how the religious ceremony would proceed, glancing at Grandfather after almost every step to be sure he wasn't saying anything that would displease him. Then he paused and asked what we would like included in his description of Grandmother Judith.

It took so long for anyone to speak that I thought no one would.

"She was always sensitive to how other people felt and eager to do what she could to ease our unhappiness," Aunt Holly said.

"Thank you. Anything else?" the reverend asked.

I watched Grandfather. He seemed mesmerized, just staring ahead. Was he thinking about Grandmother Judith?

Why wasn't Uncle Martin saying anything about his mother, either? Did he have to be sure his father would approve of this, too?

"She was as careful about how she looked and presented herself as the queen of England would be," Simon said.

Grandfather looked at him. After a beat of silence, he nodded. "That she was," he said.

Simon smiled. I thought Uncle Martin looked at him in the strangest way. It was as if he was jealous, envious of how what his own son had said pleased his father.

"My mother was a great asset for my father. She was always there when he needed her," Uncle Martin offered. He instantly looked to Grandfather for a sign of agreement or pleasure, but Grandfather had returned to that stare, that far-off look, as if he could see into his own memory and step out of the present.

It was deathly quiet again.

"Of course, you are free to use anything from the obituary I wrote," Franklin Butler said.

"I will." The reverend looked at us. I could see he was eager to end it, but after I'd gotten to know Grandmother Judith more intimately, it all felt like too little.

"She loved music, but nothing pleased her more than the sound of Grandfather's laughter," I said.

It was as if a bomb had gone off. Even the reverend looked speechless. Simon turned to me with a look of absolute terror in his eyes.

From where had I gotten that?

I shrugged. "It's just something I remember from when I was brought here as a little girl for dinner. I remember even telling my mother and her saying, 'That's very true, Caroline.'"

Simon still looked terrified, but Grandfather suddenly burst into laughter.

"She's right," he said. "From out of the mouths of babes. Feel free to include that, Reverend."

"Of course, Mr. Sutherland."

I started to breathe again. Simon's look of terror turned quickly into a smile. Everyone was smiling at me.

Except for Mrs. Lawson. She was glaring at me with those suspicious microscope eyes. I clutched the biography textbook as tightly as I could.

"Let's all rest for a while before dinner," Grandfather said. "Thank you, Reverend. We will see you at church," he said, clearly indicating that he wasn't invited to our dinner.

"I'd like to help Caroline with her hair and clothes," Aunt Holly said. "If you'd like me to, Caroline."

"Oh, yes," I said.

"Good," Grandfather said, slapping his legs and standing. "Mrs. Lawson, you'll have some time for needed rest, I'm sure. Martin, you and I will meet with Mr. Butler in the sitting room for a drink before dinner. I'm sure Simon will amuse himself. Dinner at seven thirty, then."

Like always, it wasn't until he started out that anyone else even rose to leave.

Simon leaned over to whisper, his eyes on Mrs. Lawson, whose face looked like a mask to be worn on Halloween.

"What?" I demanded, impatient and worried.

"You'll need me more than ever now," he said.

CHAPTER FOUR

"I'm so proud of you for speaking up, Caroline," Aunt Holly said when we were in my bedroom. "I was so afraid that your difficult experiences with Dr. Kirkwell and the cold glare of Mrs. Lawson every time she saw you would turn you into a frightened little bird fluttering around this mansion."

That's exactly what I am, I wanted to say.

Aunt Holly looked around my bedroom and smiled. "Your mother and I spent quite a few secret sessions up here. She was always doing little things to give it a more feminine feel. But real changes were hard to make. Your grandfather treats every inch of Sutherland as if it was some holy site—everything's a relic, a historical object. The irony is that he replaced so much of it when his father lost control. But moving a new chair into a room was like stamping it into the floor. He is remarkable when it comes to recalling where things were placed or when something in particular happened in what room or the other in Sutherland.

"Your cousin, my genius son, researched his grandfather's mind. Has he told you that?"

"No."

"Yes, well, Grandfather Sutherland is his favorite subject. He's obsessed with him," she said, grimacing like someone with a toothache. "Don't get him started. He recently gave your uncle Martin and me a lesson about hyperthymesia. It took me weeks to learn how to pronounce it."

"What does it mean? Is it a disease?"

"No. Some people apparently are able to vividly remember an abnormally large number of their life experiences—dates, times, colors, everything."

She smiled.

"I think Martin and maybe me, too, are a bit terrified of Simon. He is brilliant. He even knows how to explain things like hyperthymesia so anyone might understand. Perhaps he'll become a great teacher. When Martin challenged the idea, Simon said, 'We all write our memories in pencil. They fade. But Grandfather writes them in indelible ink.'

"It's what makes our Mrs. Lawson so important. She anticipates what would happen if some servant moves a picture or doesn't put something back in a cabinet the way it was. I'm not excusing her, but she has to be that way, or she'll be criticized. Of course, she takes it too far."

She looked at the clothes in my closet, moving through them quickly.

"This is the new wardrobe she bought you?"

"Yes."

"Do you like these things?" she asked, looking at the clothes and grimacing.

I hesitated. Finding courage in Sutherland was like chasing butterflies with your bare hands.

She smiled and tilted her head. "What?"

"Mrs. Lawson said if I complained, she'd tell Grandfather I wasn't to be trusted, and I'd be in trouble again."

Of course, I didn't really understand why I wasn't to be trusted the first time. What had I done that would even suggest it? Lived with Mommy and Nattie? What else could I do? Not that I wanted to do something else. Daddy had left with his new family. In the end, wasn't I simply guilty of loving my mother? Why wouldn't that be seen as a good thing?

I imagined that love wasn't exactly the same as cherished Sutherland loyalty, but it was just as strong, if not stronger. Would Grandfather ever believe that? Had he once and been disappointed so badly that he would never cherish it again? Was that what Simon had been trying to tell me? Was he right? No one ever really loved anyone in this house?

"She threatened you with that? Oh, that woman . . ."

She looked at the clothes again.

"None of this is proper for Grandmother Judith's funeral and funeral reception," Aunt Holly concluded, and shut the closet door. She looked at her watch. "Come on," she said. "We're going shopping. We have a good hour before the store closes."

Astonished but very pleased, I hurried after her. She practically raced us down the hall and down the stairway. Simon heard us and came out of the study. We were almost to the front door.

"What's going on?" he asked.

Aunt Holly paused. "We have to go shopping for Caroline."

"Now?"

"More than ever," she said. I followed her out, and we walked quickly through the atrium, over the slate walkway, and past the fountains. Aunt Holly opened the grand, oval-shaped copper-and-mahogany entrance doors and waved to Emerson, who was cleaning the windows of Grandfather's limousine. He quickly put everything away and drove up, stopped, and got out to open the rear doors for us.

"Where to, Mrs. Sutherland?" he asked.

"To Littlefield's. They specialize in upscale teenage girls' clothes," she replied.

Emerson smiled at me. "Yes, ma'am," he said.

"Wasn't there a song you used to sing for my mother-in-law, Emerson? You're better than the radio," Aunt Holly said when we started away.

"Yes, ma'am, 'Lovely Joan,'" he said, and began to sing.

Aunt Holly reached for my hand and smiled. "When he sings, it's like she's here with us," she whispered, and for the first time since I had heard of her passing, I felt I could cry for her and Mommy.

Our shopping spree was truly a whirlwind. Like Mommy, Aunt Holly envisioned what we should find before we found it, and once we did and I tried it on, we went right to the matching shoes. After what seemed hardly more than a half hour, if that, we were packed up and back in Grandfather's limousine to return to Sutherland.

Simon looked like he had been listening for our return the whole time. He came out of the sitting room as soon as we entered the lobby.

"That was fast," he said, his curiosity almost exploding in his eyes when he saw my bags. "New clothes?"

"You have a nice suit here to wear to dinner, Simon," Aunt Holly told him. "Be sure you do."

"Of course," he said, looking embarrassed. "I don't need to be told that."

He stood there watching us head to the stairway. Mrs. Lawson came around a corner and paused, her eyes wide when she saw us with the shopping bags. She was about to ask or say something when Aunt Holly put her hand up.

"Don't ask, Mrs. Lawson," she said. "This is just a start. I'll be looking after Caroline's personal needs from now on."

"Well, Mr. Sutherland—"

"Will be very pleased," Aunt Holly said, smiling gleefully. I hurried up the stairway with her, both of us pausing when Simon started to laugh.

While I was preparing to take my shower, Aunt Holly almost picked up the textbook that had Grandmother Judith's diary in it. As subtly as I could, I slipped it into a dresser drawer. She said she was going to get herself freshened up and left for the bedroom she and Uncle Martin used whenever they stayed over for an event. She returned to help me brush out my hair, and while she did, she talked about my mother and her memories of her even before she had married Daddy. She didn't ask me any questions about Nattie, nor did she offer any information. I was afraid to say anything that might tell her how Simon had spied on her conversations with Uncle Martin and revealed what he had heard to me. When I had dressed, we left for dinner together. Simon was waiting at the bottom of the stairway, looking at me with great suspicion, even fear, in his eyes. Aunt Holly had been with me quite a long time. I was sure he was wondering if I had blurted out anything else that might incriminate him.

"You look very nice, Simon," Aunt Holly told him. "I'm glad you brushed your hair so neatly." She turned to me. "It's the one thing he neglects."

Simon blushed, but leaning more toward anger than embarrassment. I knew he hated being envisioned as a young boy and spoken to as if he was. Aunt Holly's tone was probably the same as it had been when he was five. Despite how brilliant Simon was, I knew that a mother couldn't see her child as so much older. You were always her baby to your mother. Mommy had spoken to me often in that "baby" tone, but, unlike Simon, I had embraced the love. And also unlike Simon, I wasn't in a rush to grow up.

"I look very nice?" he said, lifting his eyebrows. "I think 'proper' is the better description, Mother. I've always thought 'nice' was one of those noncommittal words, meaningless really."

Now it was Aunt Holly who blanched. "Where's your father?" she practically snapped back at him.

"He, Grandfather, and Mr. Butler are still in Grandfather's office."

"Well, we're headed to the dining room," she said. "You can come with us or wait for them."

"I'm coming," Simon said, and walked beside me.

"Did she ask you about what you said in the Sutherland Room?" he whispered when Aunt Holly paused to tell Clara Jean something.

"No. She was just happy that I had spoken up."

"Don't get overconfident. My mother doesn't pick up on stuff as quickly as Grandfather does. I'm sure he's thinking about you."

Before I could reply, Aunt Holly rejoined us. We took our seats at the dining room table, Simon surprising me by pulling out Aunt Holly's chair for her. He then walked around the table to sit on the other side.

"Thank you, Simon," she said, and then leaned toward me to whisper, "His father often forgets, or Simon beats him to it. Maybe he likes to make him look forgetful, even incompetent, especially in front of my father-in-law."

I didn't think he heard her, but Simon sat with that smug look sitting on his face like a hen sitting on her eggs.

Moments later, Grandfather, Uncle Martin, and Franklin Butler entered, all three wearing similarly grim expressions. No one spoke as they took their seats. When Mrs. Lawson appeared in the doorway and Clara Jean followed with a tray carrying our salads, Grandfather put his hand up.

"Give us a few minutes, Mrs. Lawson," Grandfather said.

She nodded at Clara Jean, who backed up as if she had approached a wall of fire and disappeared. Mrs. Lawson remained. Grandfather looked at her but did not ask her to leave. I imagined that, by now, for him she was part of the scenery.

"Now, then," Grandfather began, "as I mentioned earlier, Mrs. Sutherland did not have a formal will as such, but she did jot down a few things she wanted to be sure were passed on according to her wishes.

"Holly, she has left all her jewelry to you. It has been properly organized and packed and will be given to you tonight before you leave. With the exception of two rings," he continued, turning toward me with his eyes so focused and intense that it was difficult to tell if there was any pleasure or anger behind them, "the ring her parents gave her on her sixteenth birthday and her engagement ring. I will hold on to both rings. Her birthday ring will be given to Caroline on her sixteenth birthday. The engagement ring will be saved for Simon when he decides on the woman he wants to be his wife. All of Mrs. Sutherland's other things will be Mrs. Lawson's responsibility to transfer to the proper charities.

"Mrs. Lawson will close down Mrs. Sutherland's suite. However, she will see to it that it is kept immaculate, the furnishings dusted and polished. Its disposition will depend on whatever the next master of Sutherland decides."

He did not look at Uncle Martin when he said that. He seemed to be looking at a vision no one else could see. I glanced at Simon. He was actually smiling like a younger prince anticipating leapfrogging to the throne. His father looked more glum than he had when they had entered. Had Grandfather said something similar in his office?

"Finally," Grandfather said, "pending anything that might change the direction of this outcome, I decided to use this occasion to announce that Caroline will be visiting with her father and his new family in Hawaii this summer. Dr. Kirkwell has assured me that her schooling will be completed before the end of the month, so at the moment, I can see no delays. You will have to assure us of that your-self, of course," he told me.

"I'm sure she will," Aunt Holly said.

Grandfather turned to her. "And I'm glad you've taken her a bit under your wing, Holly," he said, but he said it with the clear implica-tion that she had done so without his approval, "looking after some of her personal things."

Aunt Holly's face reddened a bit, but she didn't look away. Mrs. Lawson appeared quite satisfied when I glanced at her.

"And so," Grandfather concluded, "after Mrs. Sutherland's funeral, I believe our Sutherland ship of state will sail along as it has always been intended. Mrs. Lawson, you can ask Clara Jean to begin our dinner service."

The dinner continued just the way it had as those I had attended while Grandmother Judith was convalescing upstairs in her suite. In fact, it was a bit eerie. It was as if she hadn't passed away at all. Like she was still just sick. As usual, Grandfather and Franklin Butler talked about the economy—with Uncle Martin seconding almost any conclusions they reached—and some business changes they were planning. I saw that Aunt Holly was still uncomfortable and ate with her eyes only on her food. Occasionally, she paused to smile at me. Simon maintained his look of self-confidence, occasionally nodding his approval as if he was the head of the table. He was so annoying that I stopped looking at him.

After dinner, I went up to my room to do my history reading. Grandfather's announcement of what Simon had revealed excited me. Maybe my father regretted the things he had done, especially in rela-tion to me. Surely he had been thinking of me, and, just like me, he recalled happier times. Anger was truly like boiling water. When the fire beneath it was turned off, it would stop bubbling and cool down and look like it had never boiled at all. I hoped when Daddy set eyes on me again, his face would be dressed only in a smile, and the heat in his eyes would be only a rekindled love.

Simon left Sutherland that night. I didn't see him again until Grandmother Judith's funeral. I came to the church with Grandfather Sutherland and Mrs. Lawson. Aunt Holly had arrived that morning with a black dress for me from Littlefield's. She had bought another pair of shoes as well. I didn't realize she had it all on order before we had left the store.

"I'll see you at the church," she told me, and hurried out.

Mrs. Lawson came in to see what Aunt Holly had bought. It was as if she had eyes everywhere in Sutherland. A fly couldn't land on a window without her knowing.

"A total waste of money," Mrs. Lawson said. "What I bought you was sufficient."

I didn't say anything. I dressed and went down to join Grandfather, who had just stepped out of his office. I held my breath, fearful that Mrs. Lawson had said something nasty to him about my new clothes. He didn't exactly smile, but his nod was reassuring.

"I'm glad to see you know how to present yourself properly," he remarked.

Mrs. Lawson came up behind me with the intent of escorting me, but I deliberately walked faster to exit beside Grandfather. When Emerson opened the limousine door for us, Grandfather gave me a most peculiar look. It wasn't exactly a look of pleasure, but there was something warm in his eyes. For a moment, I felt as if he wasn't seeing me as much as my mother at my age. I got in quickly after him.

Mrs. Lawson said nothing when she stepped in and sat beside me. In fact, no one spoke for the entire trip to the church. The sky had only puffs of clouds here and there. The blue looked deeper and maybe a little darker than usual. I stared out the window and watched the countryside go by as if it had all turned liquid and flowed. I heard Mrs. Lawson clear her throat a few times, probably suggesting I sit up straight, but I wanted to lean as far away from her as I could.

I felt quite insecure when we entered the church and so many people turned to watch us; it felt like most were looking at me. I don't know if I actually paused, but suddenly Grandfather put his hand lightly on my back. I walked beside him to the front row, where Uncle Martin, Aunt Holly, and Simon were already seated. I could almost feel the heat of anger flowing from Mrs. Lawson, who had to walk behind us and had to sit in the second row.

The part I dreaded the most came very quickly after the service. Grandfather Sutherland wouldn't stop to accept any words of sympathy from those at the church. When we arrived at the family cemetery, my heart began to pound from the mixture of fear and sadness. I was afraid that once we approached my mother's grave, Grandfather Sutherland would take one look at me and know that I knew it was empty. Simon, as if he anticipated my nervousness, stepped up beside me. "Concentrate on Grandmother Judith today," he whispered. I knew he wasn't protecting me as much as he was probably protecting himself. How else would I know about my mother's grave?

He took a step away when Mrs. Lawson deliberately moved up to be right behind us. As if she was determined to now be my protector, Aunt Holly stepped closer to me on my right. She reached down to take my hand. I saw her small, tight smile, and then we both faced forward to listen to the graveside service.

Grandfather Sutherland didn't cry, but he kept his head bowed until the service was over. Then he took a deep breath, glanced at me, and started for the limousine. I hurried to walk beside him. When I looked back, Aunt Holly was hugging Uncle Martin, who finally looked like he was mourning his mother. Simon stood there watching me with that wry smile on his face. I was beginning to wonder if I wasn't his only form of amusement. Emerson hurriedly opened the limousine door and said something to Grandfather, which I couldn't hear. Whatever it was, it was enough for Grandfather to thank him and press his arm. Mrs. Lawson nearly pushed me out of the way to get into the limousine next.

After I got in and Emerson started away, Mrs. Lawson said, "It was a very nice funeral."

Grandfather just sat there staring ahead. Then, moments after she had spoken, he looked at me.

"I think she would have been very proud of the way you carried yourself today, Caroline," he said. He nearly took my breath away with the unexpected compliment. "Come directly to my office so I can show you the ring she has bequeathed to you."

I looked at Mrs. Lawson. It was like someone had started a fire in her mouth and the flames were scorching the undersides of her eyes.

"Okay, Grandpa," I said. It just came out: "Grandpa."

His eyes widened, and Mrs. Lawson looked even more annoyed.

Then he gave me what he really hadn't given me since I had left the dark bedroom: a soft smile.

When we arrived at Sutherland and we all got out of the limousine, Mrs. Lawson caught up with me right after Grandfather entered the house. As she passed by me, she said, "I know what you're doing."

She sped up and walked into the house to get the preparations going for the funeral reception.

What was I doing? I would have asked if she hadn't rushed past me. Grandfather stopped at his office door to wait for me before he opened it. I followed him in. He went around his desk, opened a drawer, and took out a small box. When he put it on the desk, he opened it, and I stepped up to look at the ring.

"That's her birthstone," Grandfather said. "Which just happens to be yours: topaz."

I looked at the ring.

"She had small hands," he said. "Not much larger than yours. Try this on."

He handed me the ring. I slipped it over my finger with little effort, but it felt secure. He nodded and then held out his hand, and I took off the ring and gave it back. He put it in the box and put the box back in the drawer.

"When it's time," he said. "Hopefully. Okay. Go on. Get yourself freshened up, as your grandmother would say, and come down to the funeral reception."

For a moment, I thought perhaps I could tell Grandfather that all my personal possessions had been put in the basement and that I'd like to have some of them in my room. Was there even the slight possibility he didn't know? Could that have been Mrs. Lawson's doing alone? Should I risk it? What about Simon? I would surely get him into trouble, and suddenly that mattered to me.

However, whatever smile and warmth there had been in Grandfather Sutherland's face, they were snuffed out now, perhaps because of my hesitation to do what he had said.

I left quickly and finally took a deep breath.

I didn't change my clothes, but I did brush my hair and wash my hands and my face. As I was patting my cheeks with a towel, there was a knock on my door. Probably not Simon, I thought. He would just barge in again. It was Aunt Holly.

"How are you doing?" she asked.

"I'm okay." I told her what I had accidentally said to Grandfather Sutherland and how he had shown me the birthday ring. Whether I was right to or not, I trusted her. In fact, she was the only person at Sutherland I did trust.

"Well, maybe you did find a soft spot. Dr. Kirkwell just arrived," she said. "I don't think anyone but our family, the servants, and Mrs. Lawson will know who she is and what she has done. She'll be quite careful, I'm sure."

"Mommy used to say that Sutherland had pockets of quicksand."

Aunt Holly laughed and then grew serious. "I do miss her. We were kind of birds of a feather when we were here."

I followed her out and down to the reception. Many people had already arrived. Grandfather, Uncle Martin, and Franklin Butler, with Simon hovering near them, were greeting people.

"Let's get something cold to drink," Aunt Holly said.

Just as we reached the bar, Dr. Kirkwell stepped up to me. She had never worn anything other than a pantsuit, usually with a frilly white blouse, when she treated me with her aversion therapy. She had done something with her graying dark brown hair. Although it was still cut sharply at the base of her neck, it looked softer. She had never worn as much makeup as she was wearing now. Usually, she merely brushed a dull red lipstick across her lips. She had done her eyes and added more color to the rose tint in her cheeks. Her nose looked as sharp, which for me always took any warmth out of her smile.

"Hello, Caroline. I am sorry you lost your grandmother so soon." She looked at Aunt Holly, who didn't hide her disapproval. "Mrs. Sutherland, my sympathies."

"Thank you," Aunt Holly said coolly. She turned to get a glass of wine and a soft drink for me.

"I stopped in to see your workbooks," Dr. Kirkwell said. "Very well done. We'll go over a few things you answered incorrectly. I'll resume our schedule the day after tomorrow."

Aunt Holly handed me a glass of ginger ale.

"Oh, I'm sorry, did you want something?" she asked Dr. Kirkwell.

It was far from a warm comment. They glared at each other for a moment before Dr. Kirkwell smiled coolly.

"Oh, thank you. I'll be fine."

She went to the far right corner of the bar and started a conversation with an older man who looked like he could be one of Grandfather's business associates. I was sure anyone who did business with Grandfather Sutherland or was in business because of him was here. Pockets of people were having their own conversations, but no one raised his voice or laughed. They all looked unsure of a smile.

"Someday you'll tell me all about that woman and what she did to you," Aunt Holly said, nodding at Dr. Kirkwell. "But let time pass and wounds heal. We'd better join your uncle Martin for a while. He's starting to get that overwhelmed look."

Simon had stepped up behind us. "We have four second cousins from Grandmother's side of the family here," he said. "They asked about you and wanted to meet you, but I told them you were still mourning your mother as well, which was why you were being home-schooled at the moment. It was best to wait for another time. I know they're on a strict diet of gossip, especially Cousin JoAnn."

"That was wise," Aunt Holly told him.

"Of course," Simon said. "Grandfather detests them."

"That's a little harsh, Simon. I don't think he'd call them detestable."

Simon shrugged. "That's what they are."

The look on Aunt Holly's face actually frightened me. I remembered my mother believed that the strongest love was the love a parent had for his or her child, which was why the breach between her and Grandfather Sutherland had been so painful. It was only for a moment and perhaps it would become a thought that she would regret, but I read it clearly: Aunt Holly didn't like her own son. Oddly, she would surely protect him, maybe even lay down her life for him, but she might never approve of him.

She crossed the room almost as much to get away from Simon as to comfort Uncle Martin and help him deal with the expressions of sympathy. I looked to the right and saw Grandfather and Franklin Butler talking to more people, but I also saw Grandfather glancing at us.

"Let's eat something," Simon said. "I heard Grandfather is having his dinner in his suite tonight."

I followed him. He was like a bodyguard. Every time someone approached me, he stepped up and said, "Yes, this is my cousin. She's also mourning the loss of her mother. Thank you for your sympathies."

I don't think I said a word to anyone the whole time we were there. Many people left before Grandfather announced the reception was over by leaving it himself. Uncle Martin said something to Aunt Holly, who approached us quickly.

"We're leaving now, Simon," she said. She looked at me. "I wish we could take you home with us, Caroline, but . . ."

"It's all right," I said.

"I'm staying here tonight," Simon declared, as firmly as if his feet were cemented to the floor.

Aunt Holly started to say "No" but swallowed the thought and the word in one gulp. "Whatever," she said instead. "I'll be back in the morning, Caroline. It is going to be a nice day. We'll go for a walk, okay?"

"I'd like that, Aunt Holly."

She hugged me and hurriedly followed Uncle Martin, who was just about out the door.

Mrs. Lawson was ordering and overseeing servants who began cleaning up. Those guests who were deeply engrossed in their own conversations realized what was happening and began to leave.

"I'm getting out of these clothes," Simon said. "If you want, we can do that now, take a walk. I'm sure Mrs. Wilson will make us a light dinner later."

I said nothing but followed him out. Suddenly, I was very tired.

"I want to take a shower and take a little rest," I said when we reached the foot of the stairs. "I feel like I've been running ever since I woke."

"Emotionally, you have," he said in that older man's tone he liked to use.

At the top of the stairway, he went off to the guest room he used, and I went to my bedroom, took off my clothes, and got into the shower, where, for no reason I could say, tears began to mix in with the water running down my face. I got out and went to my bed to lie down, and moments after I closed my eyes, I was asleep. I didn't wake up for quite a while. In fact, the sun had almost gone down, but what woke me was the sense of not being alone. When I turned my head, I saw him lying beside me, leaning on his right arm and staring at me. He was in a short-sleeved white shirt and jeans. He had kicked off his shoes.

He smiled.

I realized I had lain down with just my bath towel around me. Instantly, I clutched it tighter.

"What are you doing here?"

"Just watching you sleep. You dream a lot. I could see it in the way your eyes moved under your closed lids. You even moaned a few times."

"You shouldn't be in here. What if Mrs. Lawson . . ."

"Oh, she's running around like her ass is on fire. One of the servants broke those old dishes, and someone else cracked a leg on a chair moving it back to its place in the ballroom. She already has a furniture repairman working on it. At the same time, she's overseeing the preparations for Grandfather's dinner. Apparently, some of the guests took the liberty of going into other rooms and moved some artifacts. Maybe she'll have a nervous breakdown."

I smelled something on his breath. "Have you been drinking booze?"

He leaned off the bed and brought up a bottle of bourbon. "Grandfather likes this straight up, no ice. I kind of favor it myself. Ever taste bourbon?"

"No," I said. "Only wine, really."

"I always felt wine was better with something to eat. You know, red with meat, white with fish. I'll bet your stepbrother and stepsister are familiar with alcoholic drinks. If you arrive in Hawaii totally naive, you'll be at quite a disadvantage. Maybe they'll even make fun of you. You have a lot to learn in a short time. I bet you'd like vodka. It's easier to hide it in a mix. I have a bottle of that, too. I snuck down and helped myself to some of the stock at the funeral reception. I had my book bag, but Eagle Eyes was too upset with everything to notice me anyway."

He sipped from the bottle and then held it out to me.

"Go on, taste it."

"I'd like to get dressed," I said.

"So?"

"We're not going to go through this again, Simon."

He took another sip of the bourbon and swung himself off the bed.

"I don't understand why you still don't realize I'm the only one here really helping you. My mother's got her hands full with my father. In a day or so, you'll hardly see her. You don't know the half of it when it comes to my parents. Day after day, she ends up taking pills and sleeping off her sadness. Why do you think I spend so much time here instead of at home? Our house is so full of clouds of depression that it could rain tears for weeks, months."

He took another swig of the whiskey. He appeared to be going into a rant. I realized I might be the only person he'd ever told these things. He certainly wouldn't tell Grandfather Sutherland.

"I used to play operas loudly in my room to keep from hearing the

crying through the walls. You could fit three of my houses in Sutherland. I don't know why my parents just didn't move in here. There
was room for us all, but my mother was hell-bent on their being as
independent as possible. Well, how could that be possible? My father
had no life without Sutherland Enterprises. I don't know what sort of
promises he made to my mother before they were married."

He drank more, took a much longer swig.

"Simon, maybe you shouldn't drink that much," I said, but I could
see he didn't hear me. He had his back to me and was still into his
tirade.

"When my sister was born, I was as good as invisible. Of course, I
could take care of myself at a much earlier age than most children, and
I could see my mother was too absorbed. She didn't do or care much
about anyone or anything else. She never complained about my father
being gone so much. She used to. Oh, did she used to . . . big fights . . .
louder opera."

He swayed after taking another sip and finally turned to me.

"We really do have a lot in common, you know, and I don't mean
because we're cousins and Sutherlands. You think like me. I know you
do." He stepped closer. "I can't forget that day when you undressed
for me."

"The quid pro quo?"

"Yes," he said, smiling. "But this is different. This is . . ."

He stopped when we heard the door open.

Mrs. Lawson stood there, her eyes wide but her face bursting with
satisfaction.

CHAPTER FIVE

She stepped back and slammed the door before either of us could make a sound, but the slam was like a deep-voiced scream echoing into the oblivion of shadows curling up and nesting at the end of the upstairs hallway. I imagined the framework of the great house trembling. Mrs. Lawson would bring the roof down on us and take pleasure in burying us under her accusations.

Simon turned and looked at me, and surprised me by immediately whimpering like a little boy. His adult persona, for which he carried great pride and self-satisfaction, fell to his feet like melted ice. I half expected him to cry out for his mother just the way I had cried out for mine so many times at Sutherland. I almost felt sorrier for him than I did for myself, but I could feel the strain in my face as I fell into a pool of dark terror. Every muscle in my body seemed to have frozen. I couldn't even speak. Surely every ancestor painted into immortality and hanging high on the walls of Sutherland grimaced in utter disgust.

Simon looked at the bottle of bourbon in his right hand as if he had just realized it was there; then he looked at me and screamed, "NO!" He turned and nearly ripped the bedroom door off its hinges to rush out.

"Simon!" I called, and sat up.

For a few moments, it was deathly quiet. I thought I heard Mrs. Lawson laughing, making all this seem more like a distorted dream, every sound echoing through a tunnel. I had risen and reached for my bathrobe and slippers when I heard what was clearly Mrs. Lawson's shriek. My whole body really did freeze. There was a muffled series of thumps before all became deathly quiet again. I waited, afraid to move, until I heard Clara Jean's scream. Then I put on my robe and rushed out to go to the top of the stairway.

Simon wasn't there; he wasn't in the hallway. I leaned over the railing and gazed down at the servants who were quickly gathering below. Someone apparently had sent for Emerson. He entered the house running and knelt down beside Mrs. Lawson, who lay in a twisted position, her right arm reaching over her head and her left arm folded against her side, but so awkwardly that it was surely broken.

My heart must have stopped for a moment, because I couldn't breathe.

She was looking up as if she was staring at me, her mouth slightly open. I waited for her to shout, but she didn't move or blink. Could her life be leaking out of her? I could easily be the last person she had seen. Emerson followed her gaze. After a moment, he stood, looking up at me, but before he could speak, Grandfather Sutherland's walking stick could be heard tapping on the marble floor until he appeared and stopped as the scene unfolded before him. I backed away from the railing and just listened to the voices echoing in the mansion. It was as if the walls amplified everything because the house was in a rage. Its overly protective mistress was fading away.

"I'm afraid she's gone, Mr. Sutherland," Emerson said, confirming my worst fear.

"What?"

"It looks like her neck snapped. She took quite a tumble."

One of the servants gasped in a cry that sounded more like a screaming crow. There were more footsteps and then a deep silence until Grandfather's walking stick tapped a path to the bottom of the stairs. I looked for Simon in the hallway to the right of the stairs, but he wasn't there. My heart seemed to have dropped into my stomach. There was a cavernous emptiness in my chest.

Emerson's word hovered inside my ears: *Gone?*

A wave of heat moved up through my neck and into my face. I was afraid I'd burn my fingers if I touched my cheeks.

"Call the paramedics. Nobody touch anything," Grandfather bellowed. "In fact, all of you return to your chores. Now!"

I could hear them scurrying away. Gathering all the courage I could muster, I returned to the railing. As if he had eyes on the top of his head, Grandfather immediately looked up at me.

"Get down here. Carefully," he added. "We don't need another one of these."

Emerson had rushed off to call the paramedics, and all the servants practically fled.

I started down the stairs, wondering if I would faint and, just as Grandfather predicted, tumble down and land alongside Mrs. Lawson. I tried not to look at her, but looking at Grandfather's cold stare was not any easier. Just before I reached the bottom, I paused on the stairway. I saw the thin line of blood crawling from the side of her mouth and down her chin. I clutched the railing tighter as I fought back the dizziness.

"What do you know about this?" he asked.

"Nothing, Grandfather. I was in my room, and I heard all the commotion, so I put on my robe and came out."

"Where's Simon?"

"I don't know." I really didn't.

"Do you know why Mrs. Lawson was upstairs? How she fell?"

I shook my head. So far, I had not told a lie.

Emerson appeared, coming from Grandfather's office. "They're on the way. I told them I couldn't find any sign of life, so they said they would contact the police."

"Oh," Grandfather said, more like moaned, as if he just had suffered a sharp pain in his head.

Mommy had always told me that his walking stick was more of an affectation, but right now, he looked like he was leaning heavily on it to keep himself standing. He brought his free hand to his temple.

"I'm going to call Franklin. Just make sure no one disturbs anything," he said, and started off, then paused and turned back to me. "Get dressed. The police will want to talk to everyone."

I nodded and went up the stairs as quickly as I could. When I reached the top, I paused and thought about Simon. Where was he? Why hadn't he come out, too? I glanced back down at Mrs. Lawson. Despite how much I disliked her, I wished she would get up. Emerson sat in the nearest chair and stared at her as if he was either expecting or hoping she would, too. When he looked up at me, I turned away quickly and continued to my room.

For a moment, I stood leaning against the closed door. If I wished hard enough, could I open it, go out again, and find that none of this had happened? It seemed like forever since I'd had my mother's smile, my mother's comforting kiss and hug, to wipe away unpleasant dreams or unhappy events. How could I ever feel more alone than this?

I was in a daze when I washed and dressed. My hands were shaking so hard that I had trouble fastening the buttons of my blouse. I zippered up my skirt and sat to put on my socks and shoes. I could hear the siren of the approaching ambulance, insisting that there was no way to deny what had happened, no pretending, and especially no crawling into a shell.

When I stepped out of the bedroom and looked down the hallway, I still didn't see Simon. Where was he? Wouldn't all this have made him curious? I had to find him, I thought, and make sure he knew what was happening.

I stayed as far from the railing as I could, my back practically sliding along the wall, and continued to the guest rooms. The suite Uncle Martin and Aunt Holly used when they were here was the first door on the right. Although I had never been in it, I knew that Simon used the second suite on the left. I knocked softly on the door.

"Simon?"

I waited but heard nothing, so I knocked harder and called to him louder. There wasn't a sound coming from inside. I tried the knob, and the door opened. At first, I thought that because it was unlocked, he wasn't there. The heavy, ornate curtains were closed, with barely any light seeping through. There was a king-size four-poster bed with a dark oak headboard and footboard. The chandelier that hung above it resembled a giant spider dangling on a thread. When my eyes adjusted to the shadows and shapes, I stepped in. I almost didn't see him and turned to leave, but then I realized Simon was in bed, lying facedown, the blanket drawn up to his chin.

"Simon?"

He didn't respond, but as I drew closer to the bed, I could see he was trembling and gasping for breath, his shoulders lifting and falling. I drew closer and accidentally kicked the bottle of bourbon. It rolled under the bed. I thought he would have heard it, but he didn't turn or stop gasping and trembling.

"Simon!" I cried. "Mrs. Lawson . . . she's dead. The ambulance and the police are on their way here. Grandfather is looking for you."

He didn't turn but, instead of continually struggling to breathe, he released a deep moan that sounded like a long *ahhhhhhhhhhhhhhh*. It was so deep. I thought it wouldn't stop until his vocal cords snapped. He paused slightly to capture more air and continue the sound, his body trembling so hard that it looked like the bed was shaking him. I froze. I was afraid to get any closer.

"I'll get help," I said, or thought I said, then turned quickly and rushed out of the room, terrified by what he was doing. By the time I reached the head of the stairway, the paramedics were examining Mrs. Lawson, and two uniformed policemen were standing behind them. Grandfather and Emerson were off to the right, watching. I saw Clara Jean and some of the other servants standing in doorways. Two men in sports jackets and ties came in the front entrance. Grandfather turned immediately to talk to them.

Emerson stood beside him to listen but suddenly turned and looked up at me. Whatever he saw in my face or maybe heard caused him to shake his head. I stepped back to be out of sight, and for a few moments, I was afraid to move. I think I might even have whimpered the way Simon had in my room. I didn't understand what Emerson was telling me. It was some kind of warning, but I knew Grandfather wanted me dressed and down there. *What do I do?* Simon needed help, too. Maybe the paramedics should be told to go to his room, I thought.

I heard footsteps on the stairway and decided to rush back to my bedroom. When I closed the door behind me, I remained there, listening. The voices were too low and muffled for me to understand anything.

Why was I hiding? I suddenly realized I should be trying to help Simon. Surely by now, Grandfather would be looking for me. I could hear Daddy warning me about becoming a turtle: "There'll never be a shell big enough or strong enough to shelter you from all the threats and dangers in the world. Face a challenge head-on."

I nodded as if he was standing there, sucked in my breath, and stiffened my posture before I walked out of my room. When they heard me, the two men in sports jackets and ties turned simultaneously from examining the railing.

"Who are you?" the taller of the two asked me. In the hallway light, his brown hair had a rusty shine.

"I'm Caroline Bryer, Mr. Sutherland's granddaughter," I said, surprised by how strong I sounded. I even sounded a bit arrogant about it.

"Were you out here when Mrs. Lawson fell?" the shorter man asked. He looked older, with a charcoal gray to his thinning hair and a rounder, softer face.

"No. I came out when I heard something had happened, and Grandfather told me to get out of my robe and get dressed. Who are you?"

"We're police," the shorter man said. "Detective Dickens," he said, nodding at the taller of the two, "and Detective Hanofee. Homicide," he added.

The word sent an electric shock rising from my toes up through my spine. I tried not to look frightened by it. This was no time to be a little girl, not now, maybe not ever again.

"So you heard nothing before that?" Detective Dickens asked.

What I had heard still seemed like a dream. I wasn't even sure how to describe it. Did I really hear her laugh? The dull thump was surely her toppling down the stairway.

"Any voices?" Detective Hanofee followed, sounding more demanding.

"I didn't hear anyone talking."

"What were you doing?" Dickens asked.

"Doing? I had come up to take a nap, and then I took a shower and lay down. My grandmother passed away recently," I added, hoping for some sympathy.

But neither looked like he cared. Although I wasn't lying, I wasn't telling them everything. Their eyes bored holes in me. I was tempted to start screaming about everything that was done to me. I was locked in a room for months; I was tormented. Why were they looking at me like this?

But then I thought they would think I was happy to see Mrs. Lawson lying dead at the foot of the steps. They would be even more suspicious. Secrets must be kept buried. There were so many embedded in the walls of Sutherland that a few more wouldn't matter very much. The shadows in here grew like mold. When a light was turned on, you could almost see them resisting.

"Who else is up here?"

"My cousin Simon stays up here when he stays at the house, as do my uncle Martin and aunt Holly."

"Are they here now?"

"Not my uncle and aunt."

"So your cousin is here?" Detective Dickens said.

He seemed annoyed, now even suspicious. Had they already been told that Mrs. Lawson didn't like me and Simon? Had Grandfather said anything about me? Was that why Emerson looked up at me and shook his head?

"Yes." There was no hiding it, I thought. Simon needed help. "His bedroom is the second on the left," I said, nodding at the hallway.

They both turned and headed for it. I continued toward the stairs. I was so frightened and shaken that I could feel my emotions being churned inside me. If Simon blurted out that he had been in my room, if he told them Mrs. Lawson had found us together . . . We hadn't done anything, but who would believe it? And Simon's drinking . . . maybe they'd find the whiskey bottle under the bed or whatever else he had brought up. I had no doubt that if Mrs. Lawson regained consciousness, she'd point her right forefinger at me like a pistol and shoot out accusations, claiming I was the bad influence. I got him to steal the whiskey. I tempted him to come to my room. It was all my fault. See? She was right, and Dr. Kirkwell was wrong.

Detective Dickens came out quickly and hurried in my direction. I thought he was coming for me, but without saying anything, he went to the top of the stairs and called down.

"Send the paramedics up here! We've got a situation," he shouted. He turned and looked at me so coldly that I could feel my bones turn to ice. "Is he an epileptic?" he asked.

I shook my head. This was happening too fast. It was as if the house was spinning. The paramedics were rushing up the stairs.

"I don't know," I said. Could he be? I wondered. Why wouldn't Aunt Holly have told me?

"You don't know? You said he was your cousin."

"I don't know." I started to cry.

"In here!" Detective Hanofee shouted to the paramedics, and they all hurried down the hallway.

"What the hell's going on up there?" Grandfather bellowed in that deep, demanding voice that probably made the chandeliers tremble. It certainly caused me to.

What could I say that wouldn't get me into trouble? I flicked away my tears quickly and wiped my cheeks.

"Something's wrong with Simon," I told him as I turned to descend the stairs.

Mrs. Lawson's body was still on the gurney. It had not quite been taken out the front entrance. I imagined her sitting up, turning to me, and smiling gleefully. It was all a ruse; she had faked her death to trap us.

Emerson stepped up beside Grandfather and, with great concern, searched my face for a hint.

"What's wrong with him?" Grandfather asked.

"I don't know. The detective asked me if Simon had epilepsy."

"What? Get up there and see what's happening," he told Emerson, who took the stairs two steps at a time.

Grandfather looked from Mrs. Lawson to me, stroking his mustache.

"That woman navigated these stairs for decades," he said, more to himself than to me. "There will be an autopsy. She might have had a stroke or a heart attack. Did she seem sick to you the last time you saw her?"

"No, Grandfather. But if she didn't feel well, she wouldn't tell me."

"Um. We'll get down to the truth of all this. The detectives will be asking you questions."

"They already did. I told them whatever I knew."

As my mother had often told me, Grandfather's eyes could turn into drill bits gnawing away at you until he reached your very soul.

"I don't lie to him," she had told me, "which is what he hates the most: the truth. People who wield power like it when someone lies to them. It reassures them."

"Why?" I had wondered aloud when she had told me this.

"It reassures them the liar is afraid of them. They feast on fear," she had said.

Grandfather was certainly doing that now.

We both turned as Franklin Butler entered the house. He paused and it looked like he turned white when he confronted Mrs. Lawson lying on the gurney.

"What happened to her?" he asked, hurrying to Grandfather.

"She fell down the stairs and broke her neck. Now something is wrong with my grandson. There are two homicide detectives upstairs investigating, since apparently no one saw her fall," he added, eyeing me. "You'd better call Martin and Holly."

"Right."

Franklin Butler stepped back and took out his mobile phone. Grandfather gazed down, almost as though he wanted to hide his thoughts from me. After Franklin called Uncle Martin, he turned and spoke to Grandfather, but too softly for me to hear. Emerson appeared at the top of the stairway, the two detectives right behind him. We all looked up.

"They got him sedated, Mr. Sutherland, but he'll have to go to the hospital for tests and evaluation," Emerson said while descending.

"What is it?"

"It did look like an epileptic fit," Emerson said.

"Nonsense," Grandfather said. "There's none of that in this family." He sounded like he had outlawed it for the Sutherlands.

Grandfather turned to the detectives.

"What do you make of this?"

"Too early to tell, sir," Dickens said. "We called for a forensic team to inspect the stairs and the upstairs."

Grandfather looked at me. What the detective had said really seemed to surprise him.

"If you have something to tell us, tell us now, Caroline."

I started to cry again. "I didn't see her fall, Grandfather. I was in my room when I heard Clara Jean's scream."

He nodded.

One of the paramedics started down the stairs. "We have a second ambulance on the way." He looked at Emerson. "Maybe you can help me with Mrs. Lawson. Not right to leave her there," he said, and looked at the detectives.

"I'll help," Dickens said. "Won't be the first time I helped load a corpse into an ambulance."

Both detectives followed the paramedic to the gurney carrying Mrs. Lawson.

Franklin Butler turned back to Grandfather. "They're on their way."

"Call him back and tell him to meet the ambulance carrying Simon at the hospital. They're not going to do any good here. And make sure none of this gets out. There'll be ravenous reporters camped at the gate."

"Right."

"I'll be in my office," Grandfather said. "Stand by, Emerson. Give them any help they need, and alert me if there are any other developments."

"Yes, sir," Emerson said.

He looked at me, but before he could say or ask anything, Grandfather said, "You'd best go and wait in the Sutherland Room, Caroline. They'll probably have more questions for you now."

Why? I almost asked, but stopped myself, thinking it would make him more suspicious. I wiped away the tears, nodded, and started away. My heart wasn't simply pounding; it felt like it was tossing from side to side beneath my breast. How could any of this turn out to be anything else but horrible? Would my father find out? Simon had lost control of himself. He could babble anything. In my wildest imagination, I envisioned myself being sent to some lockdown facility for wayward girls with a team of Mrs. Lawson look-alikes governing every breath I took.

I wanted to cry for my mother or my father, but I swallowed back my fear and moved like someone so hypnotized that she didn't know she was moving, let alone where she was. When I stepped into the Sutherland Room, I sat on the sofa and clasped my hands in my lap. Vaguely, I heard the moaning of a second ambulance and thought about Simon. I hated his arrogance and his self-satisfaction. He was so high and above me, which made what I had seen of him in his suite even more terrifying.

And sad.

I really had become his only friend.

I gazed out the two large windows. The late afternoon sun was slipping as if the sky behind it had turned into dark blue ice. The horizon seemed to be rising to capture and hide it. I couldn't hold my perfect posture. I sat back and closed my eyes, now vaguely hearing the sounds of excited voices and footsteps. If I tried really hard, I could hear Mommy singing in the kitchen. I would hurry to watch her dance, and she would see me standing there in the doorway.

"C'mon," she'd say. "Sweet Caroline."

And we would dance, not even noticing that Daddy had come home. Sometimes he watched us, almost forcing himself to smile, and other times he'd look in, shake his head, and go upstairs to change.

Does the past slide out of your memory and into your dreams until you wonder, *Was I ever there? Did that ever really happen?*

When does a memory become a dream?

I don't know how long I was sitting there, but I suddenly realized it was getting dark in the great room. I spun around when I heard the light switch flipped and saw Aunt Holly.

"My father-in-law told me to tell you that you don't have to wait in here any longer. The police won't be back until the morning. Clara Jean is getting your dinner out soon."

"How's Simon?" I asked.

"He's going to sleep now. There was no reason for Martin and me to remain there. Martin is in with his father, Franklin, and your grandfather's attorney, Cornell Witmor."

She paused, looked down, and then walked over to the sofa to sit beside me.

"I want you to tell me everything you know, Caroline. We already know Simon had been drinking alcohol, and I know you two have drawn a bit closer lately. Don't cry," she quickly added, and reached for my hand. "Just take a deep breath and tell me what you know. I'll be with you when the police return. But it's so important, for Simon's health as well as anything, that I know exactly what went on."

Who else was there to trust other than Aunt Holly, even now when I could be in a lot of trouble?

"I went up for a nap, and when I woke up, Simon was in my room. He had a bottle of bourbon and had already drunk a lot of it. He wanted me to drink, too. He said he had taken a few things from the bar.

"I was shocked and afraid, but before anything else could happen or be said, Mrs. Lawson opened my door and saw us. She was so happy about it, too. She didn't say anything; she slammed the door. Simon . . ."

"What?" Aunt Holly asked, her eyes now sharply bright with fear.

"He screamed 'No!' and charged out after her. I didn't see anything, but I thought I heard Mrs. Lawson laugh."

"Laugh?"

"I can't be absolutely sure. I did hear her scream and what I thought sounded like her falling down the stairs."

"What about Simon?"

"By the time I put on my robe and slippers, he was probably in his room. He wasn't there at the top of the stairs. Then I heard Clara Jean scream and went to the railing, looked down, and saw Mrs. Lawson. When my grandfather saw her, he looked up and told me to get dressed and come down."

"What did you tell him?"

"I didn't tell him about Simon in my room or Mrs. Lawson finding us together. I didn't tell the detectives, either. I just told them I had heard Clara Jean scream, and I told them Grandfather had sent me to get dressed."

She nodded. "You might have to tell them all of it," she said.

"Grandfather won't want me here, and my father won't want me, either. We didn't do anything, but . . ."

"Nobody will really believe you." She nodded again. "Mrs. Lawson wins no matter what," she said, not looking at me. Then she turned sharply to me. "Let's wait to see about Simon. For now, there is no reason to tell that part of your story. Stay with what you told the detectives.

"They're doing neurological tests on Simon, but one of the emergency room doctors I know told me there was a good chance this was something akin to a panic attack. He might have just run to his room after she saw you two, or maybe he did something that caused her fall and then ran to his room.

"Don't lie," she advised, "but don't answer questions you're not asked. I don't know if you can continue to do that. You're too honest a person. Besides, you probably have your mother's streak of defiance. I don't know what your father would tell you to do."

"He would tell me not to hide, but if I don't, I probably won't see him again, and he won't be telling me anything."

Aunt Holly hugged me. "It's Sutherland," she whispered. "It's beautiful and like a castle, but it toys with our very souls: your grandfather's, my husband's, and now my son's."

"What do we do?"

"Somehow . . . I don't know why . . . you'll know what to do when the time comes."

She squeezed my hand the way my mother would to emphasize her words of promise. Was it simply part of being a mother? Or did she really believe what she had said? Was I now the hope she had given up in Simon?

"C'mon. I'll get something to eat with you."

We rose to leave, and as we did, I heard the curtains rustle as if the house itself had trembled.

CHAPTER SIX

Aunt Holly's doctor friend was right. There was nothing neurolo-gically wrong with Simon. He awoke, and from what Aunt Holly was told, his doctor decided that it was some sort of panic issue. She said Simon claimed to remember nothing before his episode, except he did admit to drinking, and there was even the possibility that he had drunk too much and had some sort of severe reaction to the alcohol. There was no mention of his being with me before his episode.

The forensic team didn't find any evidence of foul play at the top of the stairway, and the medical examiner said there was no sign of pre-fall trauma. There was simply no proof that anyone had poked, pushed, or punched her. The detectives returned to speak with Grand-father and then, almost in a routine way, questioned me again, this time with Aunt Holly present. I tried not to make my answers sound memorized, something I could imagine Simon advising. "It'll make you look guilty of something," he'd surely say.

Was there much difference between a liar and someone who

skirted the truth by leaving out a fact here and there? My father was someone who could tell. Mommy had often said he was a sort of detective, trained to spot a critical detail. She had said he could even analyze a pilot's confidence by the tone of his or her voice. I was grateful that he wasn't in the room with the detectives.

After they had left, Dr. Kirkwell arrived. Grandfather had called her to see if I was all right, but I suspected he wanted her to find out if I knew anything more. Answering her questions was more frightening to me than answering those of the detectives again. I did my best to hide the icy feeling that shivered down my spine. She had gotten inside me so much and so well when I was in the dark bedroom under her treatment that I was afraid she could see the whole truth. She did ask if I had seen Simon before he started drinking the whiskey. I hadn't, so I could confidently say no and not seem like I was lying.

"I know you weren't fond of Mrs. Lawson," she said. Her words hung in the air for a few moments as if she was anticipating that I would admit to something.

I shrugged. "She didn't like me. She proved that when she picked me up at the school that horrible day."

Dr. Kirkwell smiled. "Well, she wasn't that fond of me, either."

She said that the best thing for me to do in order to keep my mind from thinking about the terrible event was to keep up my schoolwork. She added some assignments.

"We do want you to stay on schedule so you can leave for Hawaii when the time comes."

Days later, I found out Simon had been kept in the hospital for more observation. There was even talk of him being sent to a special clinic. Aunt Holly told me that his depression appeared to be lingering, even getting deeper, and he wasn't craving to be released. When Grandfather was told everything at dinner that night, he didn't say anything or ask a single question.

The following day, I asked Aunt Holly if Grandfather had asked questions about Simon before or after she had explained his condition at dinner. His indifference had shocked me.

"No," she said. "What's happening to Simon embarrasses your grandfather, so he'll do his best to avoid it."

"Embarrasses? Why?"

"It's like he thinks Sutherlands have super blood or something, and showing any sort of weakness diminishes the name. I'm sure he's finding a way to blame Martin and me."

Her expression collapsed into one of forlorn reminiscence before she continued in a sadder voice darkened with the underlying anger.

"Did you know he didn't come to our daughter's church service? I didn't expect him to come to her graveyard ceremony, either."

She sighed so deeply that I thought her heart had certainly cringed beneath her breast.

"Part of me is buried there now, shadows falling over the grave with the rise and fall of the Sutherland sun."

She started to cry softly, the memories of her baby's smiles and whimpers flooding her eyes. Despite how much I felt sorry for myself now, I wanted very much to be a comfort to her, but I couldn't think of anything that didn't imply forgetting. What other solution was there for sorrow, and who should know better than I did? At least she didn't have her baby's burial ashes secretly stored at Sutherland.

She wiped her eyes and smiled. "Let's think of happier things for the moment. Tell me more about your mother and her friend Nattie. Did they really enjoy being together, despite all they had to confront?"

"They were more angry than sad, especially about our house and the way it was taken away. But they were mostly happy in front of me, and they worked hard at duplicating my room in Nattie's house. We were going to go to New York City for Christmas. Although I would never say it to anyone else, they were trying to turn us into a family."

"Did you ever feel like they had?"

"Yes."

I paused and held my breath. What would Aunt Holly's reaction to that be? Even with Mrs. Lawson gone, I felt like I was always being watched and heard. Somehow the house brought it all to Grandfather. When I returned to reading Grandmother Judith's diary, especially toward the end of it, I sensed she'd had similar feelings. Everyone who worked here, every corner of the house that could capture an echo, reported things to Grandfather. I understood why Simon believed the basement was the safest place for your own secrets and why so many were kept down there.

"I understand, honey. It's not something I would tell anyone," she said, emphasizing "anyone" so hard that I was positive she meant Grandfather.

"Do you know anything about Nattie?" I asked Aunt Holly, immediately looking toward the doorway of the study. She had come in while I was completing a workbook assignment, and the door remained open.

"She's being cared for, but her prognosis isn't very good, I'm afraid."

"Oh." Never did I feel more like a child stumbling about in my grief and loss and yet terribly afraid to show it. Mrs. Lawson's early words had never left me. I was to become a new person if I was to continue in the Sutherland family, even if I was able to become part of Daddy's new family, and that meant totally wiping my memory of Nattie.

Aunt Holly was staring at me hard, but I could sense she wasn't seeing me. She was seeing something in herself. I could almost hear what she was thinking.

"Maybe, if we're very careful about it," she said, speaking each word carefully and slowly, "I can take you to visit her before you leave for

Hawaii. It would have to be the tightest, strongest secret you and I have ever kept. It would be risky, probably for both of us but far more for you. Your grandfather has tentacles out everywhere in the community. I don't have any idea how much interest he's taken in her, if at all. Martin says nothing about her, which leads me to believe that your grandfather really doesn't show any interest. Gone and forgotten is his way. Who knows? Maybe he's right. It's the best formula for survival in a world that spreads tragedy and pain like butter over our hearts and minds.

"However, I don't even know what sort of a visit it would be for you, considering her condition. She suffered serious brain damage. It might not be worth the risk."

"Oh, yes," I said after only a few seconds of thought. "I'd like that very much."

"Hmmm." She thought. "I suppose we can go on a shopping spree for your clothes for Hawaii. I'll mention it casually to your grandfather, and then we'll take a short detour. I'll see how difficult that is to arrange first, so don't hold your hopes too high."

"Okay."

"Let's not talk about it again. When it can happen, I'll tell you almost moments before we do it. And we'll have to keep track of Simon's condition, of course. I'm there every morning for a while. Martin and I have consults with the psychiatrist."

"Simon doesn't say anything about me? Even ask a question?"

"He rarely talks to anyone, even us."

"What does everyone think?" I really meant just Grandfather.

"Everyone thinks he pushed Mrs. Lawson down the stairs," she said quickly. "Even you do."

I held my breath rather than answer. I obviously didn't have to, because my eyes told her she was right. I was having nightmares about it already. I should not have worried about how I looked and gone out after him to stop him.

"I don't think it's his guilt over it as much as it is what he fears Grandfather now thinks of him. I've been after Martin to get his father to visit. Forget about last night's dinner and his making no comment about Simon's condition. Not once has your grandfather asked me how he is. Right from the start, he dropped Simon's name from his conversation, perhaps even his thoughts. Maybe Franklin Butler gives him updates just the way he does about the stock market."

"But there's no one really more loyal to Grandfather than Simon. Surely he knows that," I said.

"'Expects it' is a better way to put it," she said dryly. She rose. "Well, do your work. Try to put everything else aside for now."

She started for the door and paused.

"I think you're pretty smart about us all by now, Caroline, but think twice before you say anything to Grandfather Sutherland about Simon or make any other reference to your life with Nattie and your mother." She smiled. "Your mother used to advise me never to walk around him. Just tiptoe," she said. "I wonder if anyone ever did love him. I wonder if even Simon loves him."

"You can't love someone you fear," I said. I had recently read it in Grandmother Judith's diary.

Aunt Holly nodded. "You will be the best of us."

I watched her leave and then looked to the wall behind which my mother's ashes waited. It still gave me the feeling she was nearby and I could talk to her, easily imagining or remembering what she would say.

Of course, I did what Aunt Holly had suggested and kept things to myself. Weeks went by without much changing. Once in a while, I would pause at the doorway of the basement and consider going down to look at my personal things, but somehow, without Simon alongside me, and even without Mrs. Lawson watching my every move and breath, it did seem more dangerous.

Simon was moved to a psychiatric clinic. Apparently, Grandfather was satisfied that it had all been done very quietly. Listening hard to what was said between the lines, I understood that Franklin Butler handled the contact with Simon's schooling. Other students, who rarely saw him, certainly didn't miss him, and his teachers were clearly pressured to keep whatever they knew to themselves. I toyed with the idea of outright asking if I could visit him, but all sorts of alarm bells went off inside me at just the thought.

Of course, I didn't know exactly how the detectives had concluded their investigation, but Aunt Holly's remark about everyone thinking Simon had pushed Mrs. Lawson clearly meant Grandfather did, too. You couldn't even think the word "everyone" without including Grandfather in this house. However, because of Dr. Kirkwell's report, I was confident Grandfather didn't suspect I had anything to do with it.

It was best to leave it at that, even though I couldn't help feeling guilty about Simon. Once I really had disliked him to the point of not wanting to be anywhere near him. But what I eventually saw in him was his loneliness and how similar we really were. Loneliness was like a common, highly contagious disease at Sutherland. Who didn't suffer from it here? I was sure that pain was something Grandfather might never admit to, but in my heart of hearts, I believed it was why he worked so hard and was so hard-crusted.

The grand dinners I once recalled here were becoming a thin and distant memory. It was only Uncle Martin, Aunt Holly, and me most nights. Often Franklin Butler was there, and the discussion was primarily business-related. Once Mrs. Lawson's funeral had been held, which was another church service Grandfather didn't attend—instead, from what I understood, he sat in his limousine and watched the burial in the church cemetery—no one so much as mentioned her. The investigation of her death was apparently officially over as well. To me, it was as if the walls of the house had absorbed her. Sometimes I imagined her image in the corridor as if it was trying to pop out. Maybe people like her didn't die, I thought. Maybe no place would take them but here at Sutherland, so ultimately they'd be in some sort of in-between place forever and ever, maybe even pleading for the devil to take them.

About a week before Dr. Kirkwell announced I had completed my school year, Aunt Holly mentioned shopping for my Hawaiian clothes. It had been so long since Grandfather had taken any time to speak to me, it was as if just at that moment he remembered I was here and that I was leaving for my father's home soon.

"Yes," he said. And then, like someone who had just recalled an important thing, he pointedly added, "Dr. Kirkwell says you did very well in your work. We've sent all the information about your schooling to your father just in case."

"In case?"

"In case he wants you to stay, of course. He'd have to enroll you in a school there," he said, and then began to talk with Franklin Butler about a real estate deal.

How casual this sounded to everyone. Grandfather put as much emotion into it as he would if he said, "Tomorrow is another day," or something just as inconsequential. Aunt Holly did smile at me, but Uncle Martin looked quite disinterested. I almost felt like sticking a pin in him by asking him right now, in front of Grandfather, how Simon was. I glanced at Aunt Holly. I thought she gently shook her head. Were my thoughts written in my eyes?

Right after lunch the following day, Aunt Holly arrived to take me shopping. Grandfather was out by the garage house, talking with Emerson. He paused when he saw us, and from the way he stared, I thought he might suspect something. Aunt Holly waved. Emerson waved back. Grandfather nodded, and they started to talk again.

"We're going to see Nattie," Aunt Holly said, "but we can stay only a half hour at most and then go right to the department store."

Short of seeing my mother, discovering she didn't die, this was the most exciting thing I could have wished to hear since the day I was brought here. For the entire ride to the treatment center where Nattie was being cared for, my heart was in a drumroll. Maybe she wouldn't recognize me, I feared. Maybe Aunt Holly was right: her brain had suffered so much damage that she had lost most if not all her memory. I could be looking at a face painted with a blank stare, a face in which I had hoped I would find the lost love, the happy and beautiful times filled with music and laughter, as well as all those French words and exciting descriptions that enabled me to travel on the tail of her comet.

This could be the biggest mistake of all. "Sometimes," Mommy had once said, "it's best not to go back to happier times. If they are gone, that will just remind you of how sad you now are. Press your beautiful memories like flowers into the book you keep closed in your heart."

The treatment center where Nattie was being attended did not look at all like a medical building. It was a large Queen Anne–style house on beautifully maintained grounds, with gently rolling lawns and fountains, on which large maple and oak trees were sprawling and casting shade and splendor on an already beautiful part of the countryside.

"This is really more of a rest home for the financially well-off," Aunt Holly said, immediately explaining what looked quite unexpected. I was anticipating a stone or likewise official-looking medical building that more or less resembled a hospital, albeit a private one. "Nattie has friends in high places and was obviously quite well-liked and respected. I don't know all that much more about her arrangements."

"Probably the U.S. ambassador to France," I offered.

She smiled and nodded. "As your grandfather proves to us daily, it pays to have friends in high places."

We parked near three other cars in the front. I could see there was another, larger parking lot around the right corner and toward the rear.

"There are private nurses here attending people in their suites and I think a doctor and assistant twenty-four seven. The patients keep their identities private. That is why I thought your grandfather might know about this place. If anyone knows the secrets of the rich and powerful, your grandfather does. I'm not a hundred percent positive he doesn't keep track of the comings and goings involving Nattie.

"But I'm pretty close to a hundred percent," she added, smiling. "I have a friend who's a nurse here, and she says Nattie has only the occasional friend-in-high-places visitor but no one else showing any interest, no one asking questions or watching the house. I trust her."

We got out and walked to the front entrance, which looked like the front entrance of any house. Through the glass windows in the door, I could see sofas, chairs, and tables in the foyer. There was no one sitting at an official greeting desk. We entered. Aunt Holly took my hand, and we stood quietly waiting. After a few moments, a tall, thin nurse with very short dark brown hair appeared.

"Holly," she said, and turned to me. "This is Caroline?"

"Yes, Maggie. Thank you for this."

"There's no sign-in of any kind," she said. "Just follow me. We're going to a room on the right at the end of the hallway. The doctor just left her, and she's resting as quietly as she can. Prepare yourself. She has serious trembles."

She paused and leaned toward me.

"She's far from the woman you remember, Caroline. She shows little recognition of anyone who's come, and she cannot manage pronouncing a single word. She's lost a lot of weight. We do as best we can to keep her hair looking nice. That's the hard, cold truth."

She looked at Holly.

"Do you really want to do this?" Aunt Holly asked me.

"Yes," I said firmly.

Maggie nodded and, without another word, turned and began to walk down the corridor. Aunt Holly held tightly to my hand, or was I really holding tightly to hers? We passed other rooms with the doors either closed or partially opened through which I could see a nurse or a doctor speaking with an elderly lady. The floors and halls were immaculate. It was only once I was here, inside, that the house, which resembled an ordinary home, took on the look of an institution.

Before you meet someone whom you once knew but haven't seen in a while, you envision them the way they were when you last saw them. What I recalled the most about Nattie was how intensely she would look at you when you spoke to her or she spoke to you. She was a little taller than my mother, attractive, but her figure wasn't as perfect. She wouldn't be on the cover of *Vogue* or a similar magazine, as my father would claim my mother would. Nattie was a little wider in the hips, with a smaller bosom, and thus did not have the hourglass figure my mother had. She did have beautiful kelly green eyes that were habitually lit with intelligence. She seemed capable of being interested in anything and everything just so she wouldn't miss anything or, maybe more important for me, belittle something I was interested in or cherished. I couldn't forget how firmly she would take my hand.

Even Grandfather once said at a dinner with the family that you could judge a person instantly from his handshake. "Confidence radiates in a man's fingers and grip," he said, eyeing my uncle Martin, whose handshake always looked a bit unsure to me.

"A woman's, too," Mommy added.

Whenever she did that, tack on another thought to what he had said, Grandfather would peer at her and change the topic.

I almost stopped before we entered Nattie's room. I could hear medical machinery and immediately caught a glimpse of a nurse moving around Nattie's bed. Aunt Holly let go of my hand and put her arm around my shoulders. I heard her take a deep breath. I was holding mine.

Nattie was on her back, looking straight up, with oxygen leads in her nostrils. At the side of the bed was a device to help get needed body movement. Someone had trimmed her amber hair so that it didn't hang below her ears. Ironically, to me it looked just as bright and healthy.

There was nothing warm and homey about her room. It was as if I had just left the building we had entered and walked into a hospital. The walls, at least, were a light pinkish tone, and the windows were wide, accepting as much sunlight as they could with the wooden shades opened. There was a television mounted on the wall. I imagined the bed was lifted for her to see it, but from the way her arms lay, her hands looking frozen in a curl, I was sure she had no control of any remote. Beside her bed was a pitcher of something she could drink with a straw.

What struck me the most, perhaps, was the amount of weight she had lost. It was as if her body was sinking into itself. I could see bones where I never could, and her full cheeks looked like they were being pulled in at the middle. The nurse paused after checking an intravenous drip and looked at us. Nattie showed no sign of realizing someone else was there.

"Hey, Nattie," she said. "You have guests."

Nattie didn't turn her head toward us. I realized almost instantly that she couldn't. The nurse adjusted her pillow so that her head tilted in our direction. She was looking right at me now, but my heart was shriveling in disappointment. There was no recognition in her vacant eyes. Aunt Holly squeezed my shoulder gently. I stepped ahead of her, almost reaching the bed.

"Nattie," I said.

She blinked rapidly and then made a gruesome sound. Aunt Holly embraced me quickly, but I didn't retreat. I repeated her name. I could see the struggle in her face as she struggled with the sound until I was sure she was saying "Sweet."

I was crying, but I started to sing the song my mother and I would dance to: "Where it began, I can't begin to knowing . . ."

She stopped making the sound. I wouldn't say she smiled, but a soft moment of quiet and love seeped into her face. I reached for her hand and held it. Slowly, almost unsure of itself, a tear emerged from her right eye. I looked at the nurse. She was crying, too. I didn't cry.

I was Daddy: strong, determined, and self-confident.

"I'm going to be okay, Nattie," I said. "I have Mommy near me, always."

I leaned over to kiss her cheek.

"*À bientôt, ma chérie*," I whispered, and stepped back.

She started to make that guttural sound, stopped, and closed her eyes as I let go of her hand and stepped back.

"I'm sorry," the nurse said.

She wasn't apologizing for what had happened to Nattie. She was apologizing for ending this short visit. Even these minutes had clearly exhausted Nattie. I practically fell back into Aunt Holly's arms. She turned me, but at the door, I looked back. Nattie's eyes were open, and I will swear to the day I die that she was smiling.

Neither of us spoke until we were in her car and pulling away.

"I hope this wasn't a mistake," Aunt Holly said. "Not that your grandfather would find out but that it was so painful for you."

"No. I have something about her to take with me, Aunt Holly. Forever."

She smiled and nodded. "Let's get you some really fancy Hawaiian outfits, shorts, blouses, a few bathing suits, sandals—all of it," she said.

"We'll spend as much Sutherland money as we can. And you need new suitcases, a new purse, carrying bags, hats, sunglasses, and a good travel watch."

"That sounds like a lot."

"It is. So what?" she said, laughing.

I sat back. It almost seemed like I was doing something wrong by looking forward to my future with Daddy, wrong to permit an iota of happiness, with Nattie back there and Simon in a clinic, but it was too powerful a new feeling to be denied. I ramped up my enthusiasm and, like a starving panther, attacked the choices in the department store, my eyes surely showing the dazzle of new things and new hope.

When we drove up to the grand front entrance of Sutherland, Emerson came hurrying from the garage house. At first, I thought something might be wrong, but he was just so eager and pleased to help us carry all my new things into the mansion. As if drawn by our pleasure, Clara Jean and another maid rushed to the foyer to help. The commotion brought Grandfather to his office doorway.

"You could have had her buy things in Hawaii, too, you know," he told Aunt Holly.

She laughed, which surprised him.

"And miss the pleasure of my doing it?"

"Women," he said.

"Yes. Thank heaven," she replied.

He looked at me. "I've set aside an hour tomorrow for you. We'll discuss your leaving Sutherland and what I expect of your behavior. Your flight is arranged for Hawaii in the evening, so you can sleep some on the plane. You should be as fresh-eyed as you can be when you arrive.

"Get all that organized," he ordered Aunt Holly. "Martin is arriving an hour before dinner tonight. We'll be discussing Simon."

"What about him?" she fired back.

I didn't think he'd answer. He looked more like he would just step back and close his office door, but he didn't.

"His future," he said, and then stepped back and closed the door.

Aunt Holly looked at me.

And just like that.

As a pin would puncture a balloon.

All the air in our excitement and fun whooshed away and left us folded inside ourselves.

CHAPTER SEVEN

I wished I could be in Grandfather's office to hear about Simon, too, but I knew that would be difficult. If Grandfather said anything at all about Mrs. Lawson's tumbling to her death, his eyes would be on me, and it could all begin again, because I didn't know how to block out the windows in my face. I didn't want to say anything that could get Simon into trouble and hurt his self-confidence.

"You're either born with the ability to deceive or you learn it well from those who do it well around you," Daddy had told me when he was questioning me about Mommy and Nattie during those early days. I wasn't sure if he meant Mommy was teaching me how to be dishonest. It was almost impossible to lie to my father anyway.

When dinner began that night, I thought I would learn nothing new about Simon. Aunt Holly hadn't mentioned anything, so I assumed that they had talked only about Simon's condition. However, I was surprised that we had an additional guest at the table, Cornell Witmor, Grandfather's attorney. He, as well as Franklin Butler, apparently had been at the meeting with Uncle Martin and Aunt Holly. They began, like most nights, talking business and politics. We ate and, like always, Aunt Holly, Uncle Martin, and I just listened. I did notice Uncle Martin and Aunt Holly were so quiet that they didn't say a word to each other or raise their eyes from their food much.

After our dinner dishes were cleared and we were waiting for dessert, Grandfather stroked his mustache and then turned to me, clasping his hands and resting his elbows on the table. Everyone sat back. The way the others were all looking toward the ceiling, as if they didn't want to hear what he was going to say and didn't want to make eye contact with me, felt weird and made me even more nervous.

"Your cousin Simon has described something to his psychiatrist that is very disturbing for us all, Caroline. Fortunately, the doctor is someone I have assisted in building his practice and helped, as of yesterday, actually, to make good investments for him in the stock market. I am assuming that this will all be as much news to you as it has been to us, and of course, nothing said leaves this table."

I don't think I even blinked. Every part of me was frozen in place. Should I immediately begin denying? I couldn't speak even if I wanted to be emphatic about it. When it came to looking into you, Grandfather Sutherland went deeper than my father.

"Simon revealed that he was very angry at Mrs. Lawson. I knew he wasn't fond of her, but this turned different because of what happened to her."

I just stared at him. Were my eyes even blinking?

"All he has claimed about it so far is that he was drinking and she caught him. She bawled him out and was threatening to tell me. The doctor prodded his memory, and Simon recalled marching up to her to try to convince her not to tell me anything. He admitted that he might have frightened her when he got too close to her. Because of Simon's doctor's carefully worded questions, he finally admitted that she pushed at him so hard, pressing her palms to his chest, that she caused herself to fall back on the stairway and lost her footing. After that, his memory disappears. Maybe conveniently.

"Since what he's told his doctor is protected private information, the detectives will not be informed and brought back here, nor will they be permitted to question Simon any further. He was exuberant in his angry reaction to Mrs. Lawson but claims he was not lethal. Do you understand the difference?"

"Yes," I said in a voice I could barely hear myself. "He didn't deliberately push her back. She sort of bounced off him."

Grandfather looked at Mr. Witmor and then at me, intensely again. "And you have nothing to add or correct about that?"

"No, Grandfather."

"Then it remains an accident, and Simon continues on his path to recovery."

He slammed his palm on the table. The plates and silverware jumped.

"Clara Jean," he said. She was standing in the doorway. Servants at Sutherland had no ears until Grandfather permitted them. "We are looking forward to Mrs. Wilson's apple pie crumble."

"Yes, Mr. Sutherland," she said, and hurried off.

I could feel Aunt Holly's eyes on me. I was afraid to look at her, because now, more than anyone, even Dr. Kirkwell, she saw into my heart. Of course, I had more to add to what Simon had told his doctor. Mrs. Lawson had caught us together, with me naked beneath a towel and Simon slurping from a bottle of bourbon. He had charged out after her. My words would bring back the detectives. I swallowed them all back, practically choking on the thoughts, and drank some water.

Thankfully, the conversation returned to business and politics.

However, afterward, before she and Uncle Martin left, Aunt Holly came to my room. I was already there, sitting on my bed and gazing at the nearly packed new suitcases, almost in a stupor.

I looked up when she entered. She closed the door and leaned back against it.

"I don't want you leaving for a new start carrying a heavy load of guilt with you, Caroline. Simon is a force unto himself. He's my son, but I know what he's capable of doing. If you want to know the truth, the truth is I am happy he's suffering some mental anguish right now."

"Really?"

"Yes, really. It means he is permitting his conscience some air to breathe. Even as a small child, he could rationalize and explain away something he did wrong. He was as good as a lawyer before the Supreme Court every time, too. However, in elementary school, way before we permitted him to begin homeschooling and acceleration, he hurt some of his classmates. We knew he wasn't popular; he rarely was invited to birthday parties his classmates' parents gave for them, and his teachers always made a point of telling us that he'd deliberately sit in the rear of the classroom and the cafeteria, as far away from the others as he could.

"When questions were asked in class, he waited to be sure no one knew the answer and then spoke. His teachers admitted he was brilliant, but you could almost feel their wish that he wasn't, that he was more . . . average. Martin would rush over to his father with Simon's report cards and belittle or sweep away any early warnings about Simon's behavior.

"There was always this Sutherland thing, this idea that they were expected to be heads and shoulders above their peers anyway. I don't think there was anything your mother hated more. She could feel herself being judged almost as soon as she was born."

She smiled.

"At least, that was the way she described it. I didn't want her to marry your father. She almost surrendered to everything that was expected of her. I think she hypnotized herself to believe she was in love. How could she find another man as perfect as Morgan Bryer? He was and is good-looking, full of the same self-confidence required of a Sutherland, and most of all, he thought the world of your grandfather.

"She was finally pleasing her father, but to do it, she had to deny everything she really wanted in herself. I saw how committed she was to making her marriage work, especially after you were born. She didn't oppose any of it anymore. The Sutherlands have a way of getting you to accept how things are. It's just easier. I've done the same with Martin. I think once the situation with Simon has some resolution, I'm going to set sail."

"You mean divorce Uncle Martin?"

She smiled. "I think we've been divorced for many years. There's just no official document. There are many women like your mother and me. I'm hoping you won't be one of them."

"But . . . I want to be like my mother."

"Yes, but after she became who she was. That doesn't mean you should become gay, as your grandfather feared. If you do, you do, but on your own. Everything is so complicated as we get older. It's why we dream of being children so long. The world is simpler then. Someone tells you what's right and wrong, whether to go left or right, what to believe, how to dress, practically how to dream.

"But at some point it ends, and you cross over into adulthood. For Simon it ended far too early. Sutherland has no place for children. Have you noticed that there isn't a real nursery in this house? Once Martin and your mother outgrew their cribs, they were taken apart and buried in the basement along with most everything related to infancy. By the age of two, they were sleeping in adult beds.

"The same thing was true for your grandfather, by the way. He grew up a lot like Simon." She paused, forbidding the tears that were threatening. "Not liking his own father." She took a deep breath.

"I'll be all right, Aunt Holly," I said with my father's firmness. "Don't worry about me, too."

She smiled. "Good. I'll stop by tomorrow to say goodbye and wish you a great trip."

She looked at the open suitcases.

"I think it's great that you're doing your own packing."

"Clara Jean offered to help, but I said I'm fine."

"I believe you are. Okay. I'm going home. Have a good night, sweetheart."

She came over to hug me. I held on to her for a few moments longer than I should have, but when I closed my eyes, I was hugging my mother. I suspect Aunt Holly knew. She kissed me on the forehead, brushed my hair, and left before I could see her start to cry.

For a long moment, I sat there staring at the closed door. I hated that door now. It seemed to loom like some sort of an entrance in a horror movie. *One more night*, I thought, *and I'll be gone. When I close it behind me, I'll shut up all the memories.*

That thought brought a new idea to me. I rose and, as quietly as I could, slipped out of the room. I could hear Uncle Martin and Aunt Holly saying their good nights. Their footsteps, doors opening and closing, and the words of good night settled into Sutherland's walls and floors. To me, it sometimes felt like it was constructed out of a sponge that could absorb words and thoughts as well as actions. The house grew fatter. Maybe the mansion would explode someday, just come apart, and all the skeletons would crumble into the shattered foundation.

I continued down the stairs, hesitated, listened, and then hurried to the basement door. Despite my shivering inside, I opened it, turned on the lights, and descended, desperately trying to keep each step from creaking and warning my grandfather. Now, at night, there wasn't as much light from the basically necessary bulbs, but my memory of how to navigate the cartons, old furniture, pictures, and trunks was good enough to take me past Prissy's grave and to the box of my personal things. I knelt and opened it, again listening to be sure no one had heard or seen me go into the basement. It was very quiet.

I sifted quickly through the items, found the model airplane my father had given me years ago, and took it out. Just holding it replayed that day when Nattie had first come to our house and wanted me to escort her through it. My first choice of where to go was my room. I wanted her to see it, probably because I wanted her to know me better, even better than she knew my mother at the time. I remembered her looking at the model plane and pretending the woman in one of the plane windows looked like her. Maybe I'd be taking her with me as much as a valuable personal item that shouted "Daddy!" It belonged with me when I went to him. Hopefully he'd be happy about it. He'd surely think I was thinking of him more than I was of my mother, even though that would never be true.

Clutching it tightly but carefully to my side, I made my way back to the stairs, listened hard again, and went up, switching off the lights and closing the door softly. I clung to those all-too-familiar shadows in the halls of Sutherland and ascended the dreadful stairs, closing my eyes so as not to relive the sight of Mrs. Lawson, twisted and dead at the foot of them.

As soon as I had entered my room, I carefully wrapped the model plane and padded it well in one of my suitcases. Then I finally took a deep breath, prepared myself for sleep and getting through the final night and most of the final day here. Was I wrong to hope for, to even want, a new life that would not have my mother in it? Most likely, Daddy wouldn't want me even to mention her. Could I really live with that?

Truly, I was leaving her behind in that private room on a shelf in Grandfather's office. How much did my father really know about that? Did he know her grave had an empty coffin in it with what amounted to lies engraved on a stone? Did that please him? Would I hate him for that? Would it make it impossible to start a new life with him?

It took me hours to fall asleep, and I knew I was late for breakfast, a breakfast Grandfather might have wanted me to have with him, if only to hear his new warnings and threats. Surprisingly, he wasn't there, nor was he in his office. He had gone to his real estate office in Colonie. Was he just going to let me leave without saying goodbye? I completed my packing and later had lunch alone on the patio, gazing at Grandmother Judith's garden.

Sutherland, despite how much time I had spent in it these past months, still felt like a strange place to me, something as anonymous as a historical site that no longer felt it belonged to anyone. It belonged to the country. Sutherland was truly beautiful and deserved to be acknowledged for that. The groundskeepers were everywhere, trimming and mowing with obviously special care, the care of hired help who would treat the property as if it were their own.

Two men were repainting one of the coral fences as if they were re-creating the *Mona Lisa*, pausing every few minutes to stand back and look at their work. The bushes and the trees seemed to sway to their own music in the wind, and the mountains in the distance never looked more majestic, rolling like green waves to the horizon. I should want to live here, I thought. I wondered if my mother ever really had that desire. Was it always unpleasant for her? If it was, I hated even more that her ashes were locked up and hidden in it now.

As she had promised, Aunt Holly stopped by to say her final goodbye and wish me a good, safe trip, while I was still sitting on the patio.

"Martin and I are going to the clinic to have dinner with Simon," she said. "His psychiatrist thought that was a good idea and something we should do more often, even if he simply sits there and eats and ignores us."

"Are you going to tell him I'm leaving?"

"Maybe. I'll have to check it out with the doctor first."

"Perhaps I should write him a note, maybe wish him to get well."

"I'm not sure about that. Everything is so fragile at the moment."

"Okay."

"Someday I'll call you to tell you to write him a letter. How's that?"

"That's good."

"You write and call me, however, whenever you want, Caroline. I'll always be there for you."

She hugged me for the final goodbye. I felt so empty and alone watching her walk away, feeling like an astronaut whose lifeline had snapped. *I'm truly dangling like those spiders in the basement*, I thought. How do you fall comfortably when you really don't know where the bottom lies?

Minutes later, Clara Jean came to tell me that Grandfather wanted me in his office. It had been a while since I was alone with him. I think I was still trembling from that last experience. I walked slowly through the house to his office door and knocked.

"Come in, Caroline," he said, as if he could see through it.

He was seated behind his desk, looking down at some papers. As always, he was formally dressed in a tweed suit. I stood there for a long moment, and then he looked up.

"Sit, Caroline."

He leaned back as I did.

"I think you have been helped to find the sufficient state of mind to help yourself start a new life. No one, me the least, expects you to forget your mother or your former life completely. We hope we have helped you choose what's important about it and what's not. The hardest thing to accept in this life is that someone you're expected to love, even worship, has deep flaws in his or her character. Accept that, and new, important decisions won't be so difficult for you. Do you understand?"

No, I wanted to say, and almost did. The word formed on my lips, but I knew if I said it, there was no telling how far back I'd fall.

It nearly choked me, but I said it: "Yes."

He nodded. "I think you do. You are a lot like your mother, of course, but fortunately, you have a good deal of your father's sense, too. I think, in time, you will make a good Sutherland."

He smiled.

"I'm sure you expected me to say 'Bryer,' but your father would probably be the first to permit you to think of yourself as a descendant of the family that has built this property, this world."

Oh, I could give him so many reasons why not, I thought. If only I could reveal what I had learned reading Grandmother Judith's diary. It was surely filled with thoughts and ideas she had never expressed to him. He'd be the last she would have told, probably.

He picked up a manila envelope.

"This has your tickets, boarding pass, and some spending money. Actually, a lot more than some. There is also a mobile phone in here with a slip of paper that has your phone number. You'll need to give the number to your father and his new family. The only name under 'contacts' is mine, but I have decided to permit Holly to call you. Can you think of anyone else you would call?"

Whom did he think—Nattie? Didn't he know how injured she was?

"I've lost contact with any school friends," I said, "and anyone else I knew."

He sat back again and looked at his watch as if what I had said about friends wasn't even important enough to acknowledge.

"You'll be leaving in about an hour and a half for the airport.

Emerson will come up for your luggage, and he will take you to the airport and see that you're checked in properly. These are first-class tickets," he said, patting the envelope. "You'll be able to sleep on the plane after you get on your connecting flight. Your father, ironically, will be handling your plane's arrival in Maui at the Kahului Airport, so he won't be there to greet you when you disembark at terminal one on level two and take you to the luggage carousel. You know what all that means, right? I don't want you looking like some waif, lost and ignorant of what she is doing and having to have someone lead her by the hand."

"Yes, I know. Daddy once took me on a tour of the airport and explained things to me. I think I was only five. We went on a vacation the following year and flew to Jackson Hole, Wyoming. I was too little to remember it all, but I do remember I was put on a horse and led around a track. Daddy rode beside me."

"I remember that. I had a friend who owns a hotel there. You know what fringe benefits are?"

I shook my head. I had an idea, but with Grandfather Sutherland, an idea wasn't good enough of an answer.

"Well, technically, it's a form of pay for performed services, something extra like my permitting Emerson to use my limousine to pick up friends at the airport. These benefits could be part of a hiring package, which is also true for Emerson and all my employees. They all get health insurance through my company. Your mother received many fringe benefits from simply being my daughter. Sutherland comes with a package," he said dryly.

I was silent.

"Your cell phone is another one of those." He stroked his mustache. "This is your last chance to ask me any questions. About anything."

An avalanche of them began pouring out of my mind, but did

I dare ask any of them? Why are my mother's ashes in your private room? Why did you have me practically tortured? Why don't you care more about Simon, even care more about your own son?

"Well?"

Was he daring me to ask?

"When did you start to dislike my mother?"

His fingers paused on his mustache. "Probably about the time she began to dislike me," he said. "It's not an easy thing for a father to accept. She was always a defiant child and not someone who hid her feelings well. Your grandmother became a shield for her for a while, and then your mother, in her defiance, began to stand out from behind. We did argue often, but I don't recall her crying and moaning. I'll say that much of Sutherland wouldn't let go of her. Eventually, we had a sort of truce, and I put her to work. She met your father, and for a while things went well between us.

"Your father was actually the one who first saw she was only going through the motions. He wasn't complaining to me so much as he was warning me. Yes, you probably recall your mother being deliberately cantankerous. My father used to call me that. He was right, and I was right. Sometimes I think she finally did what she did solely to drive a stake through my heart."

"No," I said, and almost bit my tongue afterward.

"Yes," he said, and stared at me.

Was he going to rescind everything? I held my breath, something I had done too often in this house. Probably all of the Sutherlands breathed less here, I thought.

"Well, there is no need for us to agree on everything before you leave. Let me finally tell you that this remains a test for you. You have to decide within yourself whether you want to live with your father and his family. If you do, you'll have to toe the line. You know what that means?"

"Do what my father wants me to do."

"Exactly. I wish your mother had never forgotten that. Okay, okay," he said, putting up his hands. "I like what I've seen in your growth here, and I'm confident you'll do well in Hawaii."

"Will I ever come back?" I asked. I was really thinking of my mother's ashes just behind the inner door behind me.

"Whenever your father wants to visit. He has an open invitation always. So, getting back to what I said. You're going to be met at the airport by your father's new wife, Parker. I've never met her, not even talked to her, but he tells me she's a no-nonsense woman. Being as she's also an air traffic controller, only part-time now, that makes sense. People trained to be efficient and tidy usually can't tolerate sloppiness or misconduct. Keep that in mind."

"It was always in mind, Grandfather. My father was my father."

He actually laughed. "I have bad news for you, Caroline."

"What?"

"You're more like me than you think. Okay. Go get yourself ready," he said, and waved at the door with the back of his hand. Before I stood, he was looking down at his papers. "Hey," he said when I started to turn. "Your envelope."

He held it out. I took it, and when I turned again, I paused at the door to the inside room. I didn't know if he noticed, but I said goodbye to Mommy.

I changed into the outfit Aunt Holly suggested I wear to travel. Then I closed my suitcases, ran a brush through my hair, and sat for a few minutes on the bed, reviewing in my mind all the things Grandfather Sutherland had said. What surprised me was that I didn't leave his office disliking him as much as I did when I had entered. I had sensed something that I hadn't previously. What was it? Could it be that he really did like me?

Could I be more confused?

I heard a knock and opened my door to let Emerson in for my suitcases. He had a smile so bright that he made me feel happy again.

"You're on your way to a new world, missy," he said. "And don't you look like the world traveler now?"

"I don't feel like one, Emerson."

"Aye, but you will. Let's load her up, then."

He took all my suitcases, one under his arm and the other two in his hands. We started out. I closed the door behind me and stood there for a moment.

Goodbye to you, old room that could be anyone's.

Goodbye to the sounds traveling along the pipes of this mansion, maybe sounds that have never stopped but instead have been bouncing from one end to the other, sounds first made by my great-grandfather, sounds maybe even made by Prissy, and of course, sounds made by Simon.

Goodbye to the memory of that dark, dreadful bedroom at the end of a hallway most of all, the bedroom I hadn't even peered into since I was released. I wished you could flush a memory out of your mind as easily as you could flush a toilet.

I turned and hurried to catch up to Emerson, who marched down the curved staircase as if he was pounding the steps into oblivion. He waited at the bottom for me to join him for the walk out of Sutherland, through the foyer, past the hall to the Sutherland Room and the kitchen and the dining room, on to the atrium with its fountains and slate walkway, toward the grand oval-shaped copper mahogany front doors.

No one watched us leave. I glanced at some windows, but there wasn't anyone looking out. Maybe they thought it was forbidden to do so, to show even the slightest sorrow about my leaving. I was hoping to see Mrs. Wilson and Clara Jean, at least. How tight my grandfather's hold on everyone was.

When we passed through the main gate, I turned and looked back at it as it was closing, with SUTHERLAND in gold-plated scrolled letters above it. I wondered when I would see it again. I couldn't help having mixed feelings. Considering where I had spent most of my time here, the feelings of relief and escape were paramount, but I couldn't help thinking I was leaving my mother behind that gate.

"I took your mother many times to the airport and often drove her to college," Emerson said.

We looked at each other's eyes in the rearview mirror.

"And I must say, sweet Caroline, she often wore the same little-girl look of insecurity. Sutherland is like a world unto itself. And leaving it is like going to another planet. But the last time I recall driving her out, she looked quite defiant and strong. I'm sure you'll be the same. I know a very good Irish traveling song. I'll change one word for you," he said, and began to sing: "'In Dublin's fair city, where the girls are so pretty, I first set my eyes on sweet Caroline . . .'" I knew the ghost at the end of the song was his way of telling me my mother would always be with me.

He sang a few songs all the way to the airport, making it difficult for me to think of anything terribly sad.

And when he left me at the gate, he hugged me and said, "I'll see you in my dreams, sweet Caroline. Safe trip and good tidings."

I watched him walk off.

I was alone.

But I did not cry.

My father hated the sound of it. And, after all, it was his ears I had to please.

CHAPTER EIGHT

As if they all knew I was the daughter of an FAA air traffic controller, everyone working at the airport and on the plane seemed to be extra attentive to me. Of course, I suspected that my grandfather might have had something to do with it. To my eyes, it seemed he had influence over anyone and everything, even the weather. Perhaps he'd had Franklin Butler call the head of the airport to say, *J. Willard Sutherland's granddaughter will be on a flight. Be sure she is treated accordingly.*

After I boarded the plane, I was singled out and taken to the cockpit to be introduced to the captain. It was on the tip of my tongue to say, *You'll soon be hearing from my father*, but I didn't say it. If he asked how I liked Hawaii or anything about Daddy's work, I would be too embarrassed to admit that I hadn't ever been there and hadn't heard from him or seen him for so long.

Other first-class passengers looked impressed, and when I sat again, the elderly man beside me said, "I guess you're the child of someone important, eh?"

"We're all children of someone important," I said, and his un-trimmed gray eyebrows almost flew off his face.

"True, true," he said, and closed his eyes, maybe recalling his own parents.

I was happy to fall asleep soon after we took off. I didn't think that came from being tired; it came from being frightened right to the base of my stomach, where my anxiety was tied in a knot.

That was because I realized that this return to my father was real. I had truly left Sutherland, but more importantly, I'd had to leave behind almost everything that had any meaning to my life, stuffed in a carton down in the dark, cold basement, which literally, because of Prissy's grave, had become the cemetery of meaningful things. Love and the memory of it could be buried.

And yet I had so many reasons to leave it all and so many reasons to look forward to this new life. After all, how many would complain about being sent to Hawaii? They'd mock my reluctance and even a hint of dissatisfaction. *Oh, poor you, being forced to live in a tropical paradise.* They wouldn't understand how or why I thought of it as the final stages of my rebirth because who I had been was unforgivable in the Sutherland world. Hawaii, this reunion with my father, probably was the final test, the place where the rest of my life would be deter-mined.

When I awoke, I ate, but I didn't look out the window until the pilot announced we were making our approach to the Kahului Airport and all seats had to be upright and tray tables stowed away. The only beach I had been on in my life was at Lake George. I had never been to the ocean. The sight of it below and the whitecaps cresting on waves was fascinating. As we descended, I was sure I even saw surfboarders, something I had seen only on television. Almost as soon as we landed, the flight attendants were playing Hawaiian music over the plane's loudspeakers. When I looked around at other passengers, I could see how excited they were at having arrived. I wondered if they could look at me and see how nervous and frightened I was.

The elderly man beside me woke up and revealed that he was a little nervous because he was coming to Hawaii to live with his eldest son.

"Can't be on my own anymore," he said, "but I'm a fish out of water. You're going home, right?"

I wanted to say, *I don't know*, but I smiled and nodded and turned to watch the plane land. Right from the moment I had stepped onto the plane, I was afraid of questions. I certainly would be even more so now.

I was one of the first off the plane. The soft, warm tropical breeze and brightness surprised me because of the contrast with the air-conditioned plane and subdued light for so many hours. But it wasn't solely that. I had emerged from the prisonlike security and austere walls of Sutherland, where shadows ruled. I was literally dropped into a world where sunlight and moonlight chased the darkness away. As soon as I entered the airport, a Hawaiian woman in a grass hula skirt approached to put a garland of orchids over my head. "Aloha," she began to say, before a tall, dark-brown-haired woman, her hair cut almost in a man's trim, especially around her ears, shouted, "DON'T TAKE THAT! GET AWAY FROM HER!"

The Hawaiian woman stepped back as if I had the plague and turned quickly to another arriving passenger.

"Come along, Caroline," the woman, who was obviously my father's new wife, Parker, said. "They treat everyone like a tourist. Don't they realize that people live here?" she muttered loudly enough for most everyone around us, including the woman with the garlands, to hear.

Parker had barely looked at me. I had anticipated a deep study when she would measure me and guess at my character, instantly spotting my weaknesses and strengths. Was I a protected little girl, spoiled, and a new problem? When you marry a divorced man, you inherit his family issues whether you like it or not. Did she automatically resent me? It seemed that way because of how her behavior suggested she was angry at simply having to be here.

But how did she instantly know I was her husband's daughter the moment I appeared? There were other young girls on the plane with their families—one, in fact, right behind me. Did Daddy take pictures of me with him when he left for his new life in Hawaii with his new family? Had Parker seen me in Colonie before they had left New York? I didn't remember ever seeing her at the airport in Albany, even though I knew she had worked there beside my father. She was still not looking at me now as we began to walk away.

"Stay to the right," she ordered, moving me over a few inches. Her fingers felt like nutcrackers on my shoulder. "Some of these people are so oblivious when they get into an airport, they'll walk right into you, let alone a wall. They think air transportation is like going to a fun park or something. Everything about it should be taken seriously," she continued in a lecture mode that resembled my father when he instructed someone.

I glanced at her and had the crazy thought that my father had found the female version of himself. She walked with his perfect posture and held her smiles back as if they were limited investments in happiness.

"We'll get your suitcases first, and then you'll wait beside them until I drive up to the curb to load. I have a white SUV. Don't move from the spot. I can't park long, only to load and unload. I have no time to look for you if you wander off. Do you have to go to the bathroom?"

She rattled all that off like a memorized speech that had been printed on a card, titled HOW TO PICK UP A PASSENGER. Maybe she was just as anxious about meeting me as I was about meeting her, and her attitude was just similar nervousness. I was hoping that was true; it would make her less like Daddy and more like my mother, even though I wasn't here to find a new parent. Doing that would be like losing my mother again.

"No. I'm fine," I said.

I had gone just before we had to prepare for landing, something my father had instructed when we had flown to Jackson Hole. Somehow, because of the tone of his voice and the firmness of his guidelines, what he had said, among so many other lessons, was carved deeply in my mind. Anyone else's advice was a memory that could thin out with time; my father's was stamped, permanent impressions.

"Good. It would be quite embarrassing for your father or for me to get a ticket at an airport. So," she said with a pause, as if she just realized I had arrived, "how was your trip? It should have been pretty good going first class," she added, pronouncing "first class" as if that were something sinful.

I finally dared to look more closely at her. Although her hair was dark brown, her eyebrows were a good shade lighter. Contrary to what I had anticipated, she didn't have a deep Hawaiian tan, which was something I envisioned they would all have, especially my stepbrother and stepsister. Whenever we went anywhere as a family, I thought I would be the obvious standout, having had sunshine practically rationed to me for so long.

However, Parker was a shade darker than pale at most. She had one of those faces that looked carved to perfection rather than beauty. Her cheeks were taut, her copper-colored eyes so dominant that it was difficult to pick up any of her features when she looked directly or intently at you. I knew I'd be fascinated by her looks from the moment I had heard my father had found someone to be his new wife. Of course, my first thought was, how did she compare with my mother?

It was like looking at two different species. Although she, unlike my mother, would never be on a *Vogue* cover, she could be on the cover of a mechanics' magazine, holding a wrench to proudly show a woman could do anything a man could do. Her voice was nowhere near as soft as my mother's. Was she talking like this only to establish her authority, or was she just naturally bossy? Grandfather did warn me about her. He did say she was like Daddy, intolerant of the careless and the inattentive.

She was slim but definitely not thin. Her shoulders and arms were muscular. She wasn't exactly small-breasted, but she did look like she was wearing a sports bra. Nothing shook on her body as she walked quickly, almost in more of a march, to the luggage area, her eyes fixed firmly on what was ahead of her. When she spoke to me, it was as if she was dropping words, not quickly but steadily, just the way Daddy would talk sometimes like someone not easily distracted and who was confident you would catch every syllable uttered. I was afraid to ask any questions. She appeared prepared to deliver the necessary information and wait until then before saying anything that could even vaguely be considered warm, inviting, and welcoming. Finally, it came.

"Well? How was your trip? The airline you were on is supposed to be superior to the other carriers."

She asked this as if she was going to make a report to the FAA. *Here's where I sound intelligent or dull to her*, I thought. *She's going to measure every syllable I utter and lock in that first impression most people carve in stone.*

I nearly stuttered. "The . . . trip was very nice, with just a little bumpiness here and there. It was the longest airplane flight I ever had. I slept a lot. They gave me a blanket and a pillow and lots to eat and drink."

"Of course. First class. It was remarkably on time, touching down maybe thirty seconds late. Are you hungry, or can you wait to get home to have something?"

"I'm not that hungry yet. I'm not sure where we are exactly, how far from your house," I said, and wondered instantly if that was a mistake. Had she expected I'd know it all, even used a Google map or something? She did look at me oddly for a moment.

"I mean, where are we on the island? I looked at maps, but I didn't have a chance to google the address to see how far away it was from the airport."

"Google. Always thought that sounds like something an infant would make in a crib or maybe what a mother would make looking at her baby . . . Google, google."

She didn't smile—but was that supposed to be funny?

She looked at me, perhaps because I didn't laugh. "You and your father have had little contact all this time, so I don't expect you to be familiar with anything in, around, or about Hawaii. So many Americans treat Hawaii like another country. We're a state. You came from the mainland. You should know that even with your having little contact with your father."

Little? I thought. We'd had none. Didn't she know that? How much did she know? What should I reveal? What would upset him if I did?

"He spoke to me mainly through my grandfather," I said. That was true; he couldn't deny it.

"Well, be that as it may, none of that really matters now," she said, sounding like she was flipping off everything in my life that existed before my getting off the plane and entering the Kahului Airport.

"We live in Lahaina. That's approximately twenty-four road miles. I believe we won't have much traffic at this hour. Our house is about two miles above Whalers Village, the famous shopping mall. We're also close to Ka'anapali Beach, which is where my daughter, Dina, and her older brother, Boston, go with their friends most of the time."

She paused and finally looked at me for more than a split second.

"My ex-husband thought it was clever to name our son after the city in which both he and our son were born. Some of his friends in school nicknamed him 'Beans' as a result."

"Beans?"

"Boston beans, ha ha," she said with a well-carved smirk on her face. "Juvenile minds find humor in the most unfunny things. Don't you ever call him that in front of me, even if Dina does so. Mainly just to annoy me. One of a number of ways she does. Understand?"

I didn't. Why would her daughter deliberately want to annoy her? I dared not ask.

"Yes." I felt like I should do what Mommy used to do to Daddy when he spoke with authority down to us like that: salute.

She took a breath and continued walking but slowed her pace.

"Although teenagers being teenagers with their own sense of values, if you can call them that, Boston doesn't get upset when his new friends here call him Beans. I've always disliked nicknames. One of the few rights parents have anymore is naming their children, and almost as soon as they are cast into the lake of education, they begin renaming each other."

One of the few rights parents have? Few? I thought. Where I just came from, no one had more rights than my father.

We turned toward the luggage carousels.

"Your father told me how your mother and you would dance to 'Sweet Caroline.' I don't think he liked it, so if you have that tune on your phone or anything, delete it."

I sucked in a breath. Why was that so important to bring up now? Did she think I'd break out in that song as soon as we were together?

Delete it? What had he told her about my mother and me? What were the other holes and cracks to avoid?

"He used to laugh at that."

"'Used to' are the key words. What you're doing here is wiping the slate clean. Isn't that clear? I did read your letter to your father, writing in your mother's voice. It was some sort of final test, as I understand it. I thought you clearly understood what to say and not to say about your previous life."

"Yes, but—"

"Just be careful about reminding him of your relationship with your mother after she left him for a woman. As you know, it's a sensitive subject for him."

Left him, I thought. I didn't remember it that way.

"It took a long time for Hawaii to wash all those painful memories out of his mind. He's happier now. We both enjoy Hawaii very much, as do my children.

"Dina has asked for you to share her room. No one was more surprised about it than me. I thought we would be giving you the guest room," she said, highlighting the word "guest." Was that a hint that she would never accept me as a member of the family?

"We removed her bed and bought two double beds with bedside tables. The closet is big enough for both of you if you keep it neat and organized, as well as the bathroom. Dina is not the most organized person. I'm hoping you will continue the good example your father says you can be, mainly because of the example he set for you."

She practically cloaked the "he" in bright lights. It sounded like I didn't even have a mother.

"Neither of my children are in the summer-school program. Boston had his seventeenth birthday last February. He is a lifeguard at Marriott's Maui Ocean Club Ka'anapali. He became a surfer from the moment his feet hit the sand here over a year ago. Surfing was invented in Hawaii; it's practically in the blood.

"Dina, on the other hand, who's only a year older than you, thinks she's an artist and spends most of her days painting scenes or whatever. One of her grade-school teachers planted that in her head, telling her she had exceptional talent and an artist's personality. Dina is a born exploiter, taking advantage of anything and everything. I am not blind when I look at my children like most parents are. You don't do them any good when you're not honest about them."

"What do you mean, exploiter?"

She laughed. "Well, you'll find out, but if Dina forgets to do a chore or is messy, she blames it on her artistic nature. If she spent as much time on doing her work as she does making excuses why she didn't or doesn't, she'd be the best of us when it comes to taking care of things and being responsible.

"I'm sure before long she'll be having you do her share of chores, claiming she has to keep her mind on her newest masterpiece, so beware. She's very clever when she wants to be and as dramatically emotional as a pregnant woman, always blaming everything on her artistic mind. I have yet to see one completed painting, or what I would call completed. I suppose you have to be an art expert to know."

She paused and narrowed her eyelids as she looked at me.

"You're not some sort of artist or poet, too, are you? That's all I need is two absentminded dreamers."

"No, ma'am. I've drawn things, but—"

"Look, let's get this straight from the start. I don't expect you ever to call me Mother or Mommy or any such thing. You can call me Parker. Boston thinks it's funny to call his mother by her name. He has lots of jokes, like 'Where do you park, Parker?' Or 'Will you park our car, Parker?'" She leaned toward me. "I'm actually amused, but I don't let him know it."

She paused. I really didn't know what to say. Was it good or bad that she was being so honest with me?

"Okay. Luggage," she said, as if that was it: I knew enough to start a new life here.

When my bags came up, she lifted them off the carousel easily, declining the help of a polite man standing nearby, practically acting insulted that he had offered.

"What did they do, pack everything you own?"

No, I wanted to say. The words were practically slipping through my tightened lips. *Lots were left down in the basement of Sutherland. In fact, everything that was really me was left there.*

But I said nothing.

"Dina puts on a pair of shorts or one of her artist's sloppy dresses and wears it for a week streaked with dripped paint. Boston can wear his favorite shorts and T-shirt for a week, too. I don't know why I bought them anything more to wear, but again, that's life in Hawaii. Here teenagers are laid-back. They're stretched out, with windblown hair and tanned faces, and carry watches with no hands."

"What?"

"Let's get all this out to the curb," she said. "I'm going to get the car."

She started off, then paused.

"Are you all right being left alone there?"

"Yes," I said, trying to keep my lips from trembling. I didn't expect to be welcomed with open arms and kisses, but this was like meeting a drill sergeant portrayed in an army movie. Rules and warnings were being issued, not warm smiles or greetings and encouragement.

She nodded and continued on to get her car. People were rushing to and fro beside me, in front of me, and behind me, shouting and laughing, many already dressed in their Hawaiian flowery shirts and shorts. I could understand why there was so much excitement flowing around me. Despite what Parker had said, it looked to me that at least ninety percent of the passengers were similar fun-seeking vacationers escaping their jobs and responsibilities. It felt like they had all become children again.

"I can smell the pineapple!" I heard a woman scream to her friends getting into rental cars.

"See you in the hot tub," another said.

How different this was for me, confronted by so many people smiling and laughing, their voices full of almost juvenile expectations as they rattled off their plans to go whale watching, kayaking, and surfing, and attend luaus. For so long I had been surrounded by people who rationed their smiles and laughter, hid them around corners or underneath their hands, and moved through a world of shadows. At this moment I was so mesmerized by all the merriment that I was standing there and looking like a smiling fool until I heard the loud horn and turned to see that Parker had driven up.

She practically leaped out of the SUV and opened the back.

"Let's go," she ordered, and began loading my luggage as easily as Emerson had. I struggled to lift the second bag high enough for her to grasp. She whisked it out of my hands, shoved it in, and closed the door. "Get in, adjust the seat, and fasten your seat belt," she said, as if we were getting into a space shuttle. It did feel like I had left the planet.

"I asked Boston and Dina to pick up some groceries for us for our dinner tonight. Boston took her to work with him so she could paint something from that beachfront. Your father will be home for dinner," she said as we drove away from the airport. It sounded more like a warning than just information. "I expect you'll be settled in by then."

I heard her and nodded, but at the moment, I was too fascinated by everything, especially the reddish soil. It was one thing to see it in pictures and another to be here. Parker noticed how I was gazing intently.

"You've never seen dirt that color, have you?"

"Not in real life," I said.

"Real life," she said, and finally laughed. "Yes, this is real life. That's because of the hematite, the iron ore. It stains everything. Don't go rolling around in it. I can tell you that the washing machine was constantly going for Dina's clothes, especially when we first moved here. As I told you, she's oblivious with a capital *O*. I know her brother does her homework for her half the time. She's good at playing him. Like all young men, he's susceptible to smiles and tears. You are a good student, right?"

"Yes," I said. I sensed quickly that false modesty would ring bells in her head. Like Daddy, she wanted your answers lean and truthful.

"I know you've been homeschooled by a renowned professor. I saw the report on you, how advanced you are with your reading and your math. Maybe some of your new good learning habits will rub off on Dina."

New? I thought. I was always a good student. Even the vaguest reference to my life with my mother would be considered negative. I almost corrected her but swallowed it quickly. *New life*, I chanted to myself. *New life.*

I gazed at all the stores and malls as we turned onto the highway. Everything looked bright and new. Windows glittered, and the parking lots and driveways were so clean that I thought they were just made. I saw chickens roving freely around people at the front of the stores, but before I could ask, she said, "All right. Let's talk."

We were well onto the highway. Let's talk? What were we doing?

"Your father asked me to make a few things clear to you before we get to our house. He knows about the death of Mrs. Lawson, of course, and asks that you do not bring it up with Dina and Boston. When your father wants to talk to you about it, he will, privately. He especially doesn't want you talking about details of the treatment your grandfather arranged for you the day your mother died. Again, that's something that, if discussed, will be discussed privately between your father and you. As far as our children know, after your mother died, your grandfather looked after you, got you some professional grief counseling, and hired your homeschool teacher."

"But why didn't I come here with my father? Aren't they curious about that? Won't they ask?"

"They did, and we explained some of the ugly background. They know about your mother and her lover, how they carried on and lied to your father about their relationship. That you were too young to fully understand, but when it became blatant and especially when your neighborhood, school, and other family learned about it, you needed extra tender loving care. Don't ever call it treatment. Understandably, you were lost, confused. It wasn't exactly the way most parents break up, the most common cause of divorce.

"They know you had to live with your mother and her lover for quite a while. I'm sure they'll want to know how your school friends treated you then. That's all right to describe. We've been brought up to date about some of that. It was unpleasant, right?"

She looked at me. I knew I couldn't simply answer; I had to be convincing. However, it was true that my school life had been difficult, and many of my classmates had avoided me. I was aware of how some neighbors had viewed us, too. But I hated admitting to it because it made Mommy look so terrible, even selfish. Everything was more complicated than a simple yes, but I had to say it. It was almost the password to this new life.

"Yes, I was no longer invited to parties and began to hate going to school."

"Exactly. It was a big emotional weight to carry on your small shoulders. They should have been more considerate."

They were, I wanted to say, but smothered the words quickly.

"You were certainly not ready to go to a place you'd never been. Fortunately, you were homeschooled at your grandfather's home so you didn't lose valuable educational time, and when you finally, in everyone's opinion, were strong enough, we agreed to let you come here to see if you could start a new life."

She sounded like she was dictating a memo, the map I should follow. *This is the fantasy I must accept and perpetuate*, I thought.

"My advice to you is that in no way, even indirectly, must you defend your mother's actions. Everyone, including my children, of course, knows about gay people, gay marriages. We just don't want to bring that into our house. So the best thing is not to talk about it. If they ask you questions, say you'd rather not talk about it. Dina loses interest in anything but herself pretty quickly. You're lucky there. Boston is involved in his work and career goals. He's always been at the top of his class and treated more like a young man than a teenage boy. We're both very proud of him.

"However, for insurance, we have had family discussions with Boston and Dina about you, and we have insisted that they don't tease you or bring it up in any negative way. Teenagers being teenagers again, I don't for one moment believe they won't do so occasionally. How you handle it will make a very big difference. Try to be an adult about it. Is that clear?"

"Yes," I said. But it sounded like a complicated maze of emotions and thoughts to navigate. How could I not make mistakes?

"Now, of course, you should understand that this is our family's particular attitude about all this gay business. Hawaii was one of the first six states to legalize homosexuality and gay marriage and has actually banned conversion therapy, so you'd only draw unwanted attention to yourself and practically make it impossible to attend school here if you even suggest you underwent such treatment. You'd be a bit freaky to many of Boston's and Dina's friends. First impressions are more important to teenagers than they are to adults. They can't handle the complexity. You don't want that. You wouldn't last any longer in schools here than you did there."

Tears came into my eyes. I think she could see it.

"I'm sorry. It's best that I get all this out now," she said, nodding as if she was convincing herself. "Hopefully, we'll never discuss it very much again."

For a long time, I was freaky in Sutherland, and now I could be freaky here. Where did I belong?

The sight of the ocean put all this aside for the moment. I took a deep breath, swallowed my anxiety, and enjoyed the beautiful scenery. The water had shades of turquoise and deep blue. Occasionally, a section of golden beach would appear, with people on chairs and lounge chairs with umbrellas. Here and there I caught sight of surfers.

"Now, let's get back to getting you acquainted with Hawaii. I'm sure you heard it at the airport, but people here say 'mahalo' for 'thank you.' You'll hear many Hawaiian expressions. You don't have to memorize them all. Just be respectful. We turn here," she said, "and go up this hill a bit. Dina has a bike. Your father bought it for her soon after we moved here, a Schwinn Super Sport. Last week, your father bought you one, as well as a helmet. Are you used to riding a bike?"

"Not really for long rides," I said. "I mean, I had a bike when I was younger, but I never had a real bike like that."

"You do now, and your father will surely go over the rules and have you ride it until he's satisfied enough to permit you to go on the highway.

"Boston has a car that he pays for himself with the money he makes as a lifeguard. Because he has a similar build to your father, most people think he's really your father's son. They get along well. Boston is used to what I would call your father's military style. His father was in the army and eventually became a recruiter. He's remarried, and my children rarely talk to him, let alone see him."

"You are an air traffic controller, too, right?"

"I am." She smiled. "I think you knew that. Anyway, I'm sort of on call now, available in emergencies. I've even flown to Honolulu to fill in when necessary.

"Well, here we are," she said, turning onto a side road and into an immediate driveway.

It was a light pink two-story house with attached double two-car garages. Surrounding it was lush landscaping. Our house back in Colonie and even Nattie's parents' home were much smaller-looking. When we pulled into the garage, I could see a brand-new bike just below another hanging on the wall, the bright orange helmet attached to it.

"We'll take your luggage into the house, to the foot of the stairway, and give you a tour of the downstairs and the backyard and pool first."

"Pool?"

We didn't have one in Colonie. I thought only estates like Grandfather Sutherland's had one. No house in our neighborhood did.

"And hot tub," she said. "Pools for upscale homes like this are like bathrooms are back in New York, a luxurious necessity. You do know how to swim?"

"Yes, but I haven't done much of it and never in an ocean."

"Right, that is different from swimming in a pool, even a lake. Well, you're lucky. Boston is a good instructor, as well as your father. He'll teach you to snorkel as well, I'm sure. Besides surfing, it's one of his favorite things to do."

She paused and thought a moment.

"You packed a bathing suit, right?"

"Aunt Holly bought me two. I haven't worn them."

"Aunt Holly," she said in a tone that suggested my father didn't approve of Aunt Holly. "You tried them on, though?"

"Yes."

"Okay. Let's go. Just take the smaller bag," she said when she opened the back. She pulled it out and handed to me. I pulled up the handle so it would be ready to roll. She did the same with the two larger bags, pulled one to the door and then the other. Then I followed her when she brought them both into the house. The garage door opened into a pantry with what looked to be well-stocked shelves. We went through it and into the kitchen, which was at least twice the size of ours in Colonie. My eyes went everywhere. It was much nicer than our kitchen in New York and especially nicer than the one in Nattie's parents' home, which was much older.

This kitchen had a wide and long granite island with a sink. I could see there were double ovens and an impressively large refrigerator. The cabinets ran along the far wall and wrapped around to the right, with matching granite counters beneath them and another pantry closet. A large window above the sinks enabled the sunlight to make everything bright-looking and new.

"These are African mahogany floors. They're throughout the house," she said proudly. "We take good care of them and all our furniture. Everything is relatively recently redone. Morgan and I believe that if you don't respect your home, you don't respect yourself. My children at least understand that. If they didn't, they'd be sleeping on the driveway."

I had no doubt.

"We eat breakfast here at the breakfast bar, sometimes lunch, and sometimes have lunch outside. We have dinner either in the dining room or right through those sliding doors to the patio and outside dining table."

I looked in the direction she was nodding. I could see the view of the ocean. My mind spun with questions. How did my father afford all this? Did Parker have money, or did Grandfather help him finance this, too, especially after he told him about Mommy and Nattie? How long did my father keep what he knew to himself? Did Grandfather Sutherland pay him to hold the secret as long as he did?

"This is a very expensive home, isn't it?" I asked Parker.

She pulled her shoulders back. "Well, it's a drop in the bucket compared to your Sutherland."

My Sutherland?

"It's just beautiful, is what I mean."

"Yes, it is."

She looked calmer.

"My daughter takes a little too much for granted. Maybe it's good that you're impressed."

She showed me the living room and the den with the big television screen, and then we put all the suitcases at the foot of the stairway, which was maybe a third of the length of the stairway at Sutherland. The steps were made of the same mahogany as the floors. The railing was a darker wood.

"As I said, we have a downstairs guest bedroom, but Dina wanted hers to be upstairs. I'm repeating it because I'm very skeptical and suspicious. She's good at sneaking in questions, so think twice and measure twice before you leap to answer personal ones.

"We'll look at the outside now," she said. "Views are what really matter here. You can see whales from our patio."

"Really?"

Under the patio roof and to the right was an outdoor barbecue and sink. The outdoor dining table was there, as well as very comfortable-looking chairs. From almost any angle, someone could have a good view of the ocean. I saw the sailboats and what looked like people riding big, motorized fish.

"What are those?"

"Those are Jet Skis," she said. "Boston hates them, which is unusual for someone his age. He says they're not good for ocean life. He was nowhere near as into nature as he became when we moved here. As you can tell from what I've told you so far, Boston is a serious young man. He doesn't shy away from responsibility, nor does he come up with excuses for mistakes. Morgan respects him for that. You should see the two of them swim against each other. Your father still has the edge, or"—she leaned in—"Boston lets him win."

"The pool is prettier than the one at Sutherland," I said.

Although Sutherland's was probably more than twice the size, it wasn't as nice a color. There were four lounge chairs and two umbrellas, right now not open. Sutherland had more comfortable-looking lounge chairs, but I sensed it was better never to suggest Grandfather's estate was a better or more impressive place to live in even in the slightest way.

"Yes, well, this isn't that old. Let's get you settled in the bedroom you and Dina will share. You can get all your clothes hung, and I'll show you what drawers were left for your things. Just take the small bag up and wait for me," she said.

I went ahead up the stairs. She took one of the suitcases in both hands and followed. I saw she was straining a bit.

"Maybe we should wait for Daddy or even Boston," I suggested.

"Your father won't be here until dinner, and I can do this just fine. Go on up," she snapped.

I felt like I had to tiptoe around broken glass. I walked up ahead and waited for her.

"Turn right," she said. "That's where Boston and Dina and now you will be. First door on the right is your and Dina's room."

The room was half the size of my bedroom at Sutherland. The two beds were separated by a table with only a clock on it, and there were tables at the sides of each bed. To the left were two windows that looked out over the pool toward the ocean, but to the right was a sliding door and what looked like a small balcony. There was a small table and two chairs on it. The closet was immediately on the right. All the walls were papered in a light pink with squiggly lines.

If Dina was into art, I wondered, why weren't there any pictures? There was so much art in Sutherland, some of it very expensive collector's pieces. I could tell her about the great artists, but then I thought she might resent that I had lived among their works. I recited to myself, *Think first, pause, and then speak*, just as Parker had instructed.

A computer table and a computer and printer were in the far right corner, and beside that was a small table with what looked like artist's supplies. The door to the bathroom was there also.

"Morgan has a computer in a nook off the den that he said you could use. Dina has already made it clear that she won't share her computer. That's like sharing a toothbrush for teenagers, I know. I made sure she left you room in the cabinets above the sink in the bathroom. I assume you brought all you need?"

"Yes."

"If you don't like the shampoo, we'll get you a different one, but this is a very good Hawaiian brand," she said, pointing to the shower.

It was a good size, and the bathroom had pretty light pink tile, but it was not even half the size of what had been my mother's and mine at Sutherland.

"Let's look at the closet. There are three sets of drawers. You'll have to organize your things in the one set on the left. I had Dina keep those empty. As you can see, there's plenty of room for hanging clothes, and there is plenty of room on the shoe racks.

"Your bed is the one on the left," she said, facing them. The two had identical blankets and pillowcases.

"Start unpacking while I get your last bag. And then take a rest. Remember, we are five hours earlier than New York time. You'll be tired come dinnertime."

"I forgot. Okay," I said. "Thank you."

"What did I tell you was the word?"

"Oh. Mahalo."

She nodded and left. I stood for a few moments and simply stared after her. With the plane ride and the efficient, quick way I was scooped up and brought here, it truly felt as if I had been swept off to a new world and a new life on an Arabian magic carpet.

But I wasn't sure if I was welcome or not.

However, I was positive that it wouldn't be long before I knew, mainly from the expression on Daddy's face the moment he set eyes on me. There was never any lie or deception in his face when he looked at me.

Many times, I wished that there were.

CHAPTER NINE

I began to unpack, looking at Dina's clothes and shoes as I did. They weren't as colorful as mine, and I saw that she still possessed warmer clothes, obviously from New York. Maybe Aunt Holly had gone overboard with clothes solely for Hawaii. Parker's angry words about the woman offering garlands of orchids still echoed. I wasn't a tourist, although I wasn't quite a resident, either.

I was already intimidated enough by the prospect of my father's reaction to seeing me and with Parker's not-so-subtle warnings and red flags. Now I had to worry about my stepsister's reaction to my clothes? I feared her thinking that I was some spoiled rich girl who was sharing a bedroom. Would I complain about the size of this bedroom after having been used to living at a mansion? Of course, if she knew the forbidden truth, she'd realize that I was about as far from that as I was from the mainland.

"It's great to see my new sister is neat," I heard, and turned around as Dina stepped into the closet doorway.

She wore a gray, almost faded artist's smock stained with paint, as Parker had described. I didn't think she was wearing anything under it. Her auburn hair was brushed to one side and long enough to cover her right breast. She was a good two or so inches taller than I was, with a rounder face than I had anticipated because of Parker's look. She had greenish-blue eyes, a small nose, and full lips, the kind I recalled Nattie envying. She was wider in the hips and had a fuller bosom than I did. She folded her arms under her breasts and leaned against the doorjamb.

There was nothing about her smile that was tentative or unsure the way mine would surely be when I first confronted someone with whom I was about to share my personal life. She didn't appear to be like Simon, indifferent or arrogant, as much as she appeared amused. She was probably thinking, *So this is what my stepsister Caroline looks like*. I continued to suspect that neither she nor Parker had seen any pictures of me. After my father had packed and left us, I remembered seeing every photograph of him and Mommy and me still where they always were. He didn't take any of those with him. I couldn't recall him ever having one of us in his wallet. If he did have one of Mommy and me, I had assumed that he had torn it up or buried it in some box full of what were painful memories for him. He had left nothing of himself behind, not even the pen he always used. He had rushed out of our lives, but not in a blind tantrum. People forget things when they're in a frenzy. This break was surgically perfect. He had returned for his things and taken everything. He was completely gone, sweetly and simply. Really, how would I return to him after that sort of rupture?

"Hi," I said. "I'm Caroline."

"You'd better be, or I'd better call the police."

"What?"

She laughed and stepped into the closet. "I always wanted to have a sister. My brother says he always wanted to have a younger brother.

I got my wish; he didn't get his. I'm gonna wanna hear all about you from birth to today, and I think," she said, putting her right index finger on her chin, "I know exactly the place where I want you to pose."

"Pose?"

"I'm an artist." She held up her case containing her painting supplies. "I left my easel in the garage so we'd have more room," she said, making it sound like she had made a great sacrifice. She sighed.

"No one in the family wants to pose for me. My brother especially won't let me paint him. I once tried secretly, and when he realized it, he put his fist through the picture."

She paused, still holding her finger to her chin.

"I wonder if he's going to like you. He forms opinions instantly, and then they might as well be printed on his passport. The best thing to do is to tell me everything you can about yourself first. If I had to depend on your father to learn anything about you, I'd have to take a blowtorch to him. His one answer to almost anything is 'Wait and see.' Including you. I know your age and your name, but that's about it, really. I don't know what kind of music you like or what you like to eat. You're not on social media, which made me very suspicious. You have a mobile phone, right?"

"Yes."

"Well, I can't wait and see any longer. You'll tell me everything and anything I want to know or think is necessary to know about you. That way, I'll be aware of what you should never tell Beans. At least, anything you wouldn't want my mother to know. He's her third ear."

"He's what?"

She laughed. "Truth is," she said, standing straight and relaxing her hand to her hip, "he's the best brother you and I could have. He'll do everything for us," she whispered, "except pose for me. C'mon, you can wait to do all that. He's carrying in groceries and helping put them away. He doesn't like to be called it, but he's a momma's boy. Let's sit out on the lanai for a few minutes and get to know each other," she said, turning to the sliding door.

"Lanai? Oh, the patio."

"I used to call it that, but almost the moment we stepped off the airplane, my mother insisted I learn the Hawaiian terms for everything. 'You're in Hawaii, so get as Hawaiian as you can,'" she said, imitating Parker. "She can be fixated and turn herself into a drill sergeant. After a while you'll think she's chanting automatically, 'Learn this, learn that.' You'll hear it in your sleep. At least, I do, and that means you will. Sleeping this close to each other, we'll practically be in each other's dreams. I bet yours are so hot that I'll wake up with a sunburn."

I stared at her with my mouth opened stupidly.

"C'mon already. Beans will be up here soon, and he's like Morgan. He'll X-ray you. Here's a free tell like in poker: Beans's ears pull back when he suspects something or doesn't believe something you've said, some exaggeration or lie, so try not to do it. Or at least as much as I do. Let's go."

I put down the skirt I was hanging up and followed her out.

"There's a party on the beach tomorrow night," Dina said as soon as we sat. I saw that she was wearing a pair of homemade shorts under her smock, shorts that she must have cut from a pair of jeans. "You can meet most of my friends right away. Later I'll tell you who's more to be trusted. Beth Raymond, for example, loves to say 'between you and me.' Once something is between you and her, everyone will know it. I'm sure you had friends like that, right?"

She took a breath, but before I could answer, she said, "Beans will take us there, but I doubt he'll stay. He calls my friends seashells."

"Why?"

"You know, the one-note roar in your ear?"

"I've never listened to a seashell."

"Oh, really? We'll have to make a list of things you've never done and compare it to mine. Anyway, my brother doesn't have that many friends himself. His best friend quit school last year to work in construction. Everyone calls him Skipper, but his real name is Steve. Parker will only call him Steve. She hates nicknames."

"I know."

She leaned toward me to whisper. "Skipper's better-looking than Beans. I flirt with him when Beans isn't watching. He's got those bedroom eyes. Know what they are?"

"No."

"You can look it up on Wikipedia, but it's not the same as actually seeing a boy look at you that way. It's like reading a love scene. It's exciting, but when you're in it . . ." She paused, seeing that I wasn't following her. "Hello. Bedroom eyes means he'd like to get you in bed? And not to count sheep together, get it?"

"Oh."

"You sure you know what I'm really saying?"

"I think so."

"Think so? Anyway, when the party's over, we'll get an Uber back."

"What's that?"

"Seriously? Oh, right. I forgot: your grandfather is one of the richest people in the world. You probably always had a limo taking you places."

What should I say? Should I tell her that once I was brought to Sutherland, I never went anywhere but to the family cemetery and, eventually, some clothing stores? That would explode into more questions circling the truth. How does someone live in constant fear that she will speak without thinking the words first?

"He's rich, yes, but I didn't do much socially after my mother died," I said. "And I lost all my school friends."

"Um, I bet you did once everyone found out about your mother. What about her lover?" she asked in a whisper, her eyes on the door.

"That's what you call her, right, a lover? I mean, they never got married, right?"

"She's . . ." I stopped myself. I almost accidentally revealed that I had seen her before coming here. "No."

"Well, what about her?"

"She's not well since the accident, is all I know."

"We're not supposed to talk about it, but you can tell me anything, and I won't tell that you told. Don't trust Beans, though. He's too goody-goody to trust, no matter how he swears to keep your secret." She sat back and shook her head. "This is, like, wow."

"What is?"

"You're really here. We're going to share a room. I have a sister, and sisters are supposed to be best friends, right?"

"I don't know. I mean, I guess so."

"What *do* you know?"

She sounded annoyed. I held my breath. Was this going to be bad from the start?

She sighed. "All right. Here's what we'll do. I'll tell you one secret about myself, and you'll tell me one about yourself. Then, later, because we'll believe and protect each other, we'll tell another and another. And that will make us real sisters, okay?"

"I don't have many secrets." *Secrets I could ever tell*, I thought.

"Sure you do. We both do," she whispered. "I'll start. I'm a virgin, but I came very close to not being one any longer, inches close, just last week at a beach party. I was naked with my boyfriend, Noa, in our beach hideaway. I almost gave in, and he didn't have any protection, either. We both had a little too much tequila. His mother is Hawaiian, and his father's from San Francisco. He's got this inky black hair and blue eyes. Very handsome. He writes poetry but doesn't show it to anyone but me. Or at least he says he doesn't. We're both creative people, which is why I wanted to lose my virginity to him. He'd appreciate it more.

"Don't look so shocked. I know two girls your age who aren't virgins any longer, and they are not anywhere as pretty and as developed as you. I'm sure you have some good stories of your own."

"I've never even had a boyfriend," I said.

"Before you claim it, that doesn't count as a secret. It has to be something no one else or maybe only one other person knows. Well? It's your turn. Come up with something as good as my secret. Don't wait. Beans will be here in minutes."

I wasn't sure what to do. I did feel tired. I couldn't think as carefully as I should. If I told her something that was really a secret, I could cause a lot of trouble quickly, almost before one day had passed. But if I didn't tell her something she'd consider a secret, we wouldn't even begin to have a good relationship.

"I stole one of my grandmother's bracelets before I left Sutherland."

"She died, right?"

"Yes, not that long ago, but all her things are really my grandfather's."

She didn't look satisfied. "Is it expensive?"

"I don't know. I just liked it and took it."

"I'll look at it and tell you. I know about things like that, being an artist."

"Okay," I said.

I did have a bracelet to show, but it was really one of my own that my mother had bought me two years ago as an extra birthday present. She did tell me to take good care of it, so maybe it was expensive enough to have belonged to my grandmother.

Dina thought. She had the expression of someone whose mind was whirling with ideas and suggestions.

"Okay," she said. "For now, that will do, but taking something from a dead person isn't exactly a revelation that puts us on the road to becoming real sisters. It's a matter of trust. My friends trust me with stuff that would get them locked up."

"Locked up?"

"And the key thrown away. They all come to me with their troubles, family troubles."

"Says who?" I heard, and turned to see who was surely Boston. I had to remember never to call him Beans, even when we were all alone. With Dina doing that, it wasn't going to be easy.

"Says whom, not who," Dina said, and looked at me. "Am I right? We were told you are very smart."

In seconds, I was thrust into a crisis: back Dina or somehow not do so and risk her getting upset.

"'Says who' is actually correct, as an idiom," I said, trying desperately not to sound arrogant about it like Simon surely would. "There are rules about 'who' and 'whom,' but most people don't follow them when they speak. Even my homeschool professor says 'who' when she should say 'whom,'" I added.

"Whatever," Dina said. "This poor excuse for a brother is my brother, Boston, known worldwide as Beans."

"Aloha," I said, hoping my answer about grammar didn't offend him.

He smiled. "Whatever Dina tells you is ten percent true most of the time."

"Ha ha, Mr. Goody Two-shoes. She's going to the beach party tomorrow night. Can you take us, brother dear?"

"If Morgan says so," Boston said. "Do you need any help with anything?" he asked me.

"I don't think so. Oh, I'm not sure where to put my suitcases."

"Just leave them. I'll store them in the garage."

"Thank—mahalo," I said, and he smiled.

Parker was right about him. I could see why. Although Daddy was more handsome, they did look alike. Boston had a similar build and was almost the same height. Like Daddy, he had very good posture, what I called proud shoulders. Looking at him from behind, someone might easily mistake him for Daddy. He had hazel eyes and a firm chin. His nose was a little long and narrower, but he had my father's straight full lips, and he had the Hawaiian tan I had been expecting to see.

He wore a turquoise tight T-shirt, blue shorts, and black sandals. He had a narrow waist and a swimmer's flat, muscular stomach. He had bigger hands than Daddy, but I imagined their size helped his swimming. When he moved slightly, I could see muscles flex in his chest. His shirt was almost another layer of skin.

"Anyway, if you need something else serious or important, don't waste your time asking Dina. She makes absentminded look like an understatement. Check under your bed. She might have kicked some dirty panties down there."

"Ha ha. Beans, beans, the more you eat, the more you toot," Dina recited.

"Keep it up, and I'll tell Parker about some smoke I saw and what I smelled coming from behind a boulder two nights ago before I arrived to pick you up. Your friends are very loyal. The seashells. They practically aimed flashlights at where you and Noa were curled up."

"If you do tell Parker . . ."

"I'm going to shower and get ready for dinner. Parker's making luau stew with chicken, one of Morgan's favorites," he added, mostly for me. "We're eating outside. You might want to help set the table," he said, this time mostly to Dina.

"I have to help her get unpacked and organized."

"I think she's capable of doing that herself and doing it right," he said. He stood there staring hard at her. "Parker will expect your help, enthusiastic help. If you're lazy tonight especially, Morgan might want to make an example of you and confine you to the house for a week. You'd be setting a bad example for Caroline, and you know how Morgan feels about anything that might reflect on him, his parenting. He might put you under house arrest for two weeks."

"House arrest?" I asked. What would he call what had been done to me?

"Yeah. He's done that to her a few times lately," he said. "Dina?"

"Okay, okay." She stood reluctantly and pouted for a moment. "You have to wait almost a full two minutes to get hot water in the shower," she told me.

"No wonder you take one only once a month," Parker joked, or I think he joked.

She growled and charged past him off the lanai. He watched her go and then smiled at me.

"She's not as bad as I make her out to be," he said. "But close," he added. "She's what both Parker and Morgan call a 'work in progress.'"

Aren't we all? I thought, especially recalling how my father saw people our age.

Boston smiled. "Looking forward to getting to know you and help you feel at home," he said, and gave me a bright, warm smile before he left.

That did sound encouraging. I could certainly use a big brother looking after me. It helped me be hopeful for a few moments, but then an overriding sense of sadness washed over me. Every time I was satisfied with something, I felt I was betraying my mother.

Instead of getting up and completing my move-in, I sat there looking out toward the ocean. It was beautiful here and quite different from where I grew up, even when we lived what seemed to be eternal spring. Neighbors were closer. Sometimes I could hear laughter and voices float across the street. It wasn't a busy street, but there was traffic.

I felt like I had passed through a tunnel that took me from being trapped in Grandfather's mansion to here. Sutherland was so far away. Everything felt very far away, even early memories. It was as if they fell behind the jet that brought me. My body finally sank with travel fatigue. I certainly didn't want to look exhausted and half asleep when my father saw me. He might take it the wrong way, assuming I was too sad to ever want to be here with him.

I should probably take a shower and wake up before I did anything else, I thought. I wondered what in my new wardrobe I should wear for dinner. I didn't want to overdress, wear something expensive and cause Dina to feel bad about what she wore. Would she change her clothes and blame me for something immediately? Having someone who was expecting me to treat her like a sister and my anticipating the same thing seemed more frightening than exciting. Would I really have a sister? I often wondered what it was that kept my parents from ever trying to add a son or another daughter to our early family world. Was it all because of my mother?

And then suddenly, as if it was one of the cartoon light bulbs over a character, I realized reuniting with my father could create a new crisis. My "new" sister might very well become jealous if he showed favoritism. Sibling rivalry, I thought. I remembered feeling it when Mommy first revealed to me that Daddy had found a new wife and family that included a daughter about my age. If I felt like that without even seeing her or knowing her name, what would she feel with me sharing her room and her privacy and especially her mother's and my father's attention? Would everything I wanted and everything I said be more important than what she wanted and said? What if I was better behaved or more responsible than she was because that's who I really was? Would that cause her to hate me? Which way should I go? Who should I be, one girl for Daddy and another for her?

On the other hand, maybe she wouldn't care who I was. Maybe

she never felt like my father's new daughter. Both she and Boston were calling him Morgan, and not Dad or Daddy. But then again, they weren't calling their mother Mother or Mommy, either. They were calling her by her name, Parker. I sensed Parker's respect for Boston and how proud of him both she and my father were, but it was all sounding so formal and not sounding like family, at least from what I knew once to be family, even the Robot Family, which was what Mommy, Daddy, and I were once called in Colonie because of how perfectly we all were always dressed and how consistently we followed events in our everyday lives. Mommy blamed it on Daddy's perfection, but I think she filled her life with the same daily and seasonal chores to keep from being unhappy.

"Busy people don't have that much time to think, especially about themselves," she had once said.

At least in those early days, we looked and behaved like the faultless family, the family that seemed natural pictured on a Christmas card. I couldn't yet imagine this family on anything more than a travel brochure, a family that had been put together by an advertising firm. Maybe I would change it. Maybe that was something I would be bringing to this house: a real sense of belonging to each other, caring for each other. I was so needy that they would suddenly realize that they were, too. My smiles would become contagious, and everyone would soften.

Could I do that without Mommy? Was it arrogant of me, even stupid, to think so?

Perhaps I had simply traded the cold, dark, and proper world of Sutherland for a smaller, much smaller, version disguised in the world of beautiful flowers, turquoise water, and glistening beaches.

My home would always be in my heart, and I would never stop singing and hearing "Sweet Caroline." There was no way to disguise it, hide it, especially from my father. Deep in my stomach the realization twirled. Dina had nothing to fear. My father's love for me would forever be on a leash. There would be no sibling rivalry, not where my mother's Captain Bryer was concerned.

Nevertheless, I went to my suitcase and carefully took out the model airplane. He might still be blinded by some anger and lingering wounded pride when he looked at me, but that wouldn't be there when he looked at this, I hoped, and I placed it prominently on the table beside my bed. It was in a holding pattern, waiting for the decision to land or remain circling. That woman on the plane looking out the window wasn't Nattie after all. That was me.

Dina was right about the hot water in the shower. It took a little more than two and a half minutes at least, but it did revive me. I put my things in the drawers and hung up the remaining clothes. I left the suitcases in the closet, as Boston had instructed. In the end, I chose a solid cream-colored blouse and a blue skirt because I thought they were the least attention-grabbing. I put on socks and a pair of new dark blue loafers. Then I brushed my hair, listening for any indication that my father had arrived. I could hear that Parker had made Dina clean up the patio and the area around the pool as well as wash down some furniture. She was complaining loudly.

When she came back to the room, she paused and stared at me. I was just finished fixing my hair.

"You're not going to be a virgin long," she said.

"What?"

"Just kidding, but now I have to shower and change and look normal. Which I hate. Why does anyone want to be just like everyone else?"

She began pulling off her smock in a feigned rage.

"Oh, the sacrifices we make to please our parents. Pray that I have strength," she added dramatically, pressing her hands together and looking up at the ceiling.

She was funny. *I think I like her*, I thought, and started to laugh but stopped instantly when I heard his voice. He had just entered. She had heard him, too.

"Well, don't just stand there like a boob brain. Go meet your father," she said.

I started out, hoping I didn't look as fearful as I felt.

"Wait a minute," she called when I started through the door. "What is that? A model plane? You want to be a pilot or something?"

"It's a present from my father. When I was little," I added.

"Why don't you put up a picture of your mother? I'd like to see what she looked like. For sure, Morgan doesn't have one."

I didn't want to admit that I didn't have one, that they were all in a basement in the mansion.

"I don't think it would please my father right now."

"So?" She shrugged. "Don't put it up, but show it to me."

"I didn't bring any," I said.

"So you're mad at her, too?"

"No. I mean . . . I don't want to talk about that."

"Oh, I suppose you will . . . eventually. So this is what Morgan gave you when you were little? A plane? No dolls?"

"It was really my mother who gave me those things."

"Interesting. Well, I can tell you that the only thing Morgan likes to give me is advice."

I could hear Boston talking to him, but their voices were just a little too low to make out every word, and I thought they had gone out on the back patio.

"He was never short of that with me, either," I said.

She smiled. "I think my friends are going to like you. Well, mostly anyway, to please me."

"Then I'll like them. Mostly to please you," I said, then took a

breath and walked out and down the stairs with the sound of her gig-
gling behind me.

Maybe we would get along really well. Maybe I would have a sister.
Hope was always a dangerous thing. It was like standing on the edge
of a cliff.

I paused on the stairway, realizing that the last time I had heard my
father's voice was when he was in a rage and had just punched a hole in
the wall. He never called me after he ran out, and as far as my mother
told me, he didn't ask about me. I had the feeling that whatever he did
say wasn't something she wanted me to hear.

"Angry people say things that they didn't even know they would
think," she confirmed when I asked a short time after she had met with
lawyers.

What I had wished she wouldn't do was leave it up to my imagination. I knew what he believed about me because of the way I avoided
meeting his eyes after he asked his questions about Mommy and Nattie before he left us. I couldn't help it. I could feel his suspicions not
only about them but about me. There were lines being drawn separat-
ing my mother's side and his side. I didn't step across them the way he
had wanted me to step.

I knew he was hoping I would be as angry and as disappointed as
he was. He wanted me to dislike Nattie, but I couldn't even pretend
to. Maybe if I could have, I wouldn't have suffered as much in the dark
room at Sutherland. Ironically, the only way to escape was to do just
that, however, to pretend I was angry and disappointed. Now that I
was here, would Daddy see through it as quickly as he always could?
He often said that avoiding the truth always led to pain and disaster.
Even lying to protect someone you love would eventually bite you like
a snake.

Was that what he still thought? Had I been bitten by a snake? Or
had one whispered in my ear like one did to Eve in the Garden of

Eden? Daddy wasn't religious, but that didn't mean he didn't believe in sins. Like Grandfather Sutherland, he saw them in any violation of what he said or held as his own Ten Commandments.

I couldn't stop trembling as I continued down the stairs. Everyone was outside on the patio. I could see my father standing there, talking to Boston, who was fishing something out of the pool with a net. Daddy was dressed as I always remembered him, in a starched, clean short-sleeved white shirt, a black tie, and black slacks, with comfortable black leather loafers, polished and shiny. His cuffed pants had sharp creases.

For a moment, in fact, it felt as if no time had passed. I had awoken from a nightmare in some other place. Daddy would turn, see me, and say, *Where have you been? Where's your mother? It's time for dinner.*

But, of course, that palpable wish burst like a balloon being filled with too much dream breath, puffs of hope and denial. I was here, shocked back to reality. Parker turned to me first. I watched every move of my father, anticipating his reluctance, almost hearing him think, *Well, it's time. I have to look at her.*

"Well then," he said when he looked at me, "looks like you grew a little."

"Hi, Daddy."

Was there anything telegraphing his desire to hug and kiss me? If there was, I didn't see it. I waited.

"Settling in pretty nicely, then, huh?"

"Yes," I said.

"Well, what do you think of Hawaii?" he asked.

"I don't know. I've hardly seen it, but it's beautiful here."

He finally smiled and looked at Parker. They seemed to exchange the same thought.

"Exactly what you would have said," she told him.

He nodded.

I felt as if I had just passed the first test. How many would there be before he opened his arms to hug me and opened his heart to welcome me back?

For a moment I imagined my mother standing behind him, smiling at me to give me courage. But that vision was gone as quickly as it had come.

And I wondered.

Did I really want him to welcome me back?

CHAPTER TEN

At dinner, Dina asked me mostly questions about my time at Sutherland after Mommy's death. Of course, she had no idea that I had spent most of it locked away.

"Morgan says our house isn't even a tenth of the size."

I glanced at Daddy, wondering how much he had described. Did he mention the golf course, the tennis court, and the ballroom? He said nothing.

"Yes, it's big," I said. "It's an old mansion," I added, trying not to sound like I had been living in a famous castle.

She said she had heard of it when they lived in Albany. "It's like some historical site or something. Sounds like you were living in a museum. Probably a lot of 'don't touch this, don't touch that.'"

"Maybe if *you* lived there," Boston said.

She ignored him. She was more interested in my homeschooling than Sutherland anyway. Every time I answered a question, I first looked at Daddy. He kept his eyes on his food but clearly was listening closely. It made me extra careful about every word I used when I described the study, the library, and the textbooks. I wondered if Dina could see how cautious I was being. If she sensed it, I had no doubt it would make her even more curious, and curiosity would only lead to the truths I was supposed to leave buried behind me.

"It wasn't much different from going to a school. I was given the same textbooks, reading assignments, workbooks, but probably more homework than ordinary. Some weeks my teacher was there six days."

"Six days! Why?"

I shrugged, trying to appear casual about it. "Everyone wanted to be sure I didn't fall behind."

"Well, I guess your grandfather paid a lot to have a professor be your homeschool teacher. Some of mine look like they were just in high school last week. And besides, how can one teacher know every subject? She'd have to be some kind of genius."

"I don't know how much she was paid. I know my grandfather was satisfied with my exam scores."

"Yeah, but being at home all the time, you couldn't make new friends. Why didn't he just send you to another school, maybe one where they didn't know anything much about your mother?"

"Dina," Parker said sharply.

She looked fearfully at Daddy. He lifted his eyes slowly and glared at her. I imagined a thin layer of ice over his pupils.

"I'm just interested," Dina whined. "She can ask me anything, so why can't I ask her anything?"

"She can ask you anything?" Boston said. His ears were jerked back. "Even I wouldn't do that. Might ruin my appetite or something if you answered."

"Ha ha. She doesn't have to ask anything about you. The most exciting thing you do is brush your teeth."

"Dina," Daddy muttered again, this time without looking at her. "We've been through this clearly."

Dina bit down on her lower lip as if the words were overflowing and concentrated on her food.

Now the silence was so thick that I could hear the hum of a motor in something in the kitchen. Maybe this was like putting seashells over your ears, I thought. Parker was staring ahead as she ate, looking like she was imagining she was somewhere else. I hadn't been here long, but already it felt like I was someplace where no one really knew anyone. You stayed within your own space, terrified your arm might graze that of someone next to you.

"Dina wants me to take her and Caroline to a beach party tomorrow night," Boston told my father.

Daddy looked up and at me as if he just had realized I was there. Then he looked with scrutiny at Dina. His face was full of suspicion. What was she up to?

"I can introduce her to my friends, Morgan. All at once instead of whenever we meet one. What's she going to do if I go and she doesn't anyway?" Dina asked.

Daddy relaxed. "Let me think about it," he said, "and be sure we're not moving too fast. After dinner, you and I will take a walk," he told me.

"Why don't you go for a bike ride?" Dina said, almost sang. "You can use my bike and get her broken into her new bike."

Daddy looked at her with eyes of ice. She giggled nervously. When I looked at Parker, she had the same angry glare on her face. *Maybe she really is my father's female duplicate*, I thought. They almost breathed simultaneously. I couldn't help but wonder how much Daddy had shared with her about Mommy. What secrets did he reveal about her and me, too? According to what Mommy had told Nattie and me, he was seeing Parker before he exploded and left us. When Mommy told

Nattie and me about it after a meeting with the attorneys, it sounded more like he was getting even than that he was in love. Was he still getting even? Would he always be?

As if I closed my fist around these questions and thoughts, I shut them down and continued to eat in silence. Only Boston smiled at me.

Parker began to talk about a fill-in assignment she was asked to do at the Kapalua Airport, and she and Daddy spoke about their work as if there was no one else at the table, using technical terms I was sure Dina didn't understand. Boston seemed to be paying attention, but from the way Dina was pouting, I knew she wasn't even slightly interested. I was always intrigued with Daddy's work, especially once I understood how important it was to everyone's safety.

"Your father literally holds the lives of hundreds of people in his hands," Mommy once told me.

Boston asked them some questions, which led to a discussion about climate change. Dina raised her eyes to the ceiling and poked me, pretending to yawn from boredom. I wasn't totally unsympathetic. How different this was from the early family dinners I remembered. For one thing, there was always music that even Daddy enjoyed back then. There was lots of laughter, too. Today all that seemed almost imagined, like it was only a dream or something I had read in a fantasy book. That kind of family was the stuff of make-believe stories that always began with "Once upon a time there was a warm and wonderful family . . ."

I couldn't help looking at Daddy when I thought about this. I'm sure I appeared to be wondering if he was the same man who used to arrive home from work, shouting, "Landed!" I used to run to him and feel his firm grip on my waist when he swung me around, my arms out, pretending to be an airplane. Maybe he realized what I was thinking that moment, remembering. He turned to me with a bit of his former self and, in a much warmer, more Daddy-like voice, asked if I liked the food.

"Yes, it's very good," I said quickly.

He nodded with approval and looked at Parker. "She cooks Hawaiian dishes like she was born here," he said, and reached for her hand. They smiled at each other in a way I couldn't remember my parents smiling at each other, even during the beautiful springtime of our lives.

However, his expression of affection for Parker felt like tiny pins in my heart. Up to the moment our lives changed, I couldn't imagine Daddy looking at any other women like this. I glanced at them all. Who was this new family? I was suddenly a stranger among strangers. Was this what my life was destined to be, a life lived on the outside, tiptoeing around my past, my memories? What would it do to me? Was this what Mrs. Lawson had really meant when she told me I would have to become someone new? And who was this new me, really? Would I become more like Daddy than Mommy as he pushed every memory of her further and further into the hum? Would affection become just a word, not to mention love, which already seemed more like a distant star, a twinkling memory fading into the darkness?

How often Mommy had said it to me: "I love you, sweetheart. Love you, Caroline. Remember, I love you, darling." And every time we heard anyone say it, even when we heard it on television, we'd look at each other as if we knew the secret, the special magic in the word.

When would I hear it again? And from whom if not him?

Daddy ordered Dina to help Parker with the dishes. Boston cleared the table. I waited to see if I had a chore, but Daddy rose and nodded at me.

"We'll go for that walk while they clean up," he said.

Dina smirked when she looked at me. Did she think I was already getting special treatment? I followed Daddy out. He paused for a second or so as if reconsidering and then started down the driveway.

He walked in what I recalled was his firm, marching style. I hurried to keep up, just the way I often had. It was funny how little things like that made me happy, probably because they were part of my life before he and Mommy broke apart. It was like picking up the pieces of a broken vase and putting it back together. Daddy was returning.

Or was he?

"I don't need to repeat what Parker has already told you is off-bounds here, right?"

"I guess not," I said.

He stopped and turned to me. "This is not a guess. It's how it is."

Tears came to my eyes because I really didn't recognize him. Then it came to me: he had always bridled his anger. It was there, but not sounding as if it was coming from a stranger. When parents are angry at you, I thought, there's more disappointment than rage. His voice now was colder, sharper. I was never really afraid of my father. The night he put his fist through the wall terrified me because he had lost the self-control that he nurtured so finely to be able to do his work and be who he was, Captain Bryer, the man who walked the same number of steps to the mailbox each time and ascended and descended our stairway with such precision and care that it became annoying to my mother.

I wondered if I was different to him, too, and if I was, did that make him happy, satisfied? Had Dr. Kirkwell and Mrs. Lawson succeeded? Did they draw down a shade over the resemblances to the little girl he knew, resemblances to the woman he had come to despise?

"I'm not trying to be hard on you, Caroline. We've simply got to make a clean break from what was our lives, lives based on lies and deception," he said in a more reasonable and careful tone. "I hope that whatever occurred at Sutherland was really enough to help you come to that conclusion. This is not only a different place; it's a different world for us both. We have a different future from what we had in Colonie."

He paused, waiting for me to say something, but I couldn't stop holding my breath, because, although I didn't like the words, they were at least words with the Daddy feeling. He started to walk again. Ahead of us the road was very dark. There were no other house lights nearby. The stars did seem brighter, and there were more of them. I could hear the sounds of cars and people talking and laughing off to the right. It was warm; I could smell the ocean in the air. The sights and the scents, even the way people sounded somewhere in the darkness, were all different. Would it change me? In weeks, months, would I become different, too?

Did different places turn you into different people?

"Tell me about Mrs. Lawson," he said, more like demanded. "Did you have anything to do with that?"

"No," I quickly replied, astonished he would ask.

"But your cousin Simon might have had something to do with it?"

"I don't know for sure."

He stopped again. "Didn't your aunt Holly tell you something? Well?"

How did he know that? Did Grandfather Sutherland tell him? Surely Aunt Holly hadn't.

"I'm not supposed to say."

My lips were trembling. There were just too many promises to keep.

He surprised me. He smiled. "That's good. You keep your word. Not something your mother would have done."

He started to turn to walk again.

"Yes, she would," I said. "If she promised."

"Like the promises she made in her wedding vows to me?"

I didn't know what to say. In a moment this would be over if I continued to disagree. He'd realize the letter I wrote was entirely a lie. I wasn't sure if I'd be happy because a burden was lifted or sad because I had lost him forever and ever.

"Mommy is not in her grave," I blurted before he could express a sign of anger.

"What?"

"She's in Grandfather Sutherland's office."

Did he know, or didn't he? I could see his face in the starlight. There was surprise, and that made me feel better, safer.

"What are you talking about?"

"Her ashes are in an urn, not in the cemetery. Her grave has her name on it but not her in it."

"Who told you that? Your crazy cousin?"

"I saw it. He showed me. He snuck me into Grandfather's office closet, and I saw it on a shelf."

"You don't know whose ashes are in that urn." He thought for a moment. "What difference does it make anyway? If she had her choice, she would have been buried somewhere else but the Sutherland cemetery."

"Not locked in a closet," I said with as much defiance as I dared.

"Right," he said without any show of anger. "But all that is in the past, and I'm telling you we're going to forget it and look toward the future."

He waved his hand as if he could do that magically.

"So, I'm glad you're hitting it off with Dina," he said in a lighter tone. "And apparently Boston likes you. You're going to meet a lot of new young people. If I can be sure you won't talk about your mother and what happened, I'll approve of your starting tomorrow and let you go to Dina's beach party. Just think twice before you speak about yourself, especially to strangers here. I don't want any of it coming back at Parker and me. She certainly doesn't deserve it. She helped me get over the past. I don't need or want to put her through any more of it or relive any. That's all gone and forgotten.

"My advice to you is to embrace this new world just as I have, enjoy a new life, and start fresh. We'll do a lot of fun things together as a family. Parker and I are both determined people. You're welcome now, but never forget this is a trial period. So," he said, turning, and without taking a breath, he continued. "You saw that I bought you a new bike and bike helmet. There are some great roads to ride, but when you're on the main ones, I want to be sure you obey the rules and have complete control of yourself. And never go out without wearing the helmet."

Then he surprised me.

"Your grandfather would probably kill me if something happened to you because I put you out there too soon."

My grandfather? I thought he was happy to be rid of me. How could he care what happened to me now, after permitting, in fact hiring, Dr. Kirkwell to do all that she had done to me? Maybe Daddy was simply exaggerating. I was afraid to ask any more about it. It would be like opening a jar full of angry bees.

When we approached the house, I saw Dina on the lanai, looking down at us, smiling as if she had heard every word and knew our secrets. As young as I was, I understood why she wanted us to share them. It would give her some power over me. What she told me almost didn't matter. I certainly wouldn't run to her mother or my father to tell on her.

Daddy brought out my new bike and handed me the helmet. I put it on.

"Make sure it's snug."

I did.

"Okay. Let's get you measured."

He held the wrench in his hand. I got on the bike, and he checked where my feet were on the pedals.

"About an inch lower," he said, and I got off while he adjusted the seat. "Go on."

I sat again.

"Just ride around the driveway here first so we're sure it's right."

He watched me. I knew I was looking ridiculously serious. When I looked up at Dina, she was laughing.

"Good," Daddy said. "It has a light." He switched it on. "Go down the hill until you reach the road that takes you to the highway and pedal back up."

"Watch out for turtles," Dina shouted.

I looked at Daddy. Was that serious?

"Concentrate on what you're doing," he said, annoyed.

He glared up at Dina. She stepped back from the railing as if his eyes really did send darts up at her.

I pedaled off and down the hill through the darkness, slowing myself carefully, terrified that I would fail and he'd decide to get rid of me because I embarrassed him. It occurred to me that because I was really his daughter, his blood, my failures and successes would have a different importance. I was in a real sense in competition with my stepbrother and stepsister. I was Captain Bryer's daughter. Maybe I should have been proud of that, but if anything, that made me more nervous. Everything I did, every day, I would be judged. After all, I was supposedly the wounded victim of a failed marriage, failing because of what my father and my grandfather thought was my mother's abnormality, causing what had happened to me to become even more serious.

How could I not be damaged?

The front wheel was shaking because of my trembling. I took a deep breath and pumped the brakes, reaching back to my younger days to recall my first bike and his teaching me how to ride while my mother watched proudly. Was she watching now? The main road lay ahead. I could see the constant traffic. It did look forbidding.

I turned and started back up the hill to the driveway, practically running away from the sight of those cars. It wasn't until that moment that my travel fatigue washed over and through me. Nevertheless, I was determined to show my father I could do it, and pumped the pedals hard to get up the hill. He was standing there with his hands on his hips.

"Good," he said. "I have some time off the day after tomorrow. I'll take you and Dina to a bike path near the ocean. You can do four or five miles."

Miles, I thought. The most I had ever ridden a bike was in the neighborhood.

"Okay, put your bike and the helmet away. Taking care of our things is important because—"

"They don't take care of themselves," I finished.

He came the closest to a Daddy smile. So many of his words and instructions came from what my mother used to call his Captain Bryer lectures. They hung in my memory like apples or peaches ready to be picked.

"Go on to bed, Caroline. You're into jet lag for sure," he said.

After I put my bike and helmet away, I hurried in and up the stairs. Dina was already there, lying back on her bed in her bra and panties, her hands behind her head.

"Back to the arms of Daddy?" she asked when I paused in the doorway.

She was the first girl other than my mother and Nattie whom I saw in her underthings. It wasn't until that moment that I realized how intimate we were going to be. There was something about her smile that didn't annoy me as much as it made me nervous. Flashes of all the pictures of girls and women together that Dr. Kirkwell had used in my aversion therapy treatment rolled across my memory's eyes. I hated the feelings that brought back. I trembled but tried to hide it with an expression of exhaustion.

"I hope so," I said. "That's why I came. But that bike ride was hard because of all the traveling I did."

Her smile widened. "You can rest up tomorrow. We'll hang out at the pool, and I'll start painting you. Don't expect a photograph. What I paint is what I see with my artistic vision. I won't be sure until I start, so don't ask what that vision is."

"Okay."

"Better close the door," she said as she unhooked her bra. "Or Beans will be peeping at us. He took your suitcases. When he says he's going to do something, he does it. I hate him. He's so dependable."

"What? Why does that make you hate him?"

"When your brother is like Beans, everything wrong you do becomes breaking news in your house, even if it's just leaving a window open. You didn't grow up with it."

"Grow up with what?"

"Being compared to your brother or even your sister. He dresses neater, takes care of his things better, even eats properly. Do you have any idea what it's like never being able to say, 'Well, he did it, too'? There's never a 'too.'"

I guess the look on my face surprised her, but she was standing there naked now, and she didn't seem to be the slightest bit embarrassed. Dr. Kirkwell had shown me enough pictures of young women for me to know that Dina had a beautiful figure. Except for the time Simon looked at me, only my mother and Nattie ever saw me this undressed. Daddy avoided looking at me in my panties even when I was only four or five. It was only lately, when Mommy and Nattie began to live together, that I had stood naked in front of a mirror and thought about my developing figure. Thinking about it and touching myself the first time brought so much heat to my face that I hurried to get dressed. I felt heat now, but Dina completely misunderstood.

"Do I have to spell it out? That means it lights up your mistakes more when you have a brother that perfect. Get it?"

"Oh, yes."

"Well, you'd better not be perfect, too. I can't live with too many angels."

"Don't worry about that," I said. "I'm sure I'll make mistakes, and mine will always be more serious than yours. As I was often told, I carry a lot of baggage."

"I bet. I bet you have a lot to tell despite that look of innocence. It's probably a mask."

"It's not a mask, but it's not innocence; it's exhaustion. I'm so tired that I'm walking in my sleep. I'll get ready for bed."

"Get ready, but also get ready to come up with a new secret. It's your turn to start it off tonight," she said, and put on her nightgown.

I went into the bathroom. She stopped me from closing the door to add something.

"I think this one should be about your mother," she said in a loud whisper, and then let me close the door.

I stood there staring at it. Why didn't Daddy consider how demanding and prodding Dina would be? He knew we were going to be living so closely. Was this another way to test me? How would we get along if I had completely zipped lips?

When I came out in my nightgown and slipped into bed, she put down her mobile phone.

"Did you see them naked together?" she asked.

"Who?"

"Your mother and her lover? I'm sure you saw them kissing, but what about the other stuff?"

"Parker told me you and Boston wouldn't ask about those things. It would upset my father, and he warned me again not to talk about it."

"You think I would tell what you told?"

"No," I said, even though I wasn't sure. She might have a best friend just waiting to hear the details.

"Well?"

"If I talk about it, I can't help thinking about it, and I'm so tired. Let me sleep. We have lots of time to tell each other things we wouldn't tell other people, especially my father and Parker," I added, hoping that would make her back away for now.

"Okay. I'll wait, but maybe you'll talk in your sleep and your secrets will leak out anyway," she said, and turned off the light.

Would I?

Despite my fatigue, going to sleep with that on my mind wasn't easy. I didn't remember when I had fallen asleep, but when I woke, Dina was already up and dressed and had gone downstairs. I could hear talking. I rose quickly. Would Daddy be upset I was getting up so late? I washed and dressed as quickly as I could, choosing one of the shorts-and-blouse outfits Aunt Holly had gotten for me. But when I went downstairs, Daddy and Boston were already gone.

"Your father has an earlier shift today, so he'll be home in time for us to go to a restaurant," Parker said. "I have a number of things to do, so I'll be leaving shortly."

Dina was still at the table, texting someone on her mobile.

"I'm sorry I slept so late," I said.

"We expected it," Parker said. "What surprised us was how early Dina rose."

"What?" she said, hearing her name.

"Where's your mobile?" Parker asked me.

"Upstairs in my purse. I haven't even turned it on."

Who was I going to call or text except Aunt Holly?

"I'm sure before long it will be attached to you," Parker said. "Dina sleeps with it. I think she even showers with it."

"Very funny, Parker."

I looked at Parker. Did she really want her children to call her by her first name even if they meant it to be funny? I couldn't imagine calling my father Morgan or my mother Linsey.

"There's cereal and bananas, berries, or do you know how to make yourself eggs?"

"Yes, I used to help . . . yes," I said. "But I'll have cereal."

She nodded at the cabinet on her right.

"Just make yourself at home now, Caroline. When I go shopping for groceries, you can come along and get some things you like."

I looked at Dina, who was gazing up at the ceiling and shaking her head.

"The excitement might be too much," she said.

I poured myself a glass of juice and chose a cereal. I tried not to look at either of them as I cut the banana as carefully and as perfectly as Mommy used to and then spooned in some berries.

"We'll hang out at the pool today. I have the perfect spot for you to pose."

"Be careful with the sun," Parker warned me. "You have very fair skin, and you haven't been in the sun very much. I don't expect her to have a burn," she added for Dina, who scoffed and got up. "Did you hear me about going to a restaurant for dinner tonight?"

"No. I mean, we can't. We're going to a beach party. Beans told Morgan last night."

"He didn't approve of it."

"He said he'd think about it," she whined.

Parker sighed. "Well, maybe Morgan and I will have a night to ourselves, then. We can regain our sanity."

"I'm changing into my bathing suit and setting up at the pool," Dina told me, ignoring her mother.

When she left, Parker turned to me.

"Your father appears pleased with you so far, Caroline. Just remember to be careful among Dina and her friends. It looks like we live apart from people here, but it's a remarkably small community. All people really know is your mother was killed in a horrible car accident. They know, of course, about your parents' divorce, but that's basically it.

"I'll be gone most of the day. I have a few other errands to run," Parker said, and left to go upstairs.

Sitting there alone in a house I hadn't yet gotten used to, but that seemed filled with warnings, gave me such an empty, lost feeling that for a moment I wondered if I was better off living in a darker mansion where the memories of my mother were never gone.

As if on cue, Dina came halfway down the stairs and brought me back to Sutherland.

"Your phone was ringing," she said. "Who's Holly Sutherland?"

I rose quickly and took the mobile from her.

"My aunt," I said. I stared at her name on the small screen.

"So call her back. You know how to do it, don't you?"

"Thank you," I said.

I went out on the patio and did just that—far enough, I hoped, for Dina not to hear.

"How are you, sweetheart?" Aunt Holly said as soon as I called. "How was your trip?"

"It was good."

"And?"

"Daddy's new wife told me he was pleased with me. So far."

"Okay. Is it nice?"

"Very," I said, and described the house and the pool and my new bike.

She laughed at how fast I was talking. "Well, I'm glad," she said when I paused for a breath.

"And how's Simon?"

I looked back first to be sure Dina wasn't listening from the doorway.

"He wants to return to Sutherland."

"He does? Does he know I'm gone?"

"Yes, but I think he wants to be sure your grandfather doesn't dislike him. His doctor thinks it's okay."

"He'd rather be there than home with you and Uncle Martin?"

"He always did," she said.

Something that I feared but didn't even voice to myself stepped up.

"Isn't he afraid of the memory of the accident?"

Would I ever get Mrs. Lawson's twisted, dead body out of my mind?

"His doctor thinks it might be better for him to confront it. I don't doubt he can. He's a true Sutherland," she said.

It was hard to tell from the tone of her voice whether she was happy or sad about that. She promised to call frequently and tell me how everything was and repeated that I should call her whenever I needed someone.

I'll call you right back, I wanted to say.

I need someone now.

CHAPTER ELEVEN

After I ate my breakfast and cleaned up, I went upstairs, put on my bathing suit, and then joined Dina at the pool. She was wearing a very revealing two-piece coral-colored bathing suit. The bottom cut sharply between her legs. It wasn't so much that it left little to the imagination but more that it lit up the imagination. My floral one-piece felt more like a little girl's, unflattering and hardly as sexy. She laughed at what I was sure was an expression of shock on my face.

I should be better at hiding my feelings, I thought. It was practically the most important thing for me to do, especially here. For the first time, I wished I could be more like my grandfather. Behind his steely look lay either satisfaction or dissatisfaction, happiness or sadness, calmness or rage, but you couldn't tell until he told you.

Simon thought that was the root of our grandfather's power: being inscrutable. "How do you play checkers with someone invisible? When he wants to, he can turn his eyes into glass. All you see is your own reflection, your own thoughts and fears, not his."

"You look so surprised, Caroline. Didn't you ever see a plunge triangle bikini?" Dina asked, proudly turning to show me how it fit so snugly.

"No."

Not in real life, I thought. Dr. Kirkwell had shown me pictures of women in even more revealing bathing suits. She had asked me if my mother owned one like it. I remember being shocked at even the idea. She didn't like my answer and basically forced me to admit that I didn't know everything about my mother, especially when she was younger, in high school and college.

"Parker hates this suit," Dina said. "She says I could just wear two Band-Aids and panties and it would be the same. Like I would take her fashion advice. You should see the suit she wears. It looks like it was made in 1930. Your father looks great in a suit, almost as sexy as Beans in his lifeguard suit."

The idea of my father being sexy brought a fresh flush to my face. She interpreted my silence as my feeling sorry for myself.

"Don't worry about it," she said. "We'll find a better bathing suit for you. I know some great shops at the beach. Maybe we can get one tonight."

"We'd better ask my father first."

Especially if it's anything like yours, I thought.

"Oh, give me a break. You don't have to wear it around here. Only when we go to the beach. He'll never know. It's not lying if you don't say or show anything. You never said you didn't, and you never said you did. That's the way I think about it. Am I right?"

"We'll see," I said.

I didn't want to tell her I thought that was still dishonest and deceitful. Nattie used to tell me that most of her job in diplomacy was learning how to walk a tightrope. She'd laugh and say, "It's not lying; it's balancing."

"You just described my life," Mommy had said. Was that becoming mine?

"Whatever. I have your lounge chair positioned over there," she said, pointing to the other side of the pool. "You'll have enough shade. Just turn toward me and keep your arms on the side. Don't cross your legs. Unpin your hair. I'd like it over your shoulders. It all matters!" she emphasized before I could even think of questioning her orders. "It's my vision."

"I don't know why it's so important to paint a picture of me as soon as I arrive. I'm still half asleep."

"Freshness. Once you're here a week or so, you won't look as innocent. I talk from experience," she said, smiling proudly, as if she had climbed Mount Everest or something. "The sun and warm nights kind of make you grow up faster."

"What does that mean?"

"Use your imagination. Think of yourself wearing a bathing suit like this on the beach with some good-looking boys around you. You think they'll want to play video games with you? You'll be swatting them away like flies. Don't dare choose any of them without first checking with me."

"Oh."

The soft tropical breeze played in my hair as soon as I loosened it. It felt like soft tips of fingers exploring my face. My imagination seemed to naturally envision the eyes and smiles of good-looking teenage boys, boys I had seen in dreams when I was conceiving of my own romances. Weren't Hawaiian beaches the most natural place to find them, all of us in clothing as skimpy as could be, sexual innuendos swirling around me? Deep down, a part of me had begun longing for the flirtatious affairs Dina was suggesting. Although I never said it to Dr. Kirkwell or to Simon, I needed to affirm who I was to myself as much as to my grandfather and anyone at Sutherland, and especially to my father, affirm that I wanted to fall in love with a boy, a man, marry and have my own children. I wanted my own Robot Family, but one so entangled with love that we could never deny each other or even think of being apart.

And I wanted this without feeling guilty, feeling like I in any way condemned my mother. Her love for Nattie and Nattie's love for her was something that I felt was real. It was right for them; it gave them happiness.

"Yeah, oh," Dina said.

I had been in such a daydream for a few moments that I lost track of what she was saying.

"What?"

"Forget it, Caroline. Go on to the lounge chair. Let's get the best of the late morning. I promised Morgan I'd ride around here with you in the afternoon and give you some hints about riding in traffic. Don't think I want to do it. I'm being selfish. If he's happy, he'll loosen up the dog collars."

"Dog collars?"

"He won't be so uptight about everything we do. Jeez, Caroline, were you brought up in a nunnery or something?" She paused, staring at me. "Okay, I think I get it," she said.

"Get what?"

She sighed deeply. "The forbidden," she moaned. "You should have seen and heard the reminders both Beans and I were getting a few days before you arrived. We're all tiptoeing around hot coals on the beach. We'll figure it all out later. If you listen to me, we'll be fine.

"Go on. Lie on the lounge chair. I have to get started while I have the artistic energy. It comes and goes in waves. Like sex," she tittered.

Of course, after my experiences at school and in the neighborhood after Mommy and Daddy separated and Mommy and Nattie began living together, and after my incarceration and the terrible aversion therapy treatment, I was terrified to the bone when it came to being brought into a new world of teenage boys and girls. What would they see? What mistakes would I make? How would Daddy react? Even after only hours of being with Dina, I wasn't confident that she was my best guide to help me navigate into a new life. But if I rejected her too strongly, things could go sour anyway.

I crossed to the other side of the pool. There was a towel rolled at the bottom of the lounge chair. She stood by her easel, her drawing pencil in hand, impatiently waiting for me to prepare myself as she had described.

"So who's Simon?" she asked as soon as I was ready. "You were talking about him right under the lanai," she said, seeing the surprise on my face. "Don't worry. I didn't hear everything. You were practically whispering. I'm surprised your aunt could hear you."

"He's my cousin," I said. "Uncle Martin and Aunt Holly's son."

"How old?"

"He's sixteen, almost seventeen, but he's always been years ahead mentally."

"Is he good-looking?"

"Yes."

"Lots of girlfriends?"

"No," I said, maybe too quickly.

She paused and stared at me a moment. "No? He likes girls, doesn't he? Or what?"

"He doesn't go to a regular school. He's too far ahead. His teachers couldn't keep up with him."

"Sounds pretty boring. Look this way, please. So what was that about a memory he might have?"

"I don't think I should talk about him anymore. Daddy wouldn't like it."

"Daddy wouldn't like it," she mimicked. Then she paused and lost her smile. "So many secrets you're going to have to give up to become my sister," she warned. "You want that, right? You want to have a best friend, don't you?"

"Yes," I said, but cautiously.

"Forget about it for now. You're acting nervous, and you're ruining my vision for the painting. I have to concentrate anyway. As my art teacher told me, I have to find my vision and concentrate on it and nothing else."

For a while she worked without talking. When the sun hit my feet, I brought up my legs.

"Oh, stop worrying about getting sunburned. Parker sees trouble everywhere. It's part of her work. Come to think of it, your father's, too." She smiled. "I think they have a traffic light on the ceiling above their bed. You know, caution, coming in too fast?" She laughed.

"What's that mean?"

She paused. "What does that mean? What does this mean? You do know how people make babies, don't you?"

"We're still trying to figure out how you were made," we heard, and saw Boston in his bathing suit, a towel over his shoulder, come out of the house. He did look quite sexy, just as Dina had said.

"Why are you home?" Dina asked, clearly sounding annoyed.

"They had to close the pool for some repair on the equipment. Hi, Caroline."

He put his towel on a lounge chair and slipped out of his sandals. Then he walked up to the edge of the pool and dove in, hardly making a splash.

"He's such a show-off," Dina said. She threw down her pencil. When he popped up, she moaned. "How am I supposed to concentrate on my work?"

Boston ignored her and turned to me. "Water's perfect. It feels like liquid silk. Come on. Dive in."

I looked at Dina. She flopped onto a chair. The pool did look inviting.

"I can't dive," I said.

"Sure you can. I'll show you how."

He pulled himself up and swung out of the pool in one motion. All his muscles seemed to flex. In his swimsuit he looked like he didn't have an ounce of fat. He held out his hand, beckoning.

"C'mon, don't be afraid."

"Maybe she doesn't care to learn to dive, Beans."

"Sure she does."

He looked at me, smiling. I stood trembling, uncertain, wondering what to do that wouldn't make me seem more like a little girl. It suddenly became very important to me that Boston see me as a young teenage woman. Should I rush to take his hand, or be coy? Which was more grown-up?

He didn't wait. He seized my hand and pulled me gently to him. Then he stepped behind me and, with his hands on my waist, guided me to the side of the pool.

"We'll start from scratch. Sit here on the edge of the pool with your feet in the water. You can touch the bottom here. The pool has a fast drop-off to the left, but here we're only about three and a half feet."

I did what he asked and then looked at Dina. She turned away, folding her arms, pouting.

"Okay," he said, sitting beside me. "You line up your body, arms out, and tuck your head in like this. It's really important to line your head up. So you're just going to slide your body into the water, but it's necessary that you keep your head tucked in, otherwise your body will just smack on the water. You just fall into the water, leaning in with your head. Watch."

He did it, and then I did.

"That was good," he said. He looked toward Dina. "You could learn, too. You never did, and you belly-flop all the time. Care to join diving class?"

"Thanks, but no thanks," she said. "You've ruined my work. Not the first time."

He scoffed and turned back to me.

"Pull yourself completely out," he told me. "Now I want you to kneel at the edge of the pool so you're not standing yet but it's midway, and do the same thing I just had you do."

He demonstrated. It was a little more scary, but I tried not to show any fear and did it as he had told me.

"That's great. A quick learner. We'll do it a few times, and then I want you to only bend one leg and push out with the other. Remember to keep your head tucked in."

I don't know how many times I did it before he told me to stand. As soon as I did one, he had me out of the water and repeating. My heart was pounding. Dina was watching now, not looking upset as much as impressed. I took my first standing dive. He said I had raised my head too much, and made me do it again and again until he said I had it.

"As I suspected. You have your father's athletic ability. But let's check out your swimming," he said.

"I think I'm going to retch from all the excitement," Dina said, rising. "Don't mind me or what I came out here to do until you bullied your way into it."

She went into the house.

"She's upset," I said. "Maybe I shouldn't have taken diving lessons."

"She'll get over it. She's usually upset ten to twenty times a day," Boston said. "Let's see you swim."

I looked toward the doorway. Maybe she would blame Boston and not me, I thought. He was staring at me, his smile more in his lips because his eyes looked like he was searching, waiting for my reaction. Why had he taken such a quick interest in me? I wondered. From what Dina and Parker had said about him and Daddy, I wondered if Daddy had told him to pay more attention to me. Was he spying on me for Daddy, too? I felt like I was moving under microscopes. Every decision I made, every word I uttered, would be evaluated.

"Parents hire me at the hotel to teach their children," he said as I hesitated. "Might as well take advantage of me. I don't mind. Go ahead. Just swim to the other side."

I looked toward the doorway. Where had Dina gone? Was she coming back?

He saw where my attention was going. "Her pout lasts ten minutes, and then she's back to being Dina. Swim."

I started across the pool.

"Whoa, horse," Boston said when I reached the other side. "You're wasting effort. Let me show you how to hold your hands and take breaths. I guess you really haven't swum much at your grandfather's mansion."

"Not since I was much younger," I said. "It's been a while."

He was in the pool beside me. I kept looking toward the house, but there was still no sign of Dina. I hadn't been here twenty-four hours, and already there was tension between her and her brother because of me.

"I would have thought Morgan would have taught you. He's intense about anything he does."

"He probably taught me. I just . . . haven't done it for a while," I said. I wasn't going to criticize Daddy, not even slightly.

"Right. You'll pick it up quickly, then. This will just be a refresher."

He started the lesson. Most of the time, he had his hands on my waist and walked alongside me. He slid them down over my thighs to show me how to kick more efficiently and then let me go back and forth until I stopped to catch my breath.

"I wish all my students were as good learners. You can concentrate. That's good. That's like your father."

"Maybe she'll need to shave her face, too," Dina quipped as she returned with a beer can in her hand.

"Morgan knows exactly how many we have, Dina."

She shrugged. "So tell him you took it. He lets you."

"Morgan is not the easiest person to lie to, Dina. You know that. Your father can see right through her," he told me.

"I think you'll cover for me," Dina said confidently, "otherwise I might elaborate on my description of your giving her swimming lessons."

"What?" He looked like his face had an instant sunburn. "What's that supposed to mean?"

"Nothing, unless I give it meaning," she said. She flopped onto her lounge chair.

Boston looked at me. I knew what she was trying to imply, but I didn't want to reveal it. I clung to innocence and pretended to be confused.

"There is definitely something seriously wrong with you," he told her, and got out of the pool. "I'm going to go meet Skipper, if anyone wants to know."

He began wiping himself down and slipped into his sandals. When he started away, Dina called to him.

"What?"

"Don't forget what time you're taking us to the beach party. And," she said, smiling, "you can stay with us. Maybe teach Caroline how to count stars or something."

He glanced at me and hurried into the house.

"You're not guilty until you look guilty," Dina said.

I was tired of saying "What?" so I got out to dry myself off and lie on the lounge chair. My thoughts were caught up in a whirlwind of confusion. Why had I suddenly become the center of an argument between my stepsister and stepbrother? What was the right thing, the safe thing, to say?

"Boston has never really had a girlfriend, you know," Dina said. I noted she had called him Boston, and not Beans, this time. "And you never had any boyfriend."

"So?"

"Nothing," she said. "Or everything."

"I don't understand."

"That's all right. I'll look after you. You clearly need to be protected." She stared at me for a few moments. "Maybe I'll return to my painting. You have that half-dumb innocent look again."

Half-dumb. Did I? Thanks to Dr. Kirkwell's treatment, I probably knew more about sex than she did.

"How many boyfriends have you had?" I asked her, my voice edgy.

"Before Noa? About three, but none as serious. How about your mother before she married Morgan? Any teenage or college sweethearts—men, I mean?"

"I don't know," I said quickly.

"So she never told you?"

"No."

"Men brag more than women. Most women, that is," she added, and started on her painting.

We heard Boston drive off.

"There's a little taco place just to the right. We can go there for lunch when we practice with your bike."

"But that's on the main road."

"If you're so scared, I'll buy yours and bring it back," she said.

"I can always say I did that anyway if you went with me. I'm a pretty good liar, especially when I lie to Parker and Morgan, despite what Beans told you. Even Parker will admit that. She says I could talk my way into heaven. Speaking of lies and secrets, you forgot to show me the bracelet you stole. Maybe you should show it to me before anyone else sees it. Maybe your father would recognize it and ask you how you got it. I trust you. You can trust me, Caroline."

I looked away. She didn't care if I revealed her secrets. She wanted mine so she could hold them over me. Dr. Kirkwell had taught me well. When you're honest about yourself with someone, you set the clock of betrayal ticking. I didn't have to be with my stepsister any longer to know that when she unlocked my heart, she'd own every breath I took.

"I can show you now."

"When we go up. No rush. If it's really there, that is."

"Of course it is. I told you."

She looked at me. My voice was even sharper than before.

"Careful," she said. "You don't want to lose that innocence again before I get into my painting."

Again?

"What do you mean?"

"Please," she said. "I saw the way you were looking Beans over. That's all right. In fact, it makes me feel better about sharing my room with you."

"Why?"

"You seem normal," she said, and laughed. "Don't worry. I'll make sure everyone thinks so, too."

"Why wouldn't they?"

She paused and smiled. "Why weren't you here with us right after your mother was killed? Don't think I don't know the truth. You don't have to worry you'll slip up and reveal things Morgan and my mother told you not to reveal. I don't miss a thing.

"Guess what?" she said, looking quickly at the house as if she was afraid Parker had returned without our knowing. "I read the letter. They made such a big deal of it. I overheard them and did my little search of their room when they were gone. Don't dare ever tell them. It's another one of my secrets revealed.

"Which is why you have to unlock more of your own. You didn't really steal your grandmother's bracelet, did you? That was pathetic. Nothing like the one I told you. We don't have to rush it. We have plenty of time to really get to know each other, right? We can start today with your telling me the truth about your cousin Simon, too. I told you I didn't hear much just to see how much you would tell me. You'll tell me more, won't you?"

The threatening tone in her voice was unmistakable. And there it was. As long as my mother and Nattie's relationship was kept a private family matter, everyone I met in this new life would not think there was anything possibly wrong with or different about me. If Dina revealed it, which I felt confident she could do, even though I had known her less than a day, she could make life very difficult for me here, maybe even impossible. When someone believes he or she is superior to you or holds some power over you, you can become helpless. I learned that lesson fast at Sutherland.

"I think you'll go with me to the taco stand for lunch now, right?" she asked with a very self-satisfied smile. "Got to be sure you're not a little spy for Parker and Morgan, and the only way to do that is to put yourself in possible trouble if I tell. That's fair, sister dear."

She turned back to her easel.

"Oh, this is coming out just as I envisioned," she said. "Innocence just gushing."

When she declared it was time for lunch, she covered her easel and said I couldn't see it.

"Artists never show unfinished work. You won't understand it because you don't have my vision. Let's get our bikes."

Reluctantly, I followed her to the garage. I kept looking for ways out of it but couldn't think of anything she would accept. She was going to force me to disobey my father.

And I hadn't yet been here a complete day.

CHAPTER TWELVE

I was trembling so badly when we left the garage that I thought I might go off the road and cause a bigger problem. The ocean breeze was stronger than it had been when I rode the night before to show Daddy I could do it. I had put on the helmet but hadn't pinned up my hair. The strands fell along my neck. Right now, it felt like dozens of hairbrushes raking through the strands, my hair whipping around my face. Dina hadn't put on her helmet.

When we went downhill, the wind was so strong that I had to close my eyes momentarily because they were tearing. Opening them, I saw that Dina was riding faster and not looking back to see where I was. As soon as she reached the main road, she finally stopped and waited for me. She nodded at the highway.

"See, it's not so bad on the main road," she said. "There is no reason why you can't bike on the side of the road. It's a lot easier riding down this hill. The taco stand is less than a half mile away. Minutes. Onward," she said, and pedaled onto the main road before I could object.

The cars whizzed by, one coming so close that it put me into a small panic, my handlebars jerking right to left. I struggled to stay on the side of the road, terrified that I could fall to my left and get hit by one of those fast-moving cars coming up behind me. Some beeped, lights flickering. I heard some drivers shouting for me to get farther to the right. I thought I heard obscenities and laughter, too. How could I explain to Dina that I had never ever ridden a bike on a highway like this? I had never even walked on the side of one. It was clear she believed I was some spoiled rich girl as it was, overly protected and spoiled.

Not once did she look back to check on me. If anything, she was pedaling faster. When she reached the taco stand, she braced her bike against a pole and waited for me. I sped up. My body was so tight that I felt every little bump shoot up from the bottom of my feet to the top of my head. The ocean breeze was stronger. Palm trees swayed. I thought I felt the droplets of waves scooped up and carried by the wind. The redolent scent of the water shot up my nostrils and filled my mouth and throat with a salty taste.

"See?" she said when I arrived. "Easy. Morgan thinks we're all planes coming in for a landing and need his firm direction and approval. Morgan's touchdowns." She laughed at her own joke. "Okay, we're here. I'm starving. Look at the menu. I have plenty of money for us."

I was still so frightened that I had little or no appetite.

"I'm not sure," I said, reading the menu. "I've never had these."

"You're kidding. Morgan or your mother never took you to a taco stand?"

"Not that I remember."

"I'll order for us both. We'll eat there," she said, nodding at the bench and table. "I'll get us both a Hawaiian Sun Nectar. You'll like it," she added, which sounded more like *You'd better like it*.

When we were given the food and drinks, we sat at the table.

"You can take off the helmet to eat. Tacos aren't dangerous," she quipped.

I set it on the table and nibbled on my food, my heartbeat finally slowing.

"Don't you like it?"

"Yes, it's delicious."

I took a bigger bite and looked back at our turn onto the highway. It was probably as close as Dina had said, but to me it appeared to be miles.

"I understand that Sutherland was so big that you could put on miles riding a bike around it."

"I didn't have a bike there."

"Why not?"

"Living there was unexpected."

"You should have left the mainland with your father. Why didn't he send for you? No one really answers that question when I ask. Just a bunch of gobbledygook."

"I'm not going to talk about that."

"OMG, Caroline. If you're going to look terrified like this all the time and especially when we meet my friends, you'll make all this more difficult for me."

"All what?"

"Keeping your precious secrets, what else? Stop worrying about what Morgan said or says. You're here. What's done is done. Forget about it already. You're terrified of any reference to your past. My friends, despite what Beans thinks, are not stupid. They'll ask you things. You'd better put all the bad stuff in a drawer and lock it." She sighed as though she really had a burden on her shoulders.

"I'm sorry," I said. "I never expected I'd end up here like this."

"So don't make ending up here seem so terrible. Just keep talking about how happy you are to be here."

"Your mother had similar advice for me when she greeted me at the airport. You even sound the same."

"Don't tell me she's finally rubbing off on me. Maybe I can still get inoculated or something. I can't imagine what Parker was like at my age. She probably had two friends: herself and her."

"Don't you like your mother?"

She paused, grimacing.

"I'm only asking because you don't sound like you do," I said.

"I grew up in a war zone. My fondest memory is of my father throwing a clock into the kitchen wall. I remember it more because the clock still worked. He had a hot temper, and I understand why Parker wanted a divorce. Actually, I know he was seeing another woman already, just like your mother. But lots of times Parker deliberately lit his fuse. Now that I give it more thought, I'm sure she was already seeing Morgan on the side. What a group of hypocrites telling us what's right and what's wrong."

"Is that why you call her by her name and never call her Mother or Mommy?"

"Mommy? Does she strike you as being a Mommy? I don't know why I call her by her name. Beans started to do it more as a joke, and I kind of hooked on. It just seemed easier after my parents divorced."

"Why easier?"

"Less sadness, maybe. Jeez, you're making me think too hard. Who cares why? Are you training to be a psychiatrist or something? What's it going to change if I knew? They made their beds, but we don't have to lie in them. We have our own lives. Let's concentrate on having good times. You know what the best drug is?"

"What?"

"Pleasure, excitement. You're starting on it tonight. I can't have a self-pitying analyst lying beside me every night. Shut the door."

"What?"

"Put your past in another room and shut the door, Caroline. That's what I've done, what I do. You don't owe your parents; they owe you. Nightmares. Thank you, Mommy and Daddy, for introducing them to us, but no thank you. Just smile and nod when you have to. And look forward to the day when you don't have to do it anymore."

I'm sure I looked wide-eyed and shocked, but I couldn't help wondering, *Can I be like her? Do I want to?*

She finished eating. I ate faster. Young men were beeping horns as they drove by us. We were in only our bathing suits. I knew she'd attract attention in hers. She enjoyed it and shifted so drivers could see her more clearly. I thought one was going to stop. He slowed down but at the last minute continued on.

"Too bad. He was cute," she said. She finished her drink.

"I guess we should head back."

Just as we stood, Parker appeared in her SUV. She slowed down, gazed at us, and continued on.

"Parker!" I gasped. "She saw us."

"Don't worry about it," Dina said. "I told you I'd take care of it."

If she was frightened about Parker seeing us, she didn't show it. All the way home, she went on and on about Noa and how much he loved her. "He's very sensitive. All creative people are, you know. I try not to be. People take advantage of you when you are sensitive. Most boys don't even try to tease me. My girlfriends are envious and wish they were as tough. Maybe that's where Parker comes into it for me. Watching her survive my father helped me build a shell."

"A shell? You mean like a turtle?"

"Yes, but I don't crawl back into it." She looked at me. "Morgan often talks about being turtles. Did he used to do that with you?"

"Yes."

Funny how it bothered me that my father shared his ideas and images with her. Did she smoothly slip into his daughter slot, quickly replacing me as I had feared when Mommy first told me about his new family? What other fatherly wisdom did he share with her? Was there nothing between us that was sacredly only for me? Was I the stranger now? Was it even possible that I would think I was more at home back at Sutherland, a mansion filled with secrets and rage? Despite what Daddy had said, I believed my mother was there on that shelf. Did I somehow miss Simon, even with all he had done? I felt like a bird that had lost its sense of direction and was flapping its wings madly as winter, with its darker, colder shadows, was crawling into its world. It was crawling into mine, even here in the sun fest of Hawaii. *Where do I go?*

We put our bikes away and went into the house. Parker wasn't downstairs waiting for us when we entered through the garage as I had expected.

"Let's go back to the pool," Dina said. She saw me looking at the stairway. "She'll find us when she wants to. Parker doesn't back off confrontations. Sometimes I think she feeds off them like a vampire feeds off blood."

She returned to her easel. I sprawled out the way she wanted me. The lounge chair was totally in shade now, but I couldn't relax. Every time I heard a sound coming from the house, I anticipated Parker emerging angrily. Dina, on the other hand, looked as relaxed as she was at the start. For me, time went by very slowly. When Dina took a break, she said we should take a dip in the pool. Parker had still not come out of the house. What was she doing? Had she already told my father?

Boston arrived home first. I heard him talking, but I didn't hear Parker. She was speaking too softly. I was wiping myself off, sitting on the lounge chair, when he came out. For a moment he stood there looking at us. Dina covered her easel. Why was he simply looking at us with his hands on his hips? Moments of silence felt like minutes. Dina finally looked at him.

"What?" she said.

"You know what," he said. "It's your fault, I'm sure."

She ignored him and began putting her things away. He glanced at me as if he had to wait for my father's permission to be friendly again and then went back inside.

"Don't listen to him. He likes being the voice of doom. Let's shower and pick out what to wear for the beach party," she said. "I have good beach bags for us."

"If Parker told him, she surely called my father. What do I say?"

She crossed over to me, carrying her supplies in her art supply bag.

"You know the advice they give people when they're arrested?"

I shook my head.

"Don't you watch television?"

"Not that much."

How could I tell her I hadn't watched television since the day my mother was killed? Even my computer time had been quite restricted. I hadn't read a newspaper and hadn't seen a copy of any magazine my mother used to get. If I told her anything, she'd know I practically had been in solitary confinement for months and months. Other than Simon, I hadn't spoken to anyone my age or close to it. Even after I left the dark bedroom and moved into my mother's room, I didn't watch television or listen to music. What would I say? I didn't know contemporary music and would have to pretend I had heard of this singer or that actor. Confronted with the reality and the realizations, I wondered now how I would hold a conversation on the beach with Dina's friends. In moments they would conclude that there was something very strange about me. My secrets would begin pouring out of my ears, nose, eyes, and mouth.

Vaguely, I wondered if it wasn't better perhaps to just tell it all and let things happen now as they inevitably would. My mind wandered back to those years when we were the Robot Family. Right before what I thought were the darkening days of our endless spring, our neighborhood looked like the setting of a fairy tale. I could hear laughter then. I could mingle with other children even though they saw our home as being so perfect and pristine that they would be afraid to set foot in it. It was different on the sidewalk and streets. That was everyone's world. I yearned for the sound of other children who were running wildly, kicking balls, and trampling lawns.

Now, at this time, on this day, at this place, I regretted ever wanting to grow up and feeling that being a child was never enough. Why didn't I see and realize that being considered an adult meant being responsible for everything you had done? Consequences would always be looming now. You couldn't hide behind being too young to understand. Excuses were transparent. There was no longer a way to defend yourself against the simple accusation. You should have known better. Or you were told not to do that. What didn't you understand?

"Well then, I'll tell you how to behave. You don't offer any information," Dina said. "And if you do, you pretend you didn't realize anything you did was wrong. You can always apologize, but you never confess. So don't start by looking guilty. Look a little surprised. Get him to think you didn't believe you were doing anything so serious. Makes them feel foolish for carrying on, making mountains out of molehills. Parker actually used to say that to my father."

She laughed. How could she think any of this was funny?

"My father lets you get away with that?"

"Maybe he's different now. He gets frustrated and finds it easier to let things go sometimes. Let's wait and see."

She stared at me a moment.

"What?"

"I might come up with a nickname for you."

"What?"

"Doomsday, what else? C'mon," she said, and led the way into the house.

Parker was in the kitchen and didn't come out to greet us before we started up the stairs. Maybe I was Doomsday, but I expected her to tell us to stop and come down. I envisioned her standing there, jabbing her right forefinger at the floor as the anger and punishments poured out. She didn't. As soon as we were in our room, Dina shut the door.

"Okay. Maybe Parker felt it was enough to tell Beans. Sometimes that was enough when I did something she didn't like. Don't assume the worst. Remember, act innocent!" she said, and started to take off her bathing suit. "Let's take a shower together," she said, smiling. "There's enough room. You wash my back, and I'll wash yours."

It was as if Dr. Kirkwell had come through the window and materialized right before my eyes. The shock on my face made Dina laugh.

"Just kidding. I wanted to see if that brought back memories of conversion therapy. Looks like it might have," she said. "I'll go first. Then you. While you shower, I'll go through your clothes for you and choose what you should wear to the beach over your bathing suit. You have another suit I saw, not much better than the one you're wearing. Maybe I'll loan you one of mine. Yes, it would fit with a little tightening on top. It'll be snug and sexy."

I was surprised at how comfortable she was standing totally naked in front of me.

"Last chance," she said, moving to the bathroom door. "You do mine; I do yours."

I still saw Dr. Kirkwell and felt the electric shock from when I had seen images of women doing what she was suggesting.

Dina laughed and closed the door behind her. I got out of my suit and wrapped the swimming towel around me. Then I sat on my bed, trying to calm my racing heart. I heard heavy footsteps on the stairway and held my breath. It was obviously Boston walking by to go to his room. I lay back and closed my eyes for a moment. It might have been for longer than I thought, because suddenly I felt Dina's hand on my face. She had her bath towel wrapped around her hair and was standing naked over me, her breasts nearly touching my face. I jerked my head away.

"Your turn," she said, laughing. "Go on. I'll work on our clothes."

I got out of the bed.

"You'll have to tell me why you're so afraid to be close to me," she said right before I closed the bathroom door. I heard her laugh.

I felt like I would start to cry if I didn't get myself into the shower quickly. When I did, I was pretty sure some of the water streaking down my face was my tears anyway. Just as I stepped out of the shower and began to dry myself, I heard the banging. Dina screamed, and then after another loud bang, I heard Daddy shout, "Get something on and get downstairs now! Both of you!"

Instantly, I was thrown back to that morning when Daddy had returned from Lake George and discovered Mommy and Nattie in his and Mommy's bed. The lightning bolt that had passed through my body then passed through it again. At first, I froze, and then I began to tremble. My teeth actually chattered. Dina opened the door.

"Just put on your bathrobe, and let me do most of the talking," she said. "Morgan forgets that I had a father with twice his temper and three times as violent. I'm not his child, and whenever I tell him that, he backs off. Parker, like most divorced parents, feels guilty most of the time. A few times, I cried hysterically when he shouted at me and blamed her for marrying him. That usually works."

I stared at her, shocked at how proud she was of her power to manipulate her mother.

"Well, it *is* partly her fault!" she said. "Because of her work, she used to leave me with my father when he was in a bad mood or drinking. A few times, he beat Beans, once making him bleed. How would you like to grow up with parents like that? When I learned about your mother, I used to wish Parker had divorced early and married a woman.

"Actually, I can't wait to be old enough to be on my own," she said, turning to the closet. "Someone will discover me, and I'll make a lot of money on my art."

When I stepped out, she threw me my robe.

"I'm going barefoot. Morgan hates it," she said, opening the door.

I hurried to put on my robe and slip on my sandals.

"To the gallows," she declared, and laughed.

Stunned to the point of almost being numb, I followed her out and down the stairs.

Parker and Daddy were waiting for us in the living room. Parker was sitting on the sofa, and Daddy was standing, looking out the window, his back to us. Parker sipped a drink and glared at Dina, who folded her arms and shifted her weight to her right leg.

"What?" she said before Daddy could turn.

He turned slowly.

"How dare you two defy me and go on the main road before I say Caroline is ready for that?"

"I was hungry. I wanted a taco. Apparently, you never bought her one, so she was interested. Besides, I wouldn't call that going on the main road. It's practically ten feet from the entrance to our street."

"It's not ten feet!" he screamed.

Dina merely shrugged. I could barely breathe.

"Whatever. I told her I would bring it back to her. She followed, and we were able to sit at the table. By the time I rode back here, the taco would have been cold anyway."

He turned his eyes on me. "You've inherited that Sutherland defiance for sure."

"What defiance?" Dina asked, sounding so surprised that I almost believed her. "She just followed. I made sure she was safe. I kept well to the side, and she just rolled in my tracks."

"You're both grounded," he said. "You don't go anywhere for a week unless I take you."

"For what? Getting a taco twenty feet from our turn? I made plans for her to meet my friends. They'll think there's something very wrong about your bringing her here to live. Like we can't get along or something and our whole family is disrupted. My phone won't stop ringing. Why am *I* being punished, anyway? I can ride on the main road. I can go to the taco stand. Parker, are you going to let him do this to me?"

"You were responsible for her."

"What? No one said I was responsible for her. What am I, her guardian or something? I'm only trying to make this work. I even suggested she share my room, my things, my closets. Now you're going to punish me because she followed me down the hill and around a turn?"

I looked at her. She was placing all the blame on me.

"Isn't this familiar? You used to let my father punish me, even hit me, and when I turned to you, you looked away. Look at the things you let him do to Boston. I'm not going to be embarrassed in front of my friends."

She stamped her foot.

Daddy looked a little stunned.

"You followed her? Did she ask you to go with her?" he asked me.

"I didn't ask her, but I didn't tell her not to. I'm not her mother," Dina insisted before I could respond. "It was just a turn on the road and a few feet. She rides well enough. If you want to control how she breathes, control her, but don't include me in the same straitjacket. Parker?"

Her mother's face seemed to collapse, soften. She looked at Daddy.

He turned away. I saw his shoulders go up and then relax.

"I want the rules of this house obeyed. We have a lot to navigate here," he said, not looking at anyone in particular. It was as if he was thinking aloud.

"I don't," Dina insisted. "I did my navigation when my parents divorced and even when you two married. No one asked my opinion, and now here's where we are. If you want us to get along, you'll have to stop lumping us together. I can't stop doing what I do because she's chained to the house or something."

"She's not chained," he said. His voice, surprisingly, softened. "I want you both to think more before you do anything. I want to see more caution all around."

"Like I want to get hurt," Dina said. "Or want her to get hurt."

"I still want to check her out before you go riding on that road," he said.

"So check her out. Give her a bicycle license or something." She turned to me. "Don't follow me unless your father says it's okay."

I couldn't speak. I stared at her and then looked at Daddy.

"All right," he said. "Let this be a warning, then. The next time I'm disobeyed, the consequences will be more severe. Understand?"

"Can we go up and get dressed now?" Dina said. "And hopefully Beans is still permitted to take us."

"Go on," Parker said, "before Morgan changes his mind."

"Ooooh," Dina said, pretending to shake. "Let's go," she told me.

I looked at Daddy. He glanced at me and then looked away. I couldn't feel my heartbeat, but I turned and hurried after Dina to the stairway.

As soon as we entered the bedroom and closed the door behind us, I snapped at her.

"You blamed it all on me!"

"No kidding."

"But why didn't you tell me you were going to do that?"

"Because you wouldn't have looked so surprised and innocent, and your father would think you and I planned it. Who are you, Alice in Wonderland? Don't check with your father before you breathe. Check with me. We're going to the beach party. That's all that matters right now. Let's pick out those clothes like I said we would."

She threw off her robe and went into the closet.

"Try on this bathing suit," she said, tossing it on the bed.

It looked even skimpier than the one she had worn this afternoon.

"I can't wear this. If he sees—"

"You wear clothes over it when we leave. What's he going to do, ask you to strip for an inspection? If you don't reach for the stars, you can't even dream of touching them."

"What?"

"A line from one of Noa's poems. I like it, don't you? It means don't be such a namby-pamby wimp."

I put on the suit, and she stood behind me, tightening it.

Looking at myself in the mirror, I wondered if I really was sexy, sexier than she was. She had bigger breasts, but mine seemed firmer, and I had a narrower waist. When I turned to the side, I thought my rear looked more curvy, too. I caught the look in her face and thought that she was thinking the same thing.

"You filled that out better than I thought you would," she said, now sounding regretful. I widened my eyes, and she laughed. "Good. Get your things together. We'll change probably before we Uber home tonight. Night swimming is great. I'll pack our towels, brushes, whatever. There'll be about eight of us. Laura Ames is always in charge of the food. We kick in for the food, and Laura gets close to twenty dollars for shopping. She's a dumpy little thing who's honored to be with us. Her parents don't have anywhere near the money the rest of our parents do. She cuts her dull brown hair too short, doesn't know the first thing about makeup, and probably sleeps with her childhood doll in her arms. She wears the dullest, most unattractive clothes. I think her mother buys everything for her or she inherits what relatives wash down to bare threads.

"Okay, stop looking at yourself. Let's get going," she said.

I really was staring at myself, never before so taken by my developing figure. Simon would call me Narcissus falling in love with his own image. Being sexy had never been as important as it was at this moment. I felt excited and guilty about it at the same time.

It was probably how Eve felt in the Garden of Eden, I thought, recalling how my mother had read the biblical tale to me.

I laughed nervously and turned to Dina.

"What?" she asked. It must have been the expression on my face.

"I've never been to an ocean beach, night or day."

"All these little virginities being broken," she said, laughing. "Until you get to the big one."

Suddenly, I realized, she was very much the snake whispering in Eve's ear.

CHAPTER THIRTEEN

"I have no doubt you can get away with murder," Boston told Dina when we got into his car. "And I'm sure you talked Caroline into disobeying her father."

"Technically, she didn't disobey him, and why do you think Caroline is so innocent? She could be a serial killer. You hardly know her, Beans. Save your tears for later. You haven't heard everything. Hell, I would say you haven't heard anything."

"Yeah, but I know you," Boston said, turning to his sister. "And when it comes to tears, I'm not wasting any on you."

Dina didn't answer. She turned away and looked out the window. We rode in silence.

"I shouldn't have gone, no matter what," I said to break through the thick, angry air. The last thing I wanted to do was irritate and build any unpleasantness between them. "I knew my father's thoughts about going on the main highway too soon. I haven't even walked on a highway that busy."

"Humph," Dina said. "See?"

"It's still taking advantage," Boston mumbled, just loud enough for me to hear.

"Really? She's not as innocent as you want to believe, Beans. Something terrible happened at Sutherland before she came here," Dina said. "And she either had something to do with it or knows something. Maybe she's in the mood to tell us some of her secrets."

"What? What happened?" Boston asked. He looked at me in the rearview mirror.

How much did Dina know? How did she know it? Why had she been talking and acting as if she knew very little? I remembered that she said she had snuck into Daddy and Parker's room and read the letter I was made to write. What else did she read? What did she really overhear them say to each other? How was I to know now what I should and shouldn't say?

Her look of excitement at my arrival, her prodding questions, the way she teased me with her nudity and her suggestions, all supported the suspicion that she had been toying with me. If I had ever needed Simon beside me, I needed him now. I thought about what he would say or do. He could be so sharp and biting with his sarcasm.

"Maybe you should tell him, Dina," I said. "You seem to know everything I'm not supposed to talk about. And you just told me I should put the past behind me and think only about the future, didn't you? Why are you the one so intent on bringing up the past?"

She laughed. "She's a lot smarter than you think, Boston Beans."

"Huh? What's this all about?"

Boston turned to look at me quickly and then back at the road.

"Dina?"

"I don't know everything. All I heard Daddy tell Parker was it was best not to bring up or have me bring up someone named Mrs. Lawson. I don't even know what she did or does at Sutherland.

I don't think it's fair that we have to live in the dark. She's here and in our lives now," she whined. "It's not fun being caught by surprise. The ocean doesn't stop news from the mainland."

Suddenly, I did feel sorry for her. I wouldn't like it, didn't like all the secrets and mysteries I had to live with at Sutherland. Maybe she was more like me than I had first thought, someone afraid to walk too fast or step down too hard.

"Did your father tell you not to talk about her, Caroline?"

"Yes."

"Then let's drop it," Boston said.

"Fine," Dina said. "We'll drop it. I'm sure now I'm painting her correctly with whirling clouds so empty, they don't have the water for rain. I'd like to stop thinking about this family or families or whatever and think about the party, think about having fun. Remember having fun, Beans?"

"Very funny. You know, Dina, you are very good at making other people feel guilty for the things you do. Caroline, you'll be learning from the best."

"What of it? She won't be a victim anymore," Dina said.

I felt my body tighten up. I never liked thinking of myself as a victim despite what had been done with me after Mommy's deadly accident. It was too much like agreeing with Mrs. Lawson and Grandfather and blaming Mommy.

"I'm not going to be a victim," I muttered, but not, I'm sure, loudly enough for them to hear.

We were back to a deep silence. Fortunately, a minute or so later, Boston turned onto a side street that ran directly toward the ocean.

"You'd better not be doing any drinking or smoking something, Dina. If anything, Morgan is going to be on high alert when you come home. I will pick you guys up. I'll be right here at eleven thirty."

"Worried about me or her?" Dina asked, but then opened the car door and got out before he could respond.

"Be extra careful, Caroline," he said when I started to get out. "I'm sure she didn't tell you that she was put on probation at school in May for insolent behavior and suspicion of smoking weed in the girls' bathroom. Morgan went to school and saved her rear end, more for Parker's sake than hers."

I nodded and opened the door. He grabbed my left wrist.

"I'll be nearby," he added.

I stepped out. Dina was urging me to hurry. I heard the roar of the waves and stepped alongside her to turn onto the beach. To our left were shelves of large, shiny boulders, and to the right the beach extended for what looked like miles to me. A half dozen or so teenagers were gathered around a barbecue. The breeze carried the music toward us. A tall boy with hair the shade of the boulders broke free and started toward us.

"That's Noa," Dina said. "He lives and breathes for my happiness."

He rushed to take the beach bags from our hands.

"For a while I thought you weren't coming," he told Dina. "You're usually the first here."

She kissed him so passionately, it brought a rush of blood to my face. While she kissed him, he looked at me.

"I'm glad you worried," Dina said, finally releasing him. "It was a little misunderstanding at home. Anyway, this is my stepsister, Caroline, a recent immigrant from New York."

"Immigrant?" He laughed.

Dina was right about the contrast of his blue eyes with his dark skin and black hair, which seemed to have a light of its own, glimmering. His face looked carved in a cameo, with his high cheekbones, firm manly mouth, and perfectly shaped nose. There was something mesmerizing about his smile, the way he tucked his lips in at the corners and just slightly widened his eyes. He wasn't as muscular as Boston, but he had a surfer's slimness, his tight bathing suit almost too revealing.

"Aloha," he said.

I was still blushing from Dina's dramatic kiss. I felt like a child caught with her fingers on a forbidden cookie in the jar. Could he see how good-looking I thought he was? I hoped Dina didn't see how fascinated I was with him.

"Hi," I said, as if I had finally squeezed enough breath out to speak. "When did you arrive?"

"She arrived yesterday, Noa. I texted you about it. Did you ignore it?"

"No, no. Sorry." He turned completely toward her. "As usual, Laura bought too much, so the birds will feast."

"She's such a hepa."

"What's that?" I asked.

"'Idiot' in Hawaiian, but she is in any language," Dina said.

"Oh, she's not that bad. But close," Noa said. "I have a new poem."

"Just for me?" Dina asked, cuddling up to him but looking at me.

"Tonight, but later for the world."

"Ha. Is he arrogant or what?" Dina asked.

I looked at him. "Maybe just proud," I said. "My grandfather doesn't believe in waiting for compliments. He says that's a sign of insecurity."

Noa's face seemed to brighten even more. Dina blew air through her lips.

"I think your grandfather is right. Do you like poetry?" he asked.

"Yes. I especially love Poe's 'The Raven.'"

"Great to read aloud," he said, nodding.

"Why read someone else's poem?" Dina asked him. "And who are you reading it aloud for?"

"He's not just someone else," Noa said, looking mostly at me. "You can read it for yourself."

"I thought about writing poems after reading him," I said.

"Well, look at us. We're just a bunch of A students. Guess what? The bell rang. School's out," Dina said. "Let's get to the party."

We started toward the others. Noa smiled again at me. Dina tugged his hand.

Dina leaned back to whisper to me. I was anticipating a compliment. I thought I handled my first experience with one of her friends well.

"Don't flirt with my boyfriend," she warned.

The warmth in my face turned icy. Was I flirting?

The girl who was surely Laura broke free of the others and hurried toward us to be the next to greet us.

"Is this your stepsister you talked to me so much about?" she asked.

She had light brown hair, a puffy round face, and eyes I thought were a little too close together. A few inches shorter than either Dina or me, she was small-breasted and wide-hipped, with most of the weight of her legs in her thighs. She had the unconfident, frightened look of someone who had so little self-respect that she was grateful for being acknowledged that she existed.

"I didn't talk about her with only you, Laura. I didn't even know you were there half the time."

"I didn't mean just me. Hi," she blurted at me. "I'm Laura Ames."

"Caroline Bryer," I said, still smarting from Dina's warning.

"It's great to meet you."

"It's great for you to meet anyone," Dina said. "Noa said you bought too much again. Maybe you shouldn't be the one to shop for our beach parties anymore."

"Oh, I just thought, since there was another person . . ."

"You think she eats twice as much as everyone else?"

"No."

"Forget about it. Hey," she called to the others, and moved quickly past Laura.

I didn't think it was possible to feel sorrier for someone other than myself so quickly.

Noa looked at me and shrugged. He and I hurried after Dina. I could see that there were many other people scattered along the beach beyond Dina's friends, also at barbecues and beach parties.

It all seemed like a blast of daylight after months of dreary bruised clouds. To our left the sun was setting, painting the ocean with startlingly beautiful blue and violet colors. I saw two sailboats off to the right and a bigger boat seemingly sliding along the horizon. The warm breeze coming off the ocean patted my face gently and lifted strands of my hair. Even Sutherland, with the beautiful mountains on its horizon, didn't hold as much magic. It was exciting. Why wouldn't I want to live here and have friends here so I could do all these things?

Dina surprised me by seizing my right arm and holding it up as if I was being declared the winner of a boxing or wrestling match.

"This is my famous New York stepsister," she announced, and then let go of my arm, but took my hand and led me closer to them. There were two boys and three other girls. She stopped first in front of the taller boy. He was quite thin, with bushy light brown hair, a narrow nose, and an almost perfectly squared jaw.

"This is Peter. We call him Peter." She laughed. "Not Pete. His parents own Precious Stones and have a jewelry store in Honolulu, too. We can get discounts, so we don't shoplift at his parents' store."

"Better not," Peter said. He took my free hand for a quick shake, so quick it was as if he wasn't permitted to touch a girl.

"Peter's next year's senior class president. He bribed everybody."

"Very funny," he said.

The girl next to him was shorter than me, with small, delicate facial features. She looked doll-like and had auburn hair neatly trimmed to the center of her neck. Her bluish-green eyes caught the glimmer of the descending sun and twinkled like Christmas tree lights. "Cute" would surely be the word following her name.

"This is Beth Raymond. Her family is from San Francisco. Her father is a real estate attorney, which means they're rich, but nowhere near as rich as your grandfather."

"Hi," Beth said. I liked her smile because it was so soft and friendly. "Between you and me, we're not rich. We're well-off."

I nodded like I understood the difference. My mother had once told me that there were rich people and there were wealthy people like my grandfather. The difference lay in their power over other people. Wealthy people like him had the power.

"Nice to meet you," I said, and glanced at Dina to see if she'd repeat what she had said to Laura, that it was nice for me to meet anyone. She gave me her slightly twisted smile, which I took for approval.

It wasn't until I turned to the other girls and was only a few feet away that I realized they were twins. My first thought was they were not happy about it. Although they had identical auburn hair, one had hers long, down to her shoulders, in fact, and the other had hers cut almost as short as Parker's. One wore a two-piece black swimsuit, nowhere as bikini-like as Dina's and mine. The other wore a light blue two-piece. They looked to be the exact same height, about five foot five, with similar figures. One wore pierced earrings, and the other didn't. They were looking for ways to be different, I thought. Who'd blame them?

"This is Tweedledee and Tweedledum," Dina said.

"Hysterical," the one closer to us with the long hair said. "I'm Sophia, and this is Ava," she said. "Before Dina says something else derogatory, our parents own and operate the Lahaina Boating Company. My father is a captain. We relocated here from Oregon ten years ago. We take people deep-sea fishing and on scenic tours. We're both training to be captains."

"How fun," I said.

They both smiled. Dina groaned. I looked at her.

"Who wants to be surrounded by tourists?" she said defensively.

"Those who want to make money," Ava said.

The boy next to them was Hawaiian and about six feet tall with a bodybuilder's physique.

"Aloha, I'm Noa's cousin, Mikala," he said, stepping forward. "My parents are partners with Noa's in the Maui Sports and Fishing Company."

"We were sorry to hear about your mother's accident," Peter said. "I lost my older brother to a motorcycle accident two years ago."

"Oh, I'm sorry," I said.

"Yeah. He was captain of the football team. He surely would have won a scholarship."

For a moment there was a heavy silence, with the sound of the sea and the voices of others on the beach as the undertone.

"Will someone turn on some music?" Dina said. "Laura, get the food organized," she ordered. "Who's got the whats?" she asked, eyeing me.

Sophia revealed a bag and lowered it to show a bottle of vodka. I could see another bag at her feet.

"No one will smell vodka on your breath," Dina told me. "We mix it with Hawaiian papaya juice. If you don't want to drink any, don't make anyone else feel bad about it," she warned me.

Ava turned on the music.

"Let's get this party partying," Beth said. She turned to Mikala, and they started to dance.

"Pardon us for a moment. I have a private reading to attend," Dina told the others, then seized Noa's hand and walked farther down the beach. He looked back at me and shrugged.

"Here," Sophia said, handing me a cup with the juice and vodka. "Welcome to the party."

I looked at the drink and at her. Dina was quite a ways away on the beach. She had sprawled out, and Noa was beside her, reading from a slip of paper in his hand. I smiled. Better to just look like I was going along with everyone else, I thought, and pretended to sip from the cup.

Peter asked me to dance. Before I could say yes or no, he took the cup out of my hand and handed it to Sophia.

"Do I look like a waitress?" she asked him.

"A little," he said.

He took my hand and led us to harder-packed sand. Even so, dancing on a beach, especially to this music, was quite different from when Mommy and I would dance. But whatever I was doing appeared to please him. I could see that everyone was watching us, watching me. Noa and Dina returned and stood there for a few moments.

"She's good," I heard Noa say.

"Probably had a professional dancer give her instructions at her grandfather's mansion," Dina replied.

"Hardly," I said, but barely above a mumble.

Nevertheless, all of them watching me and Dina's comments took some of the steam out of my moves. The others thankfully lost interest and were into themselves again.

"Here," Sophia said, handing my drink back to me as soon as I had paused.

I looked at Dina, who suddenly wore a wry smile. Would I really drink it? I did sip it, more to wipe that look off her face than anything.

Noa stepped up to me. "You did great," he said. "You're a natural. It's like you've always been here."

"Thank you." I took another sip of my drink.

"So you're definitely enrolling in school here?"

"She's not sure yet," Dina said, stepping up to us. "She has many opportunities, even a private school with a dormitory."

I looked at her. Neither Grandfather nor Daddy had ever mentioned such a school. Was that something else she had secretly read?

"Well, maybe we can change your mind," Noa said.

I looked at Dina.

"You can write her a poem that will change her mind," she said.

Noa missed her sarcasm. "I could do that. Sure," he said. "I'll make this place sound great."

"It *is* great," Dina said. She turned to talk to Sophia.

"Right. There's lots to see and do. Maybe I can take you and Dina to the volcano tomorrow or the next day."

"Yeah, right," Dina said, turning back, showing she was listening in to every word Noa said to me. "We'll take this long ride to look at lava. She still has to work on moving in."

"Work on what?" Sophia asked.

"Getting used to a different life. Doing things with her father, like learning how to ride a bike."

"You don't know how to ride a bike?" Sophia asked.

"I can ride, but—"

"She's lived like a princess. Someone cuts her meat for her," Dina said.

"No," I said, laughing. "Hardly."

"Whatever," Noa said. "You guys just tell me what you want to do. I'm at your service."

Sophia stepped back to pour more from the vodka bottle into my cup. I started to pull away but stopped. Dina was staring at me.

"Thank you," I said, smiling.

I drank again and turned to the sea. The movement of the water was mesmerizing, dazzling. Maybe it was how welcoming they all were and how exciting this suddenly felt, but I drank some more and talked to the twins. Their questions were harmless, almost as if Dina had given everyone the boundaries. Despite the way Dina had described my rich life, I did sense that they felt sorry for me for losing my mother. I did like them all and was even somewhat envious of Dina. She had fun friends.

Suddenly, I felt my phone vibrate. It did both that and rang, but the ring was too low. I looked at the others. No one had realized it. Who would be calling me at this hour? Was it Daddy? I wondered, and stepped to the right to slip it out of my pocket and say hello.

"Oh, honey," I heard Aunt Holly say. "How are you?"

"I'm at a beach party," I said, unable to hide my excitement about it, "and meeting Dina's friends."

"Right, right, I keep forgetting the time difference. I'll call you tomorrow."

"No, it's all right, Aunt Holly. I'm glad you called."

I realized she had called me just a short time ago. Why would she call so soon after that?

"What is it? Is Simon all right?"

She was quiet.

"Aunt Holly."

"I didn't mean to call. I'm so sorry."

"Yes, you did. What is it?"

She was quiet.

"What difference does it make when you call if you have something to tell me, Aunt Holly?"

"You're right. I keep forgetting you're your mother's daughter. It's your friend Nattie. You knew she was very ill. It's for the best."

"Nattie? For the best? You mean . . . she's . . . she's gone?"

"It's so much better, Caroline. She was suffering so, but you saw her, and she saw you. That was surely the highlight for her."

"Oh."

"Try not to think about it. I'm so sorry. I just thought if I kept it from you, you'd be even more upset."

"Of course," I said.

"Let's talk tomorrow," she said. "Don't think about it right now. Enjoy your new friends and the party. There's plenty of time to mourn afterward. I'll call you again soon."

"Okay," I said.

I slipped the phone back into my pocket. No matter what she said, I would think about it, of course. In fact, it felt as if I was hearing about my mother's death again. Nattie was the last close connection to her. I was foolish to hope she would heal and eventually walk out of that place. I dreamed of us being together. It was going to be like getting a part of my mother back.

And now that was gone.

Forever.

"What are you doing?" Dina screamed at me. I turned to her. "The party's over here. We're going to go for a swim before we eat," she told me.

I looked toward the ocean and then at her. I was certainly not going to tell her about Nattie.

"I've never—"

"Swum in the ocean. I know. Virginities. Don't worry. There are no sharks."

"Sharks?"

"Stop teasing her," Noa said. "I'll go in alongside you. Don't worry."

"That's why she should worry," Dina said. "C'mon, everyone," she cried, and disrobed.

She looked at me. I was suddenly more self-conscious than ever, but I did it.

"Hey, sweet," Mikala said, eyeing me so intensely that I felt naked.

"Don't take your drink in with you," Dina said. She put her hand under my cup. I hesitated. She tilted her head to illustrate what I should do, or else.

Nattie's gone, I thought. *I have to put my sadness on hold.*

I downed it.

"All right," Dina said, looking pleased. "First one to the mainland gets the prize."

"Mainland?"

Dina charged into the water.

"She'll swim six feet and stop," Noa said. I felt him take my hand before Peter could. "C'mon."

Of course the water was a little cool when I stepped in. Everything was whirling about me. I screamed when a wave washed over me. Where I drew the courage from I don't know, but when my hand slipped out of Noa's, I dove into the water the way Boston had shown me to dive. Everyone was screaming and laughing. I kept thinking, *Nattie's gone; Mommy's gone.*

I swam a little ways and then realized that the sand beneath me was sliding out from under my feet. I looked for Noa and Dina, but they seemed farther away. A small panic began to build. I lashed out, but the water seemed to envelop me and change my direction.

"Get her back!" I heard someone shout.

I swallowed some salty water, gagged, and felt myself weakening. My panic grew; I tried to shout but again swallowed too much water. My arms began to ache. I went under and bobbed and went under again, the water appearing to take me farther away from the others. I flailed about, and then maybe I passed out. I don't know, but suddenly someone was lifting me around my waist and bringing me back toward the shore. I gasped and choked and was sure I had passed out again.

When I opened my eyes, I was looking up at Boston. Everything was spinning. I was still having trouble breathing.

"Why did you let go of her hand?" I thought I heard Dina ask Noa.

"I didn't. She just slipped out and dove into the water, so I thought she knew what she was doing."

"I shouldn't have depended on him to watch over her, but he was so excited to do it," Dina was saying with great sarcasm.

"What? That's not true."

I felt myself being lifted and turned my head to rest in the nook between Boston's shoulder and chest.

"Where are you going with her?" Dina screamed.

"She needs to be checked out."

"You'll get us all into deep trouble! Bring her back! You idiot!"

Boston carried me to his car, slipped me into the back seat smoothly, and drove off. I closed my eyes, and when I awoke, I was at an emergency room. I was very dizzy and nauseated. I struggled to remember what had happened. Everything was such a blur, images running into each other: water, faces, Aunt Holly and Nattie trying to talk to me, and Daddy coming home from work and shouting, "Landed!" I was running toward him as if I was running back through time, rewinding minutes, getting younger and younger. I think I passed out again and woke hours later.

There was whiteness all around me and something beating. My arm was cuffed. I turned my head and could see Daddy just outside the door of the room I was in. He was talking to Boston, who had his head bowed. A doctor approached them, and the three went off to the right.

I tried to call out, but the effort seemed to take all my strength, so I closed my eyes and waited. I opened them to see the nurse adjust something, and moments later, Daddy approached the bed. He didn't look angry as much as in deep thought. His brow was rippling.

"I don't know what happened," I said before he could ask.

He nodded. "No, you don't," he replied, which surprised me. I had been preparing myself for all sorts of accusations and threats. "And there is good reason why not. Did you accept a drink, something with alcohol in it?"

I looked past him. Was Dina nearby?

"I . . . yes," I confessed. I couldn't lie to Daddy when we were the Robot Family, and I certainly couldn't lie to him now, maybe not ever.

"There was more than alcohol in it, and I don't mean the juice. Were you aware of that?"

"No. What else?"

"Something these kids—kids, unfortunately, everywhere these days—call Ecstasy. Didn't take long for you to get into the water with them."

"I never heard of it, Daddy."

"Your mother or Nattie Gleeson never offered you anything to smoke or take?"

"NOOOO," I said.

He nodded. "I've been questioning Dina. She thinks she's so sophisticated, but I'm trained in methods of interrogation. You know that."

I shook my head. "Interrogation? No. I don't understand."

"Well, I'd have thought your mother would have given you more of my background. Anyway, there are ways to break down someone to tell the truth. Dina claims you wanted to take showers with her, told her you'd wash her back and she could wash yours. Something you saw your mother and Nattie do?"

"NO. She was the one who wanted to do it. She was the one walking around naked, not me, Daddy."

"Um," he said. "Whether she or you initiated it, it's out there. I know some girls her age like to experiment, and she thinks you've already done so."

"No."

"Mistake to have had you share a room. But some things happen almost no matter what. If they're meant to happen, that is."

"I don't know why she's saying those things. Maybe she's just afraid of you."

"I hope so. You used to be."

"Mommy always said it was better to love someone than fear him or her."

"She did enough of that. Anyway, I have already spoken with your grandfather. He and I have decided that whatever the truth is, it's too soon."

"Too soon for what?"

"For you to have left Sutherland. You have more adjusting to do, and it's better that you have the supervision Grandfather Sutherland can provide. I have"—he looked away—"I have my hands full here. The truth is, I haven't fully adjusted to it all myself. Dina, who, as is her character, claims innocence, claims her friends will testify for her. In other words, she knows nothing about this."

"But that's what's true for me. I don't know what happened, what I drank."

"Whatever. What's clear in any case is she is not the right influence on you right now. You are like a turtle without a shell, vulnerable because of all that's happened. Maybe it's my fault or even mostly my fault, but sitting around and analyzing and blaming isn't the solution.

"You see a problem, you solve it," he said with that Captain Bryer firmness. "You're impressionable, naive, innocent beyond what you should be for your age. We know the reason for that. Fortunately, until you are less vulnerable, there is a support system for you that few can enjoy."

He paused and looked so young for a moment. Or maybe it was because of what had happened to me. I felt like his little girl again, but that face quickly disappeared.

"So you told Grandfather Sutherland everything already?"

"That was the bargain we had made."

"Bargain?" I looked away. I had become something to trade?

"You were told there were conditions, Caroline."

"But . . . Boston will tell you the truth. Ask Boston."

"There's enough dissension in this broken family as it is," he said. "For better or for worse, I took it on, and things being the way they were, it became my priority."

"Not me?"

"Apparently, your grandfather wants to do more for you. He sees potential. You've impressed him, and he's not a man easily impressed by anyone. He says you're more of a Sutherland than a Bryer."

Was that good? Did I want that? What about Daddy? Wasn't that more of an insult?

"He said that?"

"Yes. He doesn't pull punches with anyone, including me. Truthfully, it would be stupid for me to keep you here, exposed to . . . whatever. I can't provide the same protection, and although Boston is quite reliable, he has his own life to pursue, his own ambitions. He can't be appointed your guardian when Parker and I are not available."

"Protection? At Sutherland? Does that mean locking me up again?"

"No, no. He has many ideas to discuss with you for your schooling. The thing is, he wants you to be involved in your future now. No one will impose anything on you. He's not rehiring Dr. Kirkwell, either. What you'll do now is spend another day or so recuperating here, during which your things will be packed and everything actually sent ahead. You'll only have to get on a plane and return when I complete the arrangements."

"But—"

"I'll keep the model airplane you brought with you. I was happy about that, but it will be here when you return, when you're ready and willing to return. I promise that then you'll have your own room, and you can visit when you want. It'll just be easier for us both when you're older. You'll have reached the maturity to handle your past well."

"I've barely been here. How do you know I won't?"

"Sometimes it doesn't take long to know what's right or wrong to do. I'm not a man who hesitates when choices become clear, Caroline. What I want most for you, what I have always wanted most for you, is a safe landing. We have to get you on the right flight path."

What? Was I hearing right? *I'm not a plane. I'm your daughter.* The words came but evaporated almost as soon as they had.

I was dizzy again. He was fading in and out. I saw his lips moving and heard him repeat his decision. "Safe landing . . . safe landing . . . just not here and now. Right choice."

Captain Bryer had spoken. Was all this just a dream?

Maybe, I thought before I drifted off again, I did drown.

I dreamed of Mommy and Nattie, both smiling, the three of us dancing until I was dancing alone.

And then I heard my name.

Someone was calling.

I opened my eyes and saw the nurse.

"Are you all right?" she asked.

"I don't know," I said.

She smiled. "Well, you slept well. It's morning. We'll get you dressed. Your father is coming to pick you up."

"And then I'll find out," I said.

"What?" She held her smile.

"Whether or not I'm all right."

CHAPTER FOURTEEN

Parker came with him to the hospital. Compared to how she looked now, she must have been overjoyed the first time I had seen her. Waves of anger seemed to flow from her scowl. Avoiding looking directly at me, she stood beside Daddy as he finished the hospital release paperwork. When she first saw me, she didn't ask how I was. She wasn't asking now, either. She had other things to say, things that would always be more important to her than my welfare, my future.

Right from the start, I couldn't imagine her even as a stepmother. A stepmother couldn't see herself in you. I understood that, but in my mind, the word "mother" had to at least mean someone who cared for you more than just an ordinary person would. You were still part of her family. Your welfare mattered to her. Of course, it wasn't love as deep as a real mother's, but shouldn't it have been deeper than concern for a stranger? I so longed for the warmth of a loving embrace, a soft kiss, the precious holding of hands. I fought so hard against seeing myself as an orphan. I still had a father, and I had a grandfather with a familial history that touched so many, but right now, that didn't seem to matter. An orphan doesn't orbit around anyone. He or she doesn't quite know where his or her roots should go. Where would mine?

When I first left Sutherland for Hawaii, I felt more like an astronaut going from one world to another. Now I felt as if my rocket had missed its target and I was sailing into the dark unknown with stars moving farther and farther away. Even they didn't want to touch me.

There is no one lonelier than someone who finds she is the only one feeling sorry for herself. Mommy tried desperately to prevent that from happening. I felt more disappointed for her than I did for myself. More and more I realized that she was the true orphan with a family. Shadows at Sutherland were always deeper and darker for her. Even her ashes were trapped in that darkness right now.

Parker's eyes narrowed. Her face looked carved in ice. She looked like she could read my angry and distraught thoughts. It set my heart pounding. Had I no secrets to keep? I wanted to be more like Simon, who could hide his displeasure so easily behind a smile or a smile behind an apparent scowl. Right now, growing up seemed more like learning how to be deceptive. Innocence was cute, adorable, but along with it came vulnerability. I was a child on that beach, but I swore to myself that I would never be again.

"Your father and I are highly respected FAA air traffic controllers. We don't wield the power your grandfather does to be able to stifle gossip. Our reputations are very important to our work and our lives. We came here to get away from the nasty, prodding busybodies."

Tears came into my eyes. *What about Dina, then?* I wanted to say. Boston told me about the trouble she had gotten into at school, but I didn't dare bring it up, even though I thought she was being unfair.

Daddy seemed not to hear a word she was saying, or if he did, he was happy she was saying it. We went out quickly, got into the car, and started for his and Parker's home. I couldn't see myself ever calling it just home.

"I'm not blaming you completely," she continued, as if her previous words were hanging in the air between us. "Dina is grounded for two months, and when we say 'grounded,' we mean it. She steps foot off our property, we'll know, and she knows we'll know.

"We're putting you on a red-eye tonight. The doctor has assured us you're fine to travel. All your things have already been packed and shipped. We've prepared the downstairs guest bedroom for you so you can continue to rest, or you can go out to a pool lounge chair. Boston will be picking up our dinner right after his work. For today, Dina is confined to her room until dinner and then after. She will not be accompanying us to the airport."

I was surprised there was even a suggestion she would come along.

"As for your new bike, Morgan has decided we will keep it. Dina, however, will not be permitted to use it."

Why was she telling me all this? I wondered. What did she want me to say? *I'm sorry*? *Please don't send me away*? Was I supposed to wail and beg?

"I shouldn't have drunk the juice with the vodka in it, but I didn't know anything else was in it," I said. "I wouldn't have gone into the ocean for the first time if I had known."

She turned to look at me. For a second, I thought she might say something sympathetic, but whatever warmth I imagined was gone quickly.

"Dina is a mess. I accept that. We both know we have a lot of work to do, but you have more opportunity than most girls your age. The first step to maturity is accepting responsibility for your own actions. So I don't want to hear about how they snuck it on you or anything. Peer pressure is the most influential. A truly independent-minded person your age is as rare as a pimple on a whale's nose. We thought—

I thought—that with all the specialized training and instruction you had, you might have been more independent-minded. Why, we even thought you'd be the stronger influence, maybe help Dina get her act together.

"If you leave here with anything, it should be the knowledge that you are your own best friend. Trust should be one of the last things you give to anyone, to anything. I know your father did his best to have you understand that, but you were under other influences."

I looked out the window.

And without knowing why, I began to hum "Sweet Caroline."

She spun around as I got louder. "Stop that!" she said.

I smiled. "I'll never stop that," I said.

"That letter you wrote was all lies."

"Not mine. I don't lie. Daddy knows that."

She moaned and looked ahead again.

Daddy had yet to speak. Where was he? I wondered. He was staring ahead as if he was watching a radar screen. He could foresee accidents; could he foresee my future? More importantly, did he care? I was in a car moving over a scenic highway. The sun was bright, creating dazzling light over the blue sea, but I felt the same as I had felt locked in that dark, empty bedroom back in Sutherland. Loneliness was an unwelcome companion who simply wouldn't let go of my hand.

"I warned you something like this could happen," Parker told Daddy. "It was just too soon."

He looked at her and nodded slightly. "We'll turn it off and on," he said, as if my life was on a computer. "Look for a fresh start again."

"How many times have we done that with Dina? It hasn't made much difference," she said, and then he said the most promising thing since I was taken to the hospital.

"She's not Dina. There's that."

"Oomph," Parker muttered. "Sometimes I think that God rains children down on you for revenge."

What a terrible thing to say, I thought, and tried to tighten my arms around myself and squeeze into the corner of the seat. Maybe Dina was the way she was because her own mother didn't like her, didn't want her, and she knew it. I wanted to be angry at her, rage at her as soon as I saw her, but all I could do at this moment was feel sorrier for her than I did for myself. At least I was getting away from all the tension and rage that swirled around this supposedly perfect new family Daddy had found.

The house was so quiet. I imagined Dina was forbidden to play any music. I was sure they had taken away her mobile phone. I knew from my own experience that prolonged deep silence could be painful for anyone. Sometimes having only your thoughts was like a rubber ball bouncing in an empty room.

Parker showed me to the guest suite. It was nicer than Dina's room; everything was done in a sea blue with soft white curtains.

"I kept the things you should change into for your flight later tonight," she said, pointing to the closet. "I'll make you something to drink and eat for lunch and let you know when it's ready. You can sit at the kitchen nook. I have some chores to do on my computer."

"What about my father?"

She raised her eyebrows. "He has some important things to get for the house. You might remember that he is very handy and knowledge-able about how to go about house repairs. Neither of us likes being dependent on repair people. Dependability is rarer than ever, whether it involves your own children or others', apparently."

"Do you and my father have any friends?" I asked.

"What?"

"I just wondered if anyone fits your standards," I said, mustering all the defiance I could.

She stared at me, looking like she would smile for a moment. "Your grandfather is right. You're more of a Sutherland than a Bryer. You can't hide your arrogance. It's why you belong there and not here."

I looked away quickly. I didn't want her to see the pain I felt being told my father was more of a stranger to me than my grandfather. A few silent seconds passed. I continued to look away.

"The doctor said you should just rest. Maybe wait until after lunch to go out by the pool," she added, her voice a little softer. "Don't leave the property, of course."

She left and closed the door. I lay there listening for Dina's voice. Did she know they had brought me back? Was she going to try to speak to me? Would she come up with excuses, swear she had nothing to do with the drug?

Ten minutes later, Parker knocked and opened the door.

"Go have your lunch," she said.

The sandwich and drink were there on the counter.

"Is Dina having lunch?"

"She's on a hunger protest," Parker said. "Not the first time. Once she lasted nearly two days. I never understood why people punish themselves as a way to get back at you, especially children."

Maybe because a daughter expects you to care, I thought, but didn't dare say.

She left, and I sat there alone, still in a bit of a daze from what had happened. It had all happened so fast, too. I was tempted to go upstairs and knock on Dina's door. I wanted to know why she had done this to me. Whatever happened to wanting a sister? After I ate a little of the sandwich, I decided I would do it. Parker hadn't forbidden it, and what difference did it make now? I was being sent back no matter what I did, what rule I broke. I picked up the plate with half the sandwich and started quietly up the stairs.

I paused at the top and listened. Parker either hadn't heard me or didn't care. I knocked softly on Dina's door. She didn't respond, so I knocked again. Suddenly, she pulled it open, looked at me, and went back to her bed. She was in her bra and panties.

"What do you want?" she asked, looking straight up at the ceiling.

"You want this half? It's the turkey you liked."

She glanced at me. "Did she send you up here?"

"No. She's in her room, working on her books or something."

"Give it to me, but don't tell her I ate it."

"I don't think she cares," I said, walking in and handing it to her.

She took it and gobbled it down. I handed her the rest of my drink, too.

"They're sending me back to Sutherland, you know."

"Poor you, going back to a mansion, servants, and just about anything you want."

"I wanted my father to want me. I actually like it here. But I don't think you really wanted me here. I think you pretended to. I think you thought I was some sort of new amusement for you."

"Really?" she said, twisting the corner of her mouth. "You came up with that all by yourself?"

"Yes. You haven't denied it."

She continued to look up at the ceiling.

"You have friends, a boyfriend, and the art talent, but I think you might be lonelier than I am, Dina. You're too angry all the time to be happy."

"Oh, really? You know, you should be more grateful to me."

"What? Why?"

"I saw the way you looked at me when I was naked. You can try to hide it, but anyone who gets to really know you intimately will know the truth. I was a little fascinated about it and thought about encouraging you even more."

I knew my face was crimson. "That's not true, no matter what lies you told them about me. I wasn't looking at you that way. I was just surprised at how unashamed you were to be stark naked."

"Why should I be ashamed? I have a figure most of the girls around me envy."

"You told them lies about me touching you. You're the one who wanted us to shower together."

"Was I? Who do you think they believe about that? My mother never had a woman for a lover."

"Eventually you would have told stories to your friends. Maybe you have already."

"Whatever," she said. "It certainly works as a reason you were sent back. Truthfully," she said, smiling, "I've often considered experimenting a bit."

She laughed, maybe at the expression on my face. Then she lowered her eyes and stared at me.

"What?" I asked.

"Who was Mrs. Lawson? What happened to her? Why was her name so forbidden?"

I didn't respond.

"What difference does it make now? You're going back no matter what. You can say whatever you want."

"Right. And right now, I don't want to say anything about her."

"See? How was I going to be your sister if you came here with a trunk full of secrets that you would never tell me anyway? You were a stranger before you arrived, and you still are. You can't blame me."

I walked to the patio door and looked out at the ocean.

"You tell someone your deepest secrets when you believe he or she will keep them sacred," I said. "You just wanted to scatter mine on the beach among your friends. What would that have been like for me? Everyone would look at me with pity or distaste. Maybe that's what you wanted. Or you would keep a few secrets to hold over me and turn me into your little personal slave."

She laughed.

I turned and looked at her. "I'm not surprised that you think that's funny, Dina. It's who you are."

"Ya-di-di, ya-di-di. What are you, thirty years old or something? You sound like someone's mother."

"Really?" I smiled. "Thank you."

"Oh," she moaned, and waved me off.

"I'm going out by the pool," I said. "Maybe you want to finish painting my portrait."

"You wish," she said as I left.

I went down and out to the pool. Parker still had not come out of her room. As soon as I lay back, my phone rang. I wasn't surprised. I was expecting Aunt Holly to call.

"Hi, Aunt Holly," I said, and almost immediately started to cry. I tried to suck back my tears, but my voice was betraying me.

"Oh, honey, I'm so sorry. Grandfather Sutherland called me this morning."

"I guess he was very angry."

"No. Surprisingly, he wasn't. He was very Grandfather Sutherland. All business, what he expects me to do and what he wants done for you. You'll return to the same room, of course. We'll have a family meeting the day after tomorrow to discuss your educational future. Martin and I are going to move back into Sutherland ourselves for a while. There is still Simon to look after, and the doctor doesn't want us forcing him to do anything but take basic care of himself. As you know, he's always been more comfortable at Sutherland than at home."

"Doesn't he want to go on to college? He could probably get accepted anywhere in that accelerated program, right?"

"He's not quite ready to think about it. I told him about you just a little while ago."

"And?"

"It was practically the only thing that made him happy."

"Really? Is that good, his being happy that I got into trouble here?"

"Don't be so hard on yourself. Starting anew under these circumstances wouldn't have been easy for anyone. Anyway, as far as Simon's reaction, the good thing is he's thinking about someone else besides himself. He's been wallowing in self-pity and been unproductive. Grandfather Sutherland doesn't have the patience for all that. I think he's hoping you'll make a difference."

"Really? But what if I can't? Will Grandfather Sutherland be more disappointed in me?"

"Let's not worry about it now. We'll both work on Simon. He'll be our project."

"Simon would hate to be known as anyone's project."

"See? You know him better than I do already."

I had to laugh.

"I'll be at the airport with Emerson. Your things are being taken care of today. Grandfather Sutherland has replaced Mrs. Lawson with a new housekeeper, Claudia Fisher. She is from one of his properties in England. She and her husband ran it, but her husband died recently, and your grandfather decided to hire her for Sutherland and sell that property. I only spent a few minutes with her, but I know she is not as stern as Mrs. Lawson. I will say she seems to be just as efficient and dedicated to her work. She practically radiates it, and the staff knows to follow her orders. Grandfather Sutherland laid down the law on that, and your grandfather certainly does command respect.

"In fact, Mrs. Fisher talks about him as if he's British royalty. I never traced the Sutherland heritage that far back. Maybe he is."

"Does she know about me?"

"Oh, I'm sure your grandfather has given her information about us all to make sure everything runs smoothly. You'd think this was a battleship and not a home," she added, and then laughed. "I'm sorry about Hawaii and your father. I know you're disappointed, but I'm so looking forward to seeing you."

"Thank you, Aunt Holly."

"Have a good trip," she said. "Think of it this way, Caroline. Maybe it was too soon for you to start with a whole new family in a very different place. Sutherland was your mother's home."

"I'm not sure she really ever accepted it as a home."

"There's no choice when it comes to that. Sutherland is too powerful to be ignored. You're your mother's daughter. If anyone can change it more to her liking, you can. Just concentrate on how proud of you she was and will be."

"Okay. Thank you, Aunt Holly. Bye."

I sat there trying not to keep crying. A shadow caught my eye, and I looked up to see Dina on her lanai, looking down at me.

"You could come down," I said.

She turned and went back inside. I watched the door, but she didn't appear on the rear patio. I thought I heard Parker in the kitchen. Then I looked across the pool and saw the easel and the covered canvas. I rose and walked to it, watching the door. No one appeared, so I uncovered the canvas and looked at what Dina had painted.

There was what I would call a childish image of me lying on the lounge chair, with lines drawn for legs and arms. Instead of a face, there was a blob of pink and greenish paint full of swirls. Those clouds she had described were there, but more like smudges. How was this a portrait, or even a painting? And she had seemed to spend so long on it. It was more like an expression of some kind of madness. Maybe that was why Parker ignored her art. She wanted to ignore what was storming inside her daughter.

Not that she would listen to my advice, but I could tell her that trouble doesn't go away because you pretend it isn't there. It only grows stronger. I didn't want to be this wise. I wanted to be a child in the Robot Family. But I never would again.

I covered up the painting and returned to the lounge chair. I think I dozed off, because there were different shadows moving across the pool and over the house when I opened my eyes. A while later, Boston appeared. I sat up as he approached. Without saying anything, he sat on the end of the lounge chair and looked down.

"I think what happened to you and what's happening now are unfair," he began, "but when those two make up their minds about something, there's no point in trying to get them to change. They just shut down and go forward. Morgan is even more like that than Parker. Dina thinks her tantrums and howls will get them to reconsider a punishment. Our real father would give in sometimes, which only made matters worse between Parker and him. She doesn't believe in taking the easy way out. You were always going uphill here, even before you arrived."

"You warned me at the beach. I didn't listen," I said.

"Yeah, but you were excited to meet new friends and do new things. Dina might pout and rage for a while, but she'll wake up one day and regret throwing you right into the stupid swing of things. She really needs a sister. I don't have the patience, and besides, soon I'll be on my own, move out."

"Where will you go?"

"I'm not sure yet. Working things out. I'm considering becoming a Navy SEAL."

"What is that?"

"An elite military force that carries out direct raids or assaults on enemy targets. It requires the most difficult training and tests to pass, but if I do . . . I know Morgan, for one, would be very proud of me, not that that's a reason to do it."

"Sounds scary."

He laughed. "I'll get the training to handle Dina for them."

We both laughed.

"I'm sorry you're leaving, Caroline. Really."

He touched my hand, and then he took it in his, and we sat quietly for a while.

"I do hope I'll see you again. Maybe I'll come visit you at Sutherland one day."

"Really?"

"Why not? You have pools and lakes to swim in, right?"

"Yes. I'll practice diving."

"Good." He leaned over and kissed me on the cheek. I could feel my face light up. "Don't ever underestimate yourself, Caroline. You're a bright, beautiful girl. And I should know. I see tons of them at the pool."

I was speechless.

"Getting hungry?"

"Yes," I said, and told him how I had given Dina half my sandwich.

"Parker's right about her. For all we know, she has food stashed up there."

We heard my father arrive.

"Okay, let's go in. We'll act like nothing's changed," he said, smiling.

"Act" would be the word for it, I thought, and followed him into the house.

And along with me came all the conflict I felt inside my heart: wanting Daddy's forgiveness and the love he had once showed me, glad to be leaving Dina and her anger and resentment, sad to leave Boston before I had a chance to really get to know him, but happy to escape Parker's sternness and suspicions.

Despite all that had happened to me and been done to me there,

Sutherland loomed as a world of possibilities. Perhaps it was foolish of me even to think it, but in the end, Grandfather might prove to be less of a challenge than my own father. Why I should think that, I did not know.

I just thought it and then realized, *Of course I should think it.*

It was what my mother would have wanted, would have said. I heard her speak.

Don't be afraid to return, Caroline. I'm there.

I'm waiting for you.

EPILOGUE

Daddy was so silent on the way to the airport that I thought he wouldn't even say goodbye. Boston said sweet things and hugged me. Parker said, "Have a safe trip," and stepped back.

Daddy stood there looking at me with his hands on his hips like a drill sergeant. I kept thinking, *Captain Bryer, you step back, too, and let Daddy say goodbye.*

"Your grandfather will keep me informed," he said. "Things will clear up here in due time, and it will be a lot easier when you return to visit or whatever."

"Whatever?"

"Whatever," he repeated.

"I am who I am, Daddy. I'm not going to become another person."

"You're not a person yet," he said.

"What am I?"

"Training to be a person."

"I never did anything deliberately to hurt you," I said. "If you really loved me, you would know that."

"Love isn't enough, Caroline. Life's too hard to require only that from you or anyone."

"Maybe that's why you never found it, Daddy," I said.

I hugged him before he could step away. He touched my hair, and when I let go, he said goodbye. I watched them walk away. He paused and looked back. I held up my hand. He nodded and walked on.

I should have saluted, I thought, and walked onto the plane.

Everyone was just as nice to me as they were when I had first come. I had the exact same seat, making it seem as if it all had been a dream. I fell asleep and slept most of the trip, waking to eat breakfast. It was so much easier than being awake and realizing I was heading back to Sutherland, rebounding like some tennis ball that had hit a wall.

But after all, wasn't that what I actually had done? Hit a wall, a wall that had no forgiveness, not an inch. Boston was right to say I was doomed from the start. My Captain Bryer and Parker had assumed so much about me. Living with Mommy and Nattie, going through the horrendous aversion therapy, being involved somehow with Mrs. Lawson's death—all of it had somehow in their minds made me un- suitable for what they considered a "normal" life. I wasn't ready to face the challenges of being a teenager, and with the heavy and difficult load of Dina's and Parker's own past, it was all simply too much right now, maybe forever.

And what awaited me at Sutherland? I truly felt untethered; my feet didn't touch the ground. Like some balloon resembling Caroline Bryer, I floated off the plane and into the airport. Aunt Holly and Emerson were there as she had promised. I loved and needed them both, but I didn't feel like someone coming home. I had yet to find a home.

So who was I? Who was anyone who didn't feel like she belonged anywhere or to anyone? And yet when I saw Sutherland come up ahead of me, I did feel something. It wasn't exactly like returning home; it was more like I was returning to Mommy. She was there. She had grown up there; she slept there. And realizing that suddenly gave me a purpose. It was as if she had awoken inside me. I could hear her singing along with Neil Diamond. A wave of warmth overcame all my dread and fear.

Both Aunt Holly and Emerson never stopped talking all the way from the airport to Sutherland. I knew they were nervous for me and were worried about me. When the grand gate with the gilded Sutherland letters appeared directly ahead, Aunt Holly turned to me. Of course, she wanted to see my reaction. She smiled, and I realized I was smiling. How funny it was not to know what I was doing until that moment.

"You're going to be just fine," she said.

"Of course she is," Emerson seconded. He sang a few bars of "Lovely Joan," and Aunt Holly laughed the way Mommy would.

The gate opened, and we entered the estate.

"Well, I'll be," Aunt Holly said at the sight of Simon waiting at the front door. "He hasn't been out and about since you left."

He didn't smile when I got out of the limousine and approached him.

But his eyes were electric, dazzling with excitement.

"Hi, Simon," I said.

He leaned toward me and whispered, with his eyes on his mother and Emerson behind us.

"I've discovered a new and very important secret," he said, and stepped aside so that I could enter his world.